AMOR AND MORE

LOVE EVERAFTER

Also edited by Radclyffe & Stacia Seaman

Erotic Interludes 2: *Stolen Moments*

Erotic Interludes 3: *Lessons in Love*

Erotic Interludes 4: *Extreme Passions*

Erotic Interludes 5: *Road Games*

Romantic Interludes 1: *Discovery*

Romantic Interludes 2: *Secrets*

Breathless: *Tales of Celebration*

Amor and More: *Love Everafter*

Women of the Dark Streets: Lesbian Paranormal

Visit us at www.boldstrokesbooks.com

AMOR AND MORE

LOVE EVERAFTER

edited by

RADCLY*f*FE and
STACIA SEAMAN

2013

Credits
Editors: Radclyffe and Stacia Seaman
Production Design: Stacia Seaman
Cover Design by Sheri (graphicartist2020@hotmail.com)

Contents

INTRODUCTION

We love romance novels. When we want—or need—to escape from our daily lives, we know that we can open a book and join the characters on their journey toward romance and love, culimating in happily ever after. By the end, we know these women. We've laughed with them, cried with them, and cheered for them when they rode off into the sunset together.

But sometimes…sometimes we want a little more. Join seventeen of your favorite Bold Strokes Books authors as they revisit your favorite characters for *Amor and More: Love Everafter*.

—Radclyffe and Stacia Seaman, 2013

Nell Stark is the Chair of English, Philosophy, and Religious Studies at a college in the SUNY system. She and her partner live, write, and parent their rambunctious child and dog a stone's throw from the historic Stonewall Inn in New York City.

This story features characters from *The Princess Affair*.

A ROYAL ENGAGEMENT
NELL STARK

Her Royal Highness Princess Alexandra Victoria Jane—better known to her subjects as Sasha—peered around the stage and into one corner of the Throne Room. Strobe lights illuminated a small cluster of people centered on one of her cousins and his date. She sighed in frustration, even as she waved to them. Where on earth had Kerry gone?

Turning in a slow circle, she surveyed the stateroom turned nightclub. Her brother Arthur and his wife Ashleigh were up onstage, dancing with a knot of their closest friends. The newlyweds had changed into evening attire for this reception, and Sasha had no doubt that the tabloids would be thrown into paroxysms of joy at their fairy-tale perfection. Ashleigh looked stunning in her floor-length white evening gown, and Arthur had ditched his Royal Air Force uniform for a tuxedo.

Sasha watched as he twirled his wife expertly in time to the music. They looked so happy. They *were* so happy. For years, she had secretly despaired of ever falling in love, not to mention finding someone to share her life. Thankfully, Kerry had changed all that, and now Sasha was ready to take the next step. But first, she had to find her.

After several more minutes of hunting, Sasha saw her standing near one of the tables set around the periphery of the room. She was sharing it with Sasha's sister Lizzie and a few of her Cambridge friends, and as Sasha watched, Kerry tipped her head back and laughed. Her wavy red hair was artfully mussed, and her silver tux showed off both the breadth of her shoulders and the swell of her breasts.

Sasha hurried over and slipped one arm around Kerry's waist. "You're looking quite handsome tonight, Ms. Donovan."

"Your Royal Highness." Kerry's eyes twinkled. "What an unexpected pleasure."

"Unexpected?" Sasha arched one eyebrow. "You should always expect me."

"No one expects the Spanish Inquisition," quipped a clearly tipsy Lizzie, which set Kerry to laughing again.

"Nerds. The lot of you, nerds." Sasha turned her face up to Kerry's for a swift kiss. "I'm sorry I've had to spend so much time away today."

"Don't apologize. Maid of honor is a big job." Kerry pulled her closer and said quietly, "Everything okay? You seem a little tired."

"I'm fine." Sasha rested her cheek against Kerry's shoulder as they whispered. "The day went off well, I think. That's all that matters."

"You should feel pleased." Kerry kissed her again. "And I meant what I said earlier—your speech was amazing."

"You're biased."

"No. Just honest."

Sasha pulled back to meet her eyes. It was the same response Kerry had given the night they'd met, in the moments before their first kiss. The kiss that had changed everything. Suddenly, Sasha resented every other person in the room. "I've had enough of speeches. I just want to spend time with you."

"Shall we take a walk? Get out for a little while?" Kerry looked toward the stage. "I don't think the party will slow down anytime soon."

"That sounds perfect." She turned to her sister. "We're going to take some fresh air."

Lizzie narrowed her eyes. "You're not running off to—"

"Hush." Sasha embraced her before she could finish the sentence. "We'll be back. Keep the dance floor warm."

She tugged at Kerry's hand but was forced to wait until she had exchanged cheek-kisses with Lizzie. Over the past several months, Kerry had developed strong relationships with both of Sasha's siblings. She talked football with Arthur and sat between them in their box at Manchester United games. She talked literature and history with Lizzie and had gone over to Cambridge once to support her at a debating competition.

Now, as they made their way through the crowd in search of freedom, Sasha felt her anticipation grow. Tomorrow she would formalize Kerry's place in her family. In the morning, they would all retreat to Balmoral Castle in Scotland for a few more days of private celebration before Arthur and Ashleigh embarked on their honeymoon. Once they had settled in, Sasha planned to invite Kerry to ride with her into the mountains, as they had done on their first real date. This time, in addition to producing breakfast at the ruins, she would produce a ring.

"Let's walk along the park." Kerry interrupted her reverie. "If Ian will let us, of course."

The throng that had gathered outside the palace for the nuptials that morning had since dispersed to their own celebrations in pubs and homes across the city, making Sasha's protection officer amenable to their plan. He followed them from a discreet distance as they strolled hand in hand along the mostly deserted sidewalk. The light breeze blowing through the trees felt wonderful on her face after the heat of the party.

"I still can't believe Father let us turn the Throne Room into a club."

"That was a brilliant idea, and a smash hit. I heard loads of people talking about it." Kerry squeezed Sasha's hand. "Are you cold? Want my jacket?"

"I'm fine. But thank you." Kerry's solicitousness always made her feel warm inside. Cherished. "You would have made a perfect Knight of the Round Table, you know."

Kerry laughed. "If Arthur ever decides to bring back that tradition, maybe I'll apply for a seat."

They walked on for a while, chatting about their favorite parts of the ceremony and afternoon luncheon, until Sasha realized they were crossing the street. "Where are you taking me?"

"We're almost at Parliament." Kerry gestured toward the imposing façade. Big Ben's face was especially bright this evening under the light of a nearly full moon. "Since we're in the neighborhood, I thought we might duck into Westminster Hall for a minute."

Since the beginning of the summer, Kerry had been involved in a project to renovate the oldest part of Westminster Palace. Sasha had no idea why she had chosen this moment to show off her work, but she certainly wanted to be supportive. "I'd love to see how it's coming along."

On their way into the palace, they met three different pairs of security guards, all of whom were very happy to let them pass once they'd had a good look at Sasha. Several of them also knew Kerry by name. The last of the guards were positioned directly in front of the hall, and they stepped aside with a murmured, "Your Royal Highness."

Kerry took a key from her pocket and opened the lock on the thick chain binding the doors together. She threaded the links through the handles and wound the chain around her arm before handing it to the nearest guard. And then, with a grin over her shoulder, she gave the doors a strong push. They parted slowly to reveal the hall that had once been the epicenter of the English monarchy's power.

"Shall we?" Kerry extended her arm, beckoning Sasha over the threshold. As the doors swung shut behind them, Sasha took the opportunity to survey the space as she'd never done before. Always impressive, it seemed much larger when empty. She looked up at the ornate wooden roof with its arched trusses that marched the length of the hall. Moonlight filtered through the large window overlooking the dais at the far end, creating a shimmering pool of light in the center of the raised platform.

"Follow me." Kerry gently tugged at their joined hands.

"What sort of roof is that called again?" Sasha asked as she was led down the center aisle.

"It's a hammer-beam roof. Richard II had it built in the late fourteenth century. We've had to reinforce a few sections, but it's nearly finished." Kerry pointed out a scaffold that had been erected along part of one wall.

"I heard your president address Parliament here a few years ago."

"Did he do a good job?"

"I'm afraid I didn't pay close attention." Sasha felt a twinge of guilt for her rebellious past. She had felt like such an outsider in her family until Kerry had helped her see where she fit.

"I bet he was nervous. Come on, let's go stand where he did."

"Oh? Do you have presidential aspirations?" Sasha meant it as a joke—mostly. Sometimes she worried that Kerry would become homesick for her native land, or sacrifice some excellent career opportunity in the States to remain with her in the UK.

"Hardly." Kerry made a face. "What a thankless job. Besides, all my aspirations are on this side of the Pond." They reached the dais, and she gestured toward the stairs. "After you."

As soon as she had climbed up, Sasha found herself enveloped by the silvery spotlight created by the moon. She spun in a slow circle, taking in the entirety of the hall. An anticipatory hush pervaded the space, as though the wooden timbers themselves were waiting for something. Sasha turned to face Kerry…and found her down on one knee, hand outstretched, a ring nestled in the center of her palm. She gasped.

"Alexandra Victoria Jane." Kerry's voice shook slightly, and as Sasha watched in stunned silence, she moistened her lips with the tip of her tongue. "I've fallen more deeply in love with you than I ever thought possible. Before I met you, I didn't know enough to even dream of a romance like this. There is nothing I want more than the chance to make you happy every day for the rest of our lives." She had to pause to catch her breath, but her gaze never left Sasha's. "Will you marry me?"

Sasha could barely think over the roaring in her ears, but as she stared down at Kerry, one thing became clear. This whole plan—leaving the reception, their walk along the park, turning in to the palace—had been premeditated. Orchestrated. Kerry had brought her here expressly to propose. Sasha couldn't believe this was happening.

"No!"

Kerry rocked backward as though she'd been physically struck, and her face began to crumple before she ducked her head. Only then did Sasha realize exactly what she had said, and in horror, she sank to the floor, mindless of the dust.

"Yes! I mean yes! Yes, of course I'll marry you." She cupped Kerry's face and forced her to look up, wanting to slap herself when she saw the tears shimmering in those blue depths. What a bloody idiot she was.

"Yes?" Kerry's voice cracked. "Are you sure?"

Tenderly, Sasha raised her thumbs to wipe away the two tiny droplets that had escaped the corners of her eyes. "Yes. I want to marry you more than…than anything."

"Then why did you say no?"

Sasha leaned forward to press their lips together as she thought of how to reply. If she told the truth, she would ruin her surprise. But on the other hand, she had almost just ruined Kerry's beautiful proposal.

"Because tomorrow, I'm going to offer *you* a ring."

Kerry frowned. "You are?"

"Yes. I have a plan involving scones, horses, and the Scottish Highlands. Ian is in on it." Sasha stroked Kerry's cheekbones. "And now you've gotten there first."

To Sasha's immense relief, Kerry let out a small laugh. "Really?"

"Truly. I'm so sorry that 'no' leapt out of my mouth. I was just in shock that you'd managed to beat me to the punch."

Finally, Kerry smiled—that wide, open smile reserved only for her. "I'm precocious, remember?"

"How could I forget?" Sasha kissed her again. "Can you forgive me?"

"There's nothing to forgive."

They knelt together on the dais, Sasha searching Kerry's eyes until she was sure no sign of pain lingered. "May I please see my ring now?"

"Of course." Kerry helped her up and then opened her hand. Sasha plucked the ring from her palm, inspecting it in the light. It was like nothing she'd ever seen before—a tapering spiral made from a dark, heavy material, its surface inlaid with small diamonds. A flash of green caught her gaze, and she realized that an emerald had been set into the broad end of the spiral.

"I made it." Kerry sounded nervous again, her words tumbling out in a rush. "From a nail I removed from this roof. It probably belongs in a museum, but everyone insisted I should keep it as a memento." She pointed to the interior of the ring. "First, I had to forge it into the spiral shape. It's inlaid with platinum here, where it will touch your finger. The emerald at the nail head is from a ring of my great-grandmother's, which she got in Ireland. It reminded me of your eyes. And the diamonds... well, they're forever. Which is what I want us to be."

For the second time in the past several minutes, Sasha couldn't believe her ears. "You made this? How? When?"

"There's a studio at Oxford. One of the Fine Arts students helped me. Every time we had to be apart because you had something official to do, I'd lock myself in there for hours." Kerry reached out to tuck a strand of hair behind Sasha's ear. "I wanted it to represent our relationship. Strong. Enduring. Precious."

"I love it." Sasha could barely speak through the emotion constricting her throat. "I love how it looks. I love that you created it and how much thought you put into its symbolism. I love you, Kerry."

"I love you, Sasha. So much." Kerry carefully took the ring between her fingers. "Hold out your hand." When she obeyed, Kerry positioned it at the very tip of her finger and then looked down into her eyes. "A princess belongs to her people. I know that will always be true. But I also want you to be mine."

She slid the ring into place, then bent to kiss it. When she withdrew, Sasha looked down at the sparkling diamonds, made all the more brilliant by the dark surface into which they'd been set. The ring fit perfectly. It felt so *right* on her hand, just as the presence of Kerry felt in her life.

"I am yours." She threaded her arms around Kerry's neck. "You're the only one who will ever know all of me. I will always belong to you in a way I belong to no one else."

The kiss was gentle but firm, like the promises they had just exchanged. It seemed to go on forever—Kerry's mouth moving over hers with tender purpose, Kerry's arms holding her close. When it finally ended, Sasha rested her cheek against Kerry's chest, listening to the rhythm of her heartbeat. One year ago, she wouldn't have been able to imagine this moment. Now she couldn't imagine a life without Kerry by her side.

"Shall we go back?" Kerry asked after several minutes had passed in silence. "You promised Lizzie, after all."

"I did." Sasha reluctantly took a step backward. "But just so you're prepared, at the first opportunity, I am dragging you off to bed."

"No dragging required." Kerry's eyes grew a shade darker. "I want to know what it's like to make love to my fiancée."

Sasha shivered at the note of intensity lacing her voice. "That sounds so good. Every word." Together, they descended the dais, but when they reached its foot, a sudden thought gave her pause. "I just have one favor to ask."

"Oh?"

"You're the most genuine person I've ever met. I love that about you. But tomorrow…can you pretend to be surprised?"

Kerry's burst of laughter echoed through Westminster Hall, filling its dark corners with sound. "I'll certainly do my best."

"That's all I can ask." She pulled Kerry forward. "Come on. Let's tell our family the good news."

Rebekah Weatherspoon was raised in southern New Hampshire and now lives in Southern California where she has spent the last several years working in film and television production. She has a degree in European literature from the University of North Carolina at Charlotte. Her love of writing keeps her busy and, occasionally, out of trouble.

This story features characters from *Blacker Than Blue*.

HER QUEEN'S HAPPINESS
REBEKAH WEATHERSPOON

I clicked over the volume button and turned my music up a little louder. The bass pounded hard enough to make my skin vibrate, but I didn't mind. A notch higher might even do the trick, swallow up some of the noise in my head. I considered my keyboard for a second, then did just that. Cranked it up just a little bit more, setting the walls and bookshelves in the room on vibrate too. The insulated walls and reinforced concrete surrounding me would muffle the beats even if I jacked the volume up as high as it could go. Not that I would be disturbing anyone. It was the middle of July. The floors of the sorority house above were empty, the girls of Alpha Beta Omega home for the summer. A few were studying abroad and two, carrying a double major, were still in town taking summer classes but living on campus. The house was basically empty.

The music wouldn't bother Ginger either, but she was still away.

Minimizing the player, I clicked back over my email and looked at the pictures Laura had sent over from the shop, different angles of a skull she'd tattooed on an orange. Her first piece. I smiled again at the precision in her work. Her parents flipped out the moment they found out their oldest daughter had decided to leverage her fine arts degree from Maryland University into an apprenticeship at a tattoo shop. We spared them the aneurysm of knowing the shop was owned by a vampire.

I clicked on her second piece, a bleeding heart on a banana. Very good work. I wanted to show Ginger. She could see the images in my head if I thought about them hard enough, but I wanted her to see them in person, while she was sitting on my lap.

"Hey! Turn it down!"

I spun my chair around to find my sister-queen Kina standing in the doorway. Our sister-queen Faeth stood right behind her.

"Sorry." I hit the volume button in the other direction and my office stopped shaking.

"Fuck. Are you going deaf?" Kina went on, playfully digging in her ear.

"No."

"I hope you don't listen to that crap outside of the house, giving us Native girls a bad name with your shitty taste in music."

I mustered up a smile. "Dubstep's the future."

"Dubstep is crap. Sounds like someone is trying to murder a robot."

"I like it," Faeth said with a shrug and a little jolt of her straight hips. "Gets the blood pumping, yeah?"

"You're both crazy." Then Kina kicked her head back in the direction of the door. "We're taking off, so you have the whole house to yourself. You can run around naked upstairs if you want. Omi's at home with Mary, and Natasha and Rodrick are somewhere downtown handling Tokyo's need to be tied up and smacked around."

"Tempting, but I'm fine right here. Where are you going?"

"Babysit Jillian."

"Is this your first time babysitting?" I asked Faeth. Benny and Cleo had just recently caved to the idea of leaving their daughter with someone who wasn't the child's grandmother. Jillian was a sweet baby, but if my own vivid memories of motherhood served me correctly, watching an infant took some work.

"No. I used to watch my little brother. It was forty-five years ago, but the basics are fresh. Besides, our friend here will be on diaper duty." Faeth grinned, flashing her fangs as she lightly punched Kina on the shoulder.

I drummed up another smile this time and a little bit of a chuckle.

Kina turned to Faeth. "Go on without me. I'll be there in a sec."

Faeth glanced between us a moment before she nodded with her own weak smile. Then she vanished.

"You all right?" Kina asked.

There was no point in lying to her. Our sister-queen bond made us sensitive to each other's moods. That bond and the fact that Kina and I had been friends for almost a hundred years, and lovers for more than half that time, gave her a unique ability to tell when something was off with me. I rubbed my face and leaned forward in my chair.

"Ginger saw her uncle yesterday."

The air sucked through Kina's teeth, making that painfully sympathetic sound that let me know I didn't need to explain any further.

"And she's not back yet?"

"No. She's at her parents'. I don't know what to do."

"Go to her."

I shook my head. "She really wants to be alone. I don't...I don't want to barge in on her."

"Hey, listen. I know I've never experienced anything like your mating bond. What you and your na'suul have is special and strong." Both an understatement. "But I know a thing or two about women." Now, that much was true. "Go to her. She might want to be alone, but if she's hurting, she's gonna need her wife."

I wish I could deny that Kina was making sense, but I knew she was right. Ginger was hurting. I could feel her pain and her frustration and even the tears she'd shed in the hours since she'd left her uncle's home in London. It was like this every time they saw each other. Months would pass without Ginger mentioning Seamus's name. She'd only known the man existed for a few years. A horrible series of events had led to Ginger's birth and their separation. The discovery of our love, the first real sense of salvation in *my* immortal life, was soon followed by Ginger's own human life ending, abruptly. And just as abruptly Seamus had been thrust in front of her, presented by our Master as the missing piece to her past.

Ginger still hadn't figured out how she felt about him, but the emotions around their visits had formed a pattern. The hopefulness and anticipation. Somehow this time things would be less awkward. But the disappointment would settle in sometime toward the end of their time together, and then the guilt. She'd return to me...cranky, for the lack of a better word. Closed off. We'd make it a few hours, possibly feed and then make love, before Ginger would vanish to her parents' house for hours before returning with a smile on her face, all of the pain shrugged off. The complicated part was our marriage bond allowed me to feel all those emotions she pushed aside while putting on a happy façade for our girls and our sisters and for me. Each visit things got worse and worse. She hadn't come back to me cranky this time. She hadn't come back to me at all.

Maybe Kina had a point. I had to go see my Red.

"I'll give her a little more time."

"Don't wait too long. You know she needs you. But put on some pants first." After my grunt of agreement—wouldn't be a good idea to show up at my in-laws' house in underwear and a tank top—Kina squeezed my shoulder. "You know where to find us." Then she was gone.

My music was cranked back up. After all, now I really was alone. I sent Laura a text to stroke her ego a bit and lend some encouragement.

I paced.

I made it fifteen minutes. I couldn't wait any longer. After I threw on some jeans, one of Ginger's hoodies, and my sneakers, I vanished to my in-laws' and appeared on the side of their house.

It was a quiet summer night in Reading, Mass. The streetlights in the Carmichaels' neighborhood let out a low buzz only a sensitive or patient ear could detect. The crickets and other little yard creatures joined in with their tiny chirping. I let myself in through the garage door and knocked lightly on the kitchen door just inside. A special knock to let Red's family know there was a vampire at the door. Linda and Fredo were watching TV, but I didn't want to just appear in their living room.

Linda called out for me to come in. I found my mother-in-law on the couch watching *Antiques Roadshow*, her husband passed out with his head in her lap. His long legs were hanging off the edge of the arm of the couch.

"Hi, sweetheart. I'd get up and kiss you, but…" She motioned to her husband's dead weight.

"It's okay. I just came to check on Ginger."

"Is my darling daughter nearby?"

"She's on the roof."

"I told you I heard something." Fredo coughed and rolled over. "Hey, Camila. Can you go up there and get her?"

"That's the plan. If you'll excuse me."

I vanished up to the roof and appeared near the chimney. Ginger was a dozen or so feet away, looking out over the street. Her knees were pulled up to her chest and her chin rested on her arms. I could still smell her tears swirled with her light, sweet fruity scent that flared the moment I showed up.

Please go away. Her voice was clear in my head before I could take a step closer, raw and aching.

I hesitated a moment before I replied. My demon had to obey its queen, but as a wife…it wasn't so easy to just walk away. *Are you sure?*

Ginger sighed, then spoke out loud. "No."

I crossed the roof and sat down beside her, facing the backyard as our bodies touched, shoulder and side. I couldn't ignore the heat that sparked over my skin at the simple contact, even through her hoodie and the leather jacket of mine she was wearing. Red was my everything. She sighed again and moved a little closer, but kept her chin buried in her arms.

"Tell me what happened."

"Nothing," Red replied, annoyed. But not with me. "We met at his house. We went to dinner. We talked. Well, I talked and he muttered. We met up with a few of his demon friends and their feeders. They talked and then I came home. I mean, I came here."

"This is still home for you, baby."

"I know. I didn't mean it to sound like that. That's all."

This conversation wasn't going as I'd planned. Her frustration was surging all over again. I had to try something else. "Come here."

As Ginger let her feet slide lightly down the shingled roof, I wrapped my arm around her waist, under the warm leather. Her arm came around my waist just the same and she laid her head on my shoulder. I kissed her ear. Instantly her heartbeat settled.

"I just—I can't get a read on him. It's like it hurts him to look at me, but he still wants me around."

"Of course he does. Why wouldn't he?"

She peeked up at me. "You're just saying that."

"No, I'm—"

"You are."

"I'm sorry, *querida.*" It was my turn to sigh. I couldn't help encouraging her. Making Red feel loved was my job and my honor. My words and intentions were genuine, but my reassurance didn't change the truth of Ginger's experience or her uncle's. I'd barely spent any time with Seamus, but I knew the pain he carried. It was evident in his eyes every time he looked at Ginger. It wasn't a pain that just went away. I would know. It was the kind of agony that thrived on resistance. The kind of pain that would force him to keep Ginger at arm's length. He couldn't get close to her. He'd already lost a young woman he'd loved.

If I could sense that pain and reluctance from my vantage point, there was no way it didn't slap Ginger in the face every moment they spent together. It was clear from the thoughts swimming around her mind and the tears she'd shed.

"Freak act of violence ruined his life. He lost my mom forever and I'm this kid that he wanted when he was human, but I'm not even his. He hates my birth father and now I'm pain for him and he's pain for me, but we need each other. He reminds me of my mother, like this version of this person I never got to know because she was already destroyed by the time I was born. But he knew her before the drugs and the stripping. All that crap. He's the only good part of her left."

"That's not true."

"I'll let that slide because you're right. We are blood and I am pretty amazing," she replied with a heated scowl.

I tipped her chin up and kissed her soft lips. What was meant to be a peck quickly shifted to something more intense as her tongue slid into my mouth. The human side of my love was still upset and a little defensive. Our demons, though, couldn't resist their instinctual draw.

I'm not defensive, she growled, but she kept kissing me. Her hand slid up and over my breast and soon her demon took over. Mine followed suit, steadying us on the ridge of the roof as she continued to explore my body. Her hand journeyed lower, shoving its way into my pants, pushing my underwear aside. I was always wet for her, night and day, and now was no exception. I came easily, purring against her lips after only a few strokes of her fingers against my clit. That was all it took. Oftentimes, it took less. I wanted more, but instead we slowed down. This was not the right place for what else we had in mind.

I pulled back, running my fangs down the side of her neck. She arched closer and squeezed my thigh.

"Does this stop?" she asked quietly. "Actually, never mind. I've seen your thoughts. I know it doesn't."

"That doesn't mean we don't have to talk about it. Being immortal doesn't change the way you feel about certain things, like your family or your past. Being immortal just gives you more time to think about things."

"I don't want to think anymore."

"I'm not sure how well the rest of you would work if you didn't have this noodle running the show."

"You're not helping, *Mila*. I want to be sad."

I smiled at her adorable pout and brushed her long red hair off her cheek. "Have you told him how you feel?"

"It's not about how I feel. It's about how *he* feels, how *he* acts. What he's *not* saying."

"What do you want him to say?" I felt a rush of anguish flow through her as she grasped on to a few truths that not only hurt her to acknowledge, but embarrassed her as well. I kissed her again.

"I don't know." Another painful breath released.

"That may be where you find a solution. You might need to decide what you really want from him and ask for it."

"Is it that simple?"

"For your part? Yes. He may give you the answer you want or he may not, but at least you tried to bridge that gap. You can't change who he is and how he feels, but you can let him know how he is making you feel."

"You and Dalhem went through something like this, didn't you?" she asked, knowing only part of the answer.

When Ginger and I were bound as na'suul, the strongest mating bond demons like us can form, she saw flashes of my whole life, knew me in a way no one else did, but only glimpses and pieces of what my life had been before her. The details were still up for discussion. I thought of the months after my family was taken from me, my parents and my brothers. My husband and my sons. The years Dalhem mourned for his demon-bourne twin who had sacrificed himself to save me. I dredged up the memories of the time Dalhem had pushed me away.

"He sent me to live with Kina and her maker. He couldn't bear—"

"It was more than just looking at you. He couldn't deal when it came to thinking about you and your life. Knowing that you existed meant that his brother didn't."

I looked into her lovely green eyes, the emerald green she shared with her uncle. "Exactly."

"That's how Seamus feels about me. But you and Dalhem didn't talk about it."

"Because he's not now, and never was, human. Because he's Dalhem. Only his mate sees the true spectrum of his emotions, and even then, I'm not sure she gets it all."

Ginger pulled her hand out of my pants and licked her fingers. She knew exactly what that did to me. "I'm ready to go home."

We harnessed our demons and managed to say a proper good-bye to Linda and Fredo. Linda hugged us both and made us promise we'd be by later in the week for dinner. And less time spent on the roof. Then Ginger took my hand and vanished us back to our apartment.

We ended up in our bedroom. I knew what Ginger wanted, but for a moment I had to check in with her. I knew her thoughts and her motivations, but sometimes we ignore what we need in order to get what we want. She started advancing on me, shedding her clothes as we slowly circled the bed.

"Do you need to feed?" I asked her.

"No. I'm fine for another day." I knew she was telling the truth. "Is there a reason you're trying to avoid having sex with me?" She was in my mind, but she wanted me to tell her out loud.

"Uh, I think you're still upset and you're avoiding talking more about things. I don't necessarily object, I just want to make sure you're okay."

"I'll be okay when you have sex with me." Her fangs gripped onto her bottom lip, which made every logical thought I'd ever had evacuate my brain. I shed her borrowed sweatshirt and took a few steps closer.

"Promise me something."

She came to me and unzipped my jeans. With a quick tug, she yanked them down my legs. "Anything."

"Promise you'll keep talking to me. I know we can see each other's thoughts and sense each other's emotions, but—"

"I know."

I let my demon take control then, and as always the monster that shared control of my body and soul followed its queen's lead and gave into her demands. She wanted me naked first, up against the dresser with my legs around her ass, my heels pressed to her thighs. My cunt and my breasts at her disposal to lick and bite and stroke.

And then bent over the dresser where her fingers fucked me

senseless and her fangs dug into the skin of my back. She drew blood for the first time that day. I came as she licked it away.

On the bed she wanted me vocal as she straddled my crotch, grinding our pussies together as her fang pierced my knee. She wanted me to beg and plead, so I did as I gripped her leg with one hand and her breast with the other. She wanted to know exactly how I liked it, how well she was giving it to me. I gave her every truth that came to mind. I told her that I wanted more.

She collapsed on the sheets, begging for me to take control, to finish what she had started, what *I'd* started on the roof. I buried my face between her legs with my tongue lapping at her sweet slit and my fingers fucking her tight ass. She came again and again, screamed finally when my fangs latched on to her inner thigh. I didn't stop until her sweet queen's blood coated my lips.

When I woke up, Ginger was across the room in one of our oversized chairs. Her arm was wrapped around her legs again, and her phone was to her ear.

"It's Ginger."

"My caller ID's workin'."

I could hear the sarcasm in Seamus's Scottish burr.

Ginger read it as well and laughed a bit. "Sorry. I—I wanted to talk to you about my mom. About Janet."

"You want to know about her?"

"Yeah."

"Makes sense. I suppose we should have talked about her first thing, aye?"

"Yeah, maybe."

"What say you give me a little time. You know, give me a little while to figure out what I need to say."

"We can do that."

"Okay. I'll talk to ya soon."

She hung up and tossed her phone to the other chair. I took that as my cue to join her. I crossed the room and scooped Red up and sat her in my lap. Tears laced with a hint of blue shimmered in her eyes. I wiped her cheeks for her and kissed them both.

"I figured out what I needed and I asked for it," she said. "Now let's just hope he comes through with something."

"I'm sure he will."

❖

The next day a little after dark, Ginger got a call from Seamus. He was out behind the sorority house. She vanished out to see him and when she came back, she had a small bunch of envelopes in her hand. Only one of them was new.

"This one's for me, but the others are for him."

"Do you want a few minutes alone?" I asked as she tore into the first letter.

"No." She plopped down in the chair and patted the seat behind her. "I want you to read this with me."

I joined her without hesitation, pulling her tight between my legs with my arms around her waist. We read the letter from Seamus together.

Dear Ginger,

I'm glad you called me and made me man up to my shortcomings. You are very dear to me, and I apologize for being such a rotten arse these past few years. Here's the truth about your mother. You are the exact image of her I have burned in my mind, with the exception of your hair. I hate that my bastard of a brother got to claim you as his own, but I thank God every day that he and I looked so much alike that I get to see bits of me in your face. I love the parts of you that are your mother, and that is to say nearly all of you. You have the McMillan wit about you. Don't think I missed that crack you made about our waitress the other day, you wee little shit. Her teeth were boxing for the championship belt. But you've also got your mother's charm and her ease. You've got her light.

I blame myself for her death. I blame myself for the abuse she and you suffered at my brother's hand. I blame myself for the years you had to spend without a family, and even now, I blame myself for the distance between us. I'm right jealous of what you have with your Camila because I know I'll never find that love for myself again. Your mother was my queen. I know you're a Carmichael now, but you were born a McMillan and you'll always be one of ours.

I hope this helps mend things between us. Or at least starts the process.

Your Uncle, Seamus

P.S. I suppose I could have sent this in an email for you to keep electronically, but my da always taught me when you mean to really say something to someone, particularly someone you love, you write it down. These were from your mother. Ignore the X-rated bits.

We read the letters he sent along, handwritten love notes from her mother from the late '80s. Her mom and her uncle had been so in love, and Seamus was right, the voice on those pages was so much like Ginger's, it amazed me. Janet cracked inappropriate jokes. She lusted heavily for her man, and when she got especially emotional, she rambled, just like Ginger. Red had started crying about halfway through Seamus's letter, and by the time she finished her mother's words to him, she was a sobbing wreck on my shoulder. But there was happiness in those tears. A small sense of closure and reassurance that Ginger's mother had died of a broken heart and not the burden of caring for Ginger alone.

I held her until the tears stopped, until she was ready to talk again. It was everything to me to see a small smile creep across her lips.

"I forgot how funny she was. When she wasn't high or passed out, she was always trying to make me laugh, always trying to make it so we had a good time. He's right. She had this light about her."

"It's here," I told her, placing my hand over her heart. Then I kissed her forehead. "And here."

"Thank you for pushing me to talk to him. You were right."

"I don't care if I'm right when it comes to you," I told her. "I just care if you're happy."

She kissed me once more as she whispered, *I am.*

Erin Dutton lives near Nashville with her amazing partner and often draws inspiration from both her adopted hometown and places she's traveled. When not working or writing, she enjoys golf, photography and spending time with family and friends. Look for her at www.erindutton.com or at facebook.com/erin.dutton.

This story features characters from *Fully Involved*.

FAMILY FIRST
ERIN DUTTON

"Ms. Webb, you can go in now," the nurse said as she exited the hospital room and held open the door.

Reid nodded. "Thank you. I just need a minute."

The nurse gave her an understanding look and let the door swing closed. She wheeled her cart into the next room, leaving Reid alone in the hallway.

Reid stared through the window at the man lying in the bed, uncertain if she could force herself inside or if she would flee. She didn't want to be here. But even she couldn't ignore the phone call informing her that her estranged father had been admitted to the hospital.

"How long have you been standing out here?" Isabel pressed against her back and slid her arms around her waist.

"He had a visitor and then the nurse went in." Reid's excuse covered the last thirty minutes but didn't explain why she'd avoided the inside of that room for the last several hours. After getting the call, she'd left work and come to the hospital, thinking of her mother. Despite divorcing her father many years ago, her mother would no doubt be at his side now. But Reid had avoided his room, instead busying herself with speaking to his doctors and updating family members by phone.

"Are you ever going in?"

She shrugged. "I talked to his buddy when he came out. Apparently, he's also my father's sponsor."

"Am I supposed to ignore the fact that you didn't answer my question?"

"Yep. He's got four months sober."

"Wow."

"Yeah, well, liver disease will do that to you." The diagnosis wasn't unexpected, but the fact that it had been enough to stop her father's drinking surprised her. She hadn't talked to him in over a year, and the last time had been as contentious as always. She had dodged a handful of phone calls several months ago, which she now figured probably coincided with his diagnosis.

"Oh, honey." Isabel held her tighter and rested her chin on her shoulder.

"He said Pop talked about me at their meetings. When I asked what he said, he suggested I ask him."

"Maybe you should."

"I don't know if I can. It's like he's two different men. The father I grew up with, and then the drunk who abandoned us. I'd come to terms with that in my mind. And now—now I'm supposed to forget all of that because he's sick?"

"Despite his faults, you became a firefighter at least partly because of him. I know he hasn't told you in a long time, but he's proud of you. I only wish he hadn't thrown away the chance to know the woman you turned out to be, because you are pretty damn amazing."

"Yeah?"

"Yes. You're strong and faithful. And you take care of your family."

"I hope you can always say that." Reid covered Isabel's hands and squeezed. As a firefighter, she was accustomed to being strong for her crew and, at home, for Chase and Isabel. Since they were children, she'd wanted to protect Isabel. She'd loved her for as long as she could remember, but in the past four years, Isabel had returned that love in ways Reid had never dreamed possible. "I would never want you and Chase to feel as if I wasn't there for you."

"You don't have to worry about that. And maybe your dad will get the opportunity to see it, too."

Reid nodded, but she wasn't as hopeful as Isabel sounded. The liver specialist had gathered them in a conference room and laid out her father's slim chances for recovery from that point. After that meeting, Reid could see why her father had chosen him as his doctor. He delivered the news bluntly with little regard for emotions. His bedside manner sucked, but that's what her father would have needed to stop drinking—a cold, harsh wake-up call.

Apparently, her father had been seeing him for several months, since his symptoms had become too severe to ignore any longer. His sobriety had sparked some improvement, but this latest bad turn didn't bode well.

"You should talk to him." Isabel released her and took a step away, but kept hold of her hand.

"So I have to be the bigger person because he's dying?"

"Won't you regret it if you don't at least try? I think you need this more than you want to admit."

"What will I say?"

"Everything you're afraid to say—even the bits that will hurt you both." Isabel stroked Reid's jaw. "Then tell him how you love him anyway. Leave no regrets."

Could she do that? Could she tell her father how disappointed she'd been these past years, then let go of it and forgive him? Certainly their relationship hadn't turned out the way she wanted, maybe not the way he'd wanted either. But neither of them could change the past. And once she stopped trying to do that, she was left only with the simple fact that he was her father and she loved him. He tended to be even more emotionally closed off than she was, so just the thought of slogging through all of this touchy-feely stuff with him exhausted her.

"You don't have to do it all this minute. Just start the dialogue." Isabel rubbed Reid's shoulder, then pulled her in and hugged her.

"Will you stay?" Reid whispered next to her ear.

"I'll be right here waiting for you."

She touched Isabel's cheek and kissed her, letting her lips linger. She cupped the back of Isabel's neck and held her close for a moment, breathing deeply as if she could draw strength from Isabel's nearness.

When she turned and put her hand on the hospital room door, that first step away from Isabel was one of the hardest she'd ever taken.

❖

"Hi, Pop," Reid rasped as she stepped inside, surprised by the rush of emotion that choked her voice when she saw him lying there.

Over the years, she'd seen his body change as a result of his drinking. But the transformation since she'd last seen him was devastating. Her father had always been a blue-collar man, but his normally weathered, ruddy face now looked pale and waxy. The hollows of his cheeks sagged, pulling the corners of his mouth down. Just above the line of the sheet over his body, his bony shoulders poked out under the thin hospital gown.

"Reid?" He opened his eyes, but didn't quite seem able to focus on her in the dim light of the room.

"Yeah, it's me." She moved close to the bed, grasping the back of a chair to steady herself against the onslaught of feelings. Suddenly her chest ached and tears stung her eyes.

"Don't do that."

She braced for a lecture about how tears were a waste—about how she should buck up.

"I don't deserve your tears." He met her eyes. "I'm sorry, Reid."

She stared at him, taken aback by both the quick apology and his pained expression. Suddenly she couldn't find a single word to express her feelings and she struggled to recall enough of her conversation with Isabel to borrow some of hers.

"Sit down—please."

Stubbornly, she crossed to the window instead, turning her back to him. Outside in the parking lot, a man helped an old woman from a car, then handed her a cane.

He sighed deeply. "I'm supposed to make amends—as part of the steps."

Reid watched the man's halted steps as he walked beside the woman, practically feeling his impatience with her slow gait.

"Look at me when I'm talking to you." Her father's stern tone felt familiar.

She turned.

"I keep thinking about how I used to take you to the station with me. No matter how many frilly dresses your mother tried to put you in, I couldn't keep you from climbing on the engines. I finally had to tell her that for the sake of your decency, she'd better let you wear the little pants you preferred."

"I never thanked you for that, did I?"

"You loved going down there with me, and the guys loved having you there."

The guys loved it. He didn't say that he'd enjoyed it.

"I bet you have similar memories with Chase."

"You might too if you'd been around," she snapped before she could stop herself. She bit her lower lip to keep from saying anything else.

"Hell, I'm no good at this stuff." The stubble of his buzz cut rasped against his palm as he rubbed his hand over his thinning hair.

She returned to his bedside and dropped into the chair. This would have been easier if he wasn't obviously trying so damn hard. "Neither am I."

"Yeah, well, you get that from me. Your mother can talk about feelings until you'd think your ears might bleed."

"She's not that bad."

"My point is, you and I, we don't do that."

She shrugged, thinking of how Isabel had opened up her world. She glanced at the closed door, imagining Isabel waiting for her on the other side. "I'm getting better at it."

He looked at the door, too. "Your mother told me. Isabel Grant, huh?"

She nodded, sitting up straighter and pushing her shoulders back.

"Good for you. She's a good girl." He reached through the rail of the bed and picked up a shiny blue coin from the nightstand. "I want you to have this."

She took the coin in her hand and flipped it over. "What is it?"

"It's my ninety-day coin."

"I can't take this."

"Keep it. God willing, I'll live long enough to get my six-month coin. I know I'm about a decade too late. But I don't know how much time I have left—"

"Pop—"

"Let me get this out while I can. I did a lot of things wrong with you, kid. But it was my failure, not yours. What you've done—taking in Chase and making a family with Isabel. I'm proud of you. Don't ever put anything in front of them."

"I don't. If there's one thing you've taught me, it's that." Guilt stabbed through her at his stricken expression. "Shit," she hissed, propelling herself out of her chair. "I guess I've got a lot of anger that I have to figure out how to let go of. You let me down."

"I know."

She couldn't handle the resignation in his tone. Was that supposed to be enough? She couldn't dissolve years of pain simply because he apologized. She needed to blow up—to rant about what he'd cheated them out of and how much easier losing Jimmy might have been for all of them if he'd been around and been the kind of father she needed.

She paced the length of the room, then turned back toward him. He looked tired, more so than when she came in here. "I'll try, okay? That's all I can promise."

"That's all I'm asking for. We'll work on it. You're my only daughter. I've missed you."

She nodded and swallowed hard. That was the closest he'd come to saying he loved her in a long time. She hated that she still wanted so badly to hear it. "You need to rest."

"You look like you do, too. Will you come back?"

"Yeah." She strode across the room, suddenly feeling suffocated.

She stepped into the hallway and pulled the door shut without looking back. Immediately, Isabel embraced her. But the stifling sense of not being able to catch her breath didn't ease. She pulled away, meeting Isabel's confused gaze.

"I need to get out of here."

"I'll take you home."

"No. I'll drive myself."

"Are you okay? What happened in there?" Isabel reached for her, but Reid backed away.

"Can we talk about it later? I'll meet you at home."

Isabel nodded. Reid couldn't get down the hall and into the elevator fast enough. Outside, she climbed into her truck and rolled the windows down, then sped away. She hadn't run away from Isabel in a long time, but spending time with her father brought back some long-buried fears and pain. And she needed to face them herself before she was ready to bare them to Isabel.

Reid stood at the railing on her back porch, staring into the yard. She clung to the familiar sights around her—the swing set where Chase played and the hammock where she and Isabel liked to lie on clear evenings. Closing her eyes, she imagined herself in that hammock with Isabel's warmth against her body. The hammock would swing gently in a breeze that stirred the scent of dried, fallen leaves. Whenever Isabel would sneak her hand under the hem of her shirt and rest it against her stomach, she felt protected—which was rare for her.

The screen door creaked, but Reid didn't turn around, instead enjoying a moment of anticipation before Isabel appeared beside her.

"Are you okay?" Isabel asked as she pressed their shoulders together.

Reid nodded, not quite trusting her voice through a sudden rush of emotion. She'd been fighting a breakdown all day and Isabel pulled at her defenses.

"Want to talk about it?"

She shook her head slowly. "Not yet."

"Why don't you go change and put on something comfortable? I'll make you some dinner."

"I'm not hungry."

"Have you eaten anything today?"

"No." She'd been in a fog since the phone call. In fact, she still wore her BDU pants and a navy T-shirt emblazoned with the department logo that she'd put on for work that morning.

"I should go to the station." She could immerse herself in work, insulate herself from the feelings assaulting her now.

"I thought you said Megan called someone to cover for you."

"She did. But there's no need to pay overtime when I can be there."

"No."

"Iz—"

"No. When you respond to a bad call, I give you space until you want to talk about it. I've watched you work it out with your crew and I do my best not to take it personally when you seem to shut me out. But this…is personal. And you're going to let me in. Maybe not right this minute. But you won't run away from me either."

She would let her in. She shielded Isabel from many of the things she saw on the job, but not because she needed to protect herself from Isabel. She'd long ago given up on that. She would give Isabel everything and didn't need to hold anything back. She turned and draped her arms around Isabel's shoulders, sighing with relief when Isabel's arms tightened around her waist.

She felt as if she'd been fighting a five-alarm fire. The emotional beating she'd taken today magnified her physical exhaustion. And now it took every ounce of strength she had to remain upright and cling to Isabel. She fisted her hands in the back of Isabel's cotton shirt, pressed her cheek against her neck, and breathed in deeply. The light, blackberry-scented body spray Isabel preferred mixed with her chemistry to create a scent more intoxicating than any expensive perfume.

"Come inside." Isabel took her hand and led her into the kitchen. She crossed to the cabinet and got a frying pan.

"I don't think I can eat." Reid took the pan from Isabel and set it on the counter. "I told you, I'm not hungry."

Isabel laid her hand against Reid's cheek. "I just want to take care of you."

"Okay." She took Isabel's hand and led her down the hall toward their bedroom. She stopped beside their bed and held her arms out at her sides. "You may begin pampering me now."

Isabel smiled and stepped closer. She rested her fingertips against Reid's collarbones. "Your uniform still confuses me." She swept her fingers across her chest to her shoulders. "I want to hate them, but whether like this, or in your Class A's, or all sooty and sweating in your turnout gear," she grinned wide and winked, "especially then, you're so damn sexy."

"Well, I wouldn't want to confuse you." Reid grasped the hem of her shirt and lifted it over her head. She dropped it on the floor beside the bed and reached for the waistband of her pants, but Isabel shooed her hands aside.

"Let me." She opened Reid's fly and pushed the pants down her hips, taking her underwear with them. When they pooled over the tops of her boots, Isabel shoved her back onto the bed, tugged open the laces, and wedged off her boots, letting each one fall with a thud before removing her pants as well.

Reid rolled over, intent on burrowing under the covers, but Isabel grabbed her arm.

"Not yet." She pulled her off the bed and turned her toward the bathroom. "Turn on the shower."

While Reid adjusted the water, Isabel shed her own clothes. They stepped into the large tiled stall together, each easing under one of the dual showerheads Reid had installed when she'd renovated the master bath the year before. Hot water cascaded over Reid's body, washing away her will to continue fighting her fatigue.

She stood, compliant, while Isabel lathered her body and fruit-scented steam filled the air around them. Instead of Reid's usual Irish Spring soap, Isabel selected her own body wash.

"Now I'll smell like you," Reid said.

Isabel moved Reid under the water, gliding her hands over her as she rinsed away the suds. "Is that so bad?"

Reid shook her head. "Sometimes I use yours just so I can smell it throughout the day when I'm not with you."

"I wondered why I ran out so often."

"But it's not the same on me."

"Stay in here for a moment so you don't get chilled." Isabel stepped out and reached for her towel.

Reid ducked her head under the water and closed her eyes. Shortly after Jimmy died, Reid had returned from the cemetery soaking wet and freezing. Isabel had put her in the shower in much the same way as she had today. That time she hadn't gotten in with her, though Reid suspected they'd both wanted her to.

That evening had been one of the turning points in their relationship. And when Reid thought about all that they'd been through since, all of the amazing memories they'd made together, she couldn't imagine ever jeopardizing their happiness. Isabel and Chase mattered more to her than anything else in the world. Had her father ever felt that way about his family? If he had, how had things gone so drastically different?

Reid was saved from trying to answer that question when Isabel opened the shower door and stretched out a large, fluffy towel for her. Without hesitation, Reid turned off the water and stepped into her arms.

❖

Reid slid between the sheets, then held the top one up and waited for Isabel to join her. They settled comfortably together in their usual manner, Isabel tucked into the curve of her outstretched arm and resting her head on Reid's shoulder.

Isabel traced the valley down the center of Reid's chest, then circled under the swell of one breast.

"Do you have any idea how much I love you?" Reid swept her hand down Isabel's back, caressing the arch of her spine as it led into the swell of her buttocks. She'd never tire of following that line of silky skin.

"I have some idea." Isabel kissed the outside of Reid's breast, sending shivers over her skin.

"I loved you for so long, I thought I knew. But when you started to love me back—sometimes it's almost too much." Reid stumbled over the emotion that flooded her and brought a thickness to her throat.

"I know, sweetheart." Isabel's tone was meant to soothe, and her touch against Reid's skin remained maddeningly gentle. But desire swept through Reid as sure as each stroke of Isabel's fingers. She moved over her and pressed her hips between her legs, spreading them farther. "You don't have to—"

"Shh. I need to do this. I want to show you…" Though she didn't finish the sentence, she sensed that Isabel knew. She needed to feel her—to cling to her.

"Okay. But I'm supposed to be taking care of you now." Isabel rolled her over, reversing their positions smoothly. She arched back and pulled her upper body away to look into Reid's eyes.

Isabel braced her arms beside Reid's shoulders, and the long, toned muscles of her biceps flexed, carving ridges and valleys through her creamy skin. When they worked out together, Reid lifted heavier weights, intent on building mass and strength, while Isabel chose lighter weights and knocked out twice as many reps. Reid kissed Isabel's upper arm and stroked the taut muscle, appreciating her quiet power.

Isabel captured her mouth in a kiss that began tenderly, then flared as her lips parted and she stroked her tongue against Reid's. As Isabel rose back up, the sheet fell down her back. Reid grabbed it and pulled it tight around her waist, bringing their lower bodies flush. She spread her legs and pressed her knees to the sides of Isabel's hips. When Isabel thrust against her, Reid lifted her own hips to meet her, seeking more. She slid her hands up Isabel's back, urging her down until their chests rested together.

"I love you like this," Reid whispered, reveling in the feel of Isabel against her, the hard points of Isabel's nipples against the soft curve of her breasts. She slipped her hand under the curtain of Isabel's hair and pressed her hand to the back of Isabel's neck. "You're the only one to ever make me feel this way."

"What way?" Isabel murmured against Reid's throat.

"Weak. And strong at the same time." She'd never given herself to anyone as she did Isabel, trusting her to keep her safe when she let her guard down.

"Hmm, is that why you fought us so hard in the beginning?"

"That's one of many reasons I fought us."

"Aren't you glad now that you gave in?" Isabel rubbed her finger over Reid's nipple.

"It's working out so far."

Isabel pinched and Reid pulled in a breath at the shot of pleasure. Isabel smiled and started to slide down Reid's body, dropping kisses on her chest, then her stomach.

"No. Stay with me." Reid pulled her back up. Isabel's mouth was certain to get her off quickly, but right now she didn't care if she even finished as long as she could stay wrapped up in Isabel's loving gaze.

"I'm right here," Isabel said as she covered her once more. "Whatever you need."

"God, is it too much of a cliché to say I want you to hold me?"

Isabel laughed softly. "No, it's been a long day." She shifted and stretched out beside Reid. "Come here."

Reid turned into her embrace. She rested her cheek against Isabel's breast and focused on the steady beat of Isabel's heart instead of on the emotions of the day that threatened to swamp her once more. She slowed her breathing to match the rise and fall of Isabel's chest.

"He was my hero."

"I know." Isabel threaded her fingers through Reid's hair.

"Emphasis on the *was*, I guess."

"When he got hurt and retired, it broke something in him and he never recovered." Isabel's response painted her father as a victim, and something about that didn't sit well with Reid. She'd always placed the blame squarely on her father's shoulders. "I know you've held on to a lot of anger. But don't you have some good memories of your childhood—times when he was there for you, lessons he taught you? Do his mistakes erase all of those things?"

"We've talked about this before. I don't forgive as easily as you do."

"You can. After Jimmy died, I said some pretty horrible things to you. You forgave me."

"I was trying to get in your pants," Reid joked, though she knew Isabel made valid points.

"You and Jimmy idolized him when we were kids, and his withdrawal took that from you. But he's lost a lot, too. It sounds like he's been making some big changes."

"He didn't have much choice, once he got sick."

"But he did. He could have kept drinking himself to death. Even under those circumstances, I'm sure quitting wasn't easy for him. He's not perfect, but none of us are."

"It's not fair." If in fact her days with him were numbered, possibly the only thing she could control was how she spent that time. "I'm not ready to lose him."

"We're never ready to lose our parents, honey."

"So what do I do?"

"You sleep for a while." When Reid lifted her head to protest, Isabel held her in place. "You're exhausted. Nap for at least an hour. Later we'll go back to the hospital. Maybe he'll be awake and you'll be able to talk to him some more."

Reid snuggled closer to Isabel, fatigue overtaking her now that she'd starting letting go of some of her emotional baggage. She wrapped her arm around Isabel's waist and held tight. They would go together, and maybe this time she would ask Isabel to go in the room with her.

With Isabel at her side, she could say what she needed to say. She could get her father back, for however long she had him.

Don't ever put anything in front of them. Her father's words wavered through her head as she closed her eyes. She took several deep breaths, but her mind refused to quiet.

"Isabel?"

"Yeah?"

"I'm ready to tell you about my conversation with him today."

D. Jackson Leigh grew up barefoot and happy, swimming in farm ponds and riding rude ponies in rural south Georgia. Her passion for writing led her to a career in journalism and North Carolina, where she edits breaking news at night and writes lesbian romance stories by day. Friend her at facebook.com/d.jackson.leigh, on Twitter @djacksonleigh, or at www.djacksonleigh.com.

This story features characters from *Long Shot*.

THE POND
D. JACKSON LEIGH

Willie Greyson sat on the weathered dock and extended her long legs out over the water. She dipped her heels, then immersed her feet in the sun-warmed pond. She wiggled her toes and frowned.

It seemed like she'd spent a lifetime at this small oasis hidden on the back part of Lori's father's farm, a lifetime of long minutes waiting for Lori to appear on the path across from the dock. They'd begun meeting here when they were just girls, Lori's hair in pigtails and Willie's in a single long braid. They were best friends. Willie fished and Lori talked. Damn, she could talk the paint off the side of a barn.

Then things changed. While Willie grew tall and lanky, Lori remained petite, her body softened with lush, womanly curves. Their relationship changed, too.

They discovered they wanted more.

Their first kiss had been at the beach. She'd borrowed Papa's truck and they spent the day sitting on the sand and wading in the surf hand in hand. They explored a rock outcropping, then stopped to rest in the secluded shade of a large boulder. They sat shoulder to shoulder and Lori trembled against her. It was much too warm to be chilled, but Willie wrapped an arm around her shoulders and pulled her closer. Lori looked up, their faces a hairsbreadth apart. Before Willie had time to change her mind, she lowered her head and kissed her. Lori's lips were soft and warm and tasted faintly of the salt spray.

She drove home with Lori pressed against her side, until she pulled off onto a tractor path near Lori's house and stole another long, exploring kiss. That kiss left her breathless and hungry. But for what? Did other women have the same feelings for each other? She instinctively knew this was something they must hide, but it didn't stop them.

The kiss was followed by weeks, months, of more stolen kisses, tentative touches, and frustrated partings.

Willie wanted more.

She had a pretty good idea what "more" meant after one of their long make-out sessions had led her to a stunning discovery. She'd been confused by the dampness in her crotch afterward and surprised when it reappeared that night as she lay in bed and relived their kisses. She smoothed her hand down her belly and slid her fingers into her stiff curls. Yes, she was wet again. Was she ill? She didn't feel bad. In fact, it felt pretty good, really good when her fingers slid across her swollen tissue. A few more strokes and she experienced her first toe-curling, eye-opening orgasm. Wow. What had she done? Could she make it happen again? Did Lori know about this?

"More" became her new mission.

Lori was so beautiful. One look as she appeared at the edge of the pond's clearing and Willie wanted to bury her fingers in her thick mahogany curls. She wanted to stare into those sable-brown eyes framed by long, dark lashes and soak up the strength and shy affection she saw there. She wanted to feather kisses across the freckles that dotted Lori's otherwise flawless skin and to taste those soft lips.

She wanted that, but today she planned to have more.

Lori paused and their eyes locked. Willie was already wet from the anticipation, and seeing Lori standing in the sunlight, barefoot and clothed only in a simple sleeveless gingham dress, made her stand to relieve the uncomfortable pressure building in her loins. The wood dock was hot against her bare feet as she trotted to the pond's grassy bank and skirted the water to meet Lori under a huge shade oak.

Willie kissed her shyly, and the question in Lori's eyes told Willie that her nervousness was showing.

"I brought a blanket and I swiped a jar of Papa's scuppernong wine," she said.

Lori smiled at the small feast Willie had spread out for them—wine, cheese, and soda crackers—and they sat with the food between them.

"Oh, Willie, this is wonderful. You won't get in trouble for the wine, will you?"

Willie grinned at her. "No, but one of my brothers might. Papa would never believe I did it."

Lori shook her head, but smiled. "You're such a scamp. Your poor brothers, always taking the blame."

"They've all done it before, so they'll be too busy blaming each other to think it could be me." She uncapped the mason jar, handed it to Lori, and watched her take a sip.

"It's sweet," Lori said.

"Sweet like you." Willie followed Lori's pink tongue swiping across her lips to gather all of the grapes' nectar. Her cheeks heated when she realized Lori caught her staring, and she began to ramble nervously. "It won a blue ribbon at the county fair last year. Papa says this year's batch is even better, and he's going to enter the fair again next month."

Lori handed the jar back to Willie and lowered her eyes, toying with the hem of her dress.

Willie frowned. "What's the matter? Is the wine too sweet?"

"No, the wine is perfect." She looked at Willie, affection softening her gaze. "You're perfect." Her expression turned to frustration. "It's just that, well, Earl Montgomery asked Daddy if he could take me to the fair next month. I told Daddy I was going with you, but Mama said it's time for me to start paying some attention to boys."

Willie took a big gulp of the wine and swallowed it down. "Is that what you want to do?" She stared at the blanket and picked at a loose thread near her knee.

"No." Lori crawled around the food and took Willie's face in her hands. "I want to go with you, Willie."

Willie searched her eyes and saw the truth of her declaration. "I told Papa that I don't want to get married. I want to go to the university and get a degree and then a good job. I'll buy a house and you can come live with me. They'll call us old maids, but I don't care. I just want to be with you. I love you, Lori."

Lori's eyes filled. "I love you, too, Willie. Only you."

Her lips, her tongue, tasted of the wine and Willie drank her in. She gathered Lori in her arms and eased her down until they were lying side by side. She was careful, though. Lori's tiny, delicate frame always made her feel big and clumsy. But Lori rolled onto her back and drew Willie down on top of her.

"I'll crush you," she murmured.

"No, you won't," Lori said. "I love the weight of your body on mine. I love your strength."

Willie kissed her way down Lori's neck and sucked at her pulse because she'd discovered that it made Lori hum with pleasure. She hummed now and Willie reflexively pressed her tingling crotch against Lori's hip. She captured Lori's mouth, pouring all the passion, all the feeling that was welling up in her, into a long kiss as she inched her hand up to cup Lori's breast. They'd done this before, and Willie anticipated Lori's whimper when she circled her thumb around the rigid bump of her nipple.

She broke their kiss and stared into Lori's eyes as she slowly unbuttoned her dress. They hadn't done this before. They'd only groped and pressed together fully clothed. But Lori didn't stop her. Instead, she reached for the buttons of Willie's shirt, too.

Lori's chest was flushed, but her skin was cool. Willie slipped her hand under the stiff white cotton of Lori's bra, then closed her eyes and moaned at the supple flesh that filled her palm.

"Oh, Willie." Lori wiggled beneath her. "Let me up."

"I'm sorry, I'm sorry." She withdrew her hand and sat up abruptly. "I didn't mean—"

"No, it's okay." Lori sat up, too. "I just—" She unfastened the last button on Willie's shirt and dropped her gaze to take her in.

Willie had never needed to wear a bra under the work shirts she always wore. She was glad for that now. She shivered when Lori pushed the shirt back and trailed her fingertips lightly across her collarbone, then downward to touch her small breasts.

"So strong, but so soft," Lori said, pushing the shirt off Willie's shoulders. She stopped. "Is this okay?"

"Yes."

"I want…I want to feel your skin on mine, Willie. Take this off and unhook my bra for me."

Willie shucked off her shirt and leaned into Lori, kissing her again as she reached around to work the hooks loose and pull the straps from Lori's shoulders. Lori lay back and drew Willie down with her. Their moans mingled as their breasts brushed together.

"Willie." Lori's hands explored her back, her arms tightening around her.

Willie kissed her again. Their tongues danced sensuously, then desperately.

Lori squirmed. "Willie, God." Her tone went from breathless to desperate. "I want...I want—"

Willie knew what Lori wanted. "More," she said, smoothing her fingertips along Lori's cheek. "I want it, too. Do you trust me to show you?"

Lori trembled. "Yes. Yes, please, before I break into a million pieces from wanting you."

No one ever came to the pond except them, so Willie didn't hesitate as she rolled onto her back and unbuckled her belt. She could feel Lori watching as she stripped off her jeans and underpants, and when she rolled to face her again, Lori was wiggling out of her panties, too.

Clothes cast aside, no barriers between them, they both stared. Willie thought she was going to faint at the sight of Lori completely naked, then she remembered to breathe. "You are so beautiful," she whispered.

"Show me," Lori said softly.

She bent her head to taste Lori's lips, then her neck and chest. She flicked her tongue against one pink nipple, and Lori arched upward.

"Harder, Willie." Her hands were on Willie's breasts, massaging and tweaking her sensitive nipples. "Harder like this."

Willie gently bit the nipple in her mouth and cupped Lori's other breast with her hand, lightly pinching. She smiled at her shy little Lori's full-throated moan.

She slipped her leg between Lori's thighs. Lori was slick and hot, and Willie groaned at the pleasure of knowing they were together in their desire. She kept teasing Lori's breast with her hand, but rose to claim her mouth again. Her hips bucked and her sex slid easily against Lori's leg as their tongues moved together. Holy Mother, that felt good. Too good. Another stroke, and she'd be beyond holding back.

She skimmed Lori's soft belly to part her folds, and Lori whimpered as Willie found her swelling flesh. She'd had some practice now with her own body and used that knowledge to find the spot that made Lori wrench away from their kiss and gasp. She was careful to keep the pressure light, but it was difficult. Lori's thigh pushed harder into Willie's crotch, making it almost impossible to concentrate as her own need rode her hard, racing against her determination to bring Lori to orgasm first.

Lori sucked in an abrupt breath and her eyes widened. "Oh, God, Willie, oh." Lori's body bowed beneath her, and Willie gave in to her own climax.

She didn't remember rolling onto her back and pulling Lori on top of her, but she was thankful. Her heart surely would have pounded right out of her chest if it wasn't for Lori's cheek pressed against it. They panted, perspiration sheening their naked bodies.

Lori shuddered, her body tensing and releasing with the residual of her climax. Her words were a breathy whisper. "I never knew."

"Yeah. Me neither." Willie stroked Lori's back, still marveling at the intimacy of touching her bare skin. She chuckled. "I sort of found out by accident one night after you got me all worked up with your kisses."

Lori lifted her head to hold her gaze. "I love you, Willie."

"I love you, Lori, more than I thought I could love anyone. It makes me crazy to think about you being with anyone else."

"I'll never love anyone but you."

Willie hugged her tightly and swore she'd never let Lori go. They'd find a way to be together.

"Lorraine?"

They both jerked up as Lori's mother called out.

"Where are you?" Her voice came from the edge of the clearing.

"Shit." Willie looked for their scattered clothes.

"There's no time." Lori's eyes were wide with panic.

"Jump in the pond."

They both ran to the water and dove in. When they surfaced, Mrs. Caulder was standing next to their blanket.

"Lorraine Caulder, what on earth?"

Lori bobbed in the water. "We were just swimming to cool off, Mama. Is something wrong?"

Mrs. Caulder stared down at their picnic and scattered clothes. "I'll tell you what's wrong." She put her hands on her hips and gave Willie a murderous glare that made her want to duck back under the water. "Your tomboy days of traipsing around the woods and skinny-dipping are over. You are much too old, young lady."

"But, Mama—"

"No buts, Lorraine. Get up to the house. Now."

Lori gave Willie a beseeching look.

"Go ahead," Willie said, her voice low. She was beyond miserable that their perfect afternoon had been shattered, but Lori's dilemma was what mattered. "I'll talk to you tomorrow."

Lori swam to the shore and quickly dressed. When she turned back to Willie, Mrs. Caulder swatted her on the butt. "Git. Now. Earl Montgomery has come calling and is waiting in the parlor. You need to get cleaned up before he sees you looking like a wild ragamuffin."

Willie lifted her hand in a silent wave when Lori glanced back for one last look before disappearing down the path.

Mrs. Caulder lingered, glaring at Willie until she wondered if the woman expected her to get out of the water and dress in front of her.

"Y'all aren't children anymore, and you need to leave my daughter alone." She looked down at the blanket, and Willie felt suddenly exposed, as if Lori's mother could see what they had been doing. Her eyes were hard when she looked up at Willie again. "I don't want to talk to your parents, but I will if you come around again."

Willie stood in the water for a long time after Mrs. Caulder left. She was scared, really scared. Could they keep her from seeing Lori? She waded out of the pond and dressed. Lori loved her. They would find a way to be together.

She waited at the pond every day for three long weeks—the worst weeks of her life. She closed her eyes against the hollow ache that slowly choked her as she sat on the dock every day, waiting, wondering, and waiting more.

Desperate, she finally went to Lori's house, determined to talk to her. They could run away to another town and get jobs. She didn't have to go to the university. She'd do anything as long as she didn't lose Lori.

But when she walked into the yard, she could hear the angry voices inside. She knocked, but no one came to the door. She knocked again, and Lori finally appeared. Her eyes were red from crying, and she refused to look at Willie as she told her that she was going to marry Earl Montgomery next month.

Willie hung around until the day of the wedding and stood across the street from the church. When Lori arrived, she got out of the car and looked right at Willie, then walked into the sanctuary. Willie drove to the bus station, bought a ticket to Richmond, and joined the army.

❖

She never thought she'd find herself back at this pond, waiting once again for Lori. She squinted in the bright sunlight, searching the tree line again as if she could will her to appear. Every moment without her still seemed like a millennium.

Army life had been good to her, but even sweeter was their reunion and the years they'd finally spent together. The years of waiting had been more than worth it. So there was no doubt that she would wait for Lori again…as long as it took. But then time had no relevance here in this oasis that was theirs.

The water shimmered around her and Willie closed her eyes against the glare. When she opened them, Lori stood on the bank across from her. Her smile was soft. "Somehow, I knew I'd find you here."

Willie sprang to her feet and dove into the water, swimming across the small pond in strong, sure strokes. Lori waded in to meet her and they were in each other's arms again. Lori's kiss was as sweet as she remembered.

Then Lori's hands were on Willie's face, smoothing down her shoulders and arms to cup Willie's hands in her smaller ones and examine them. She felt her own face, then looked up at Willie in wonderment.

"We're young again."

"Yes." Willie held up her hands. "No more arthritis."

"I never minded. I was too glad to find you after all those years apart."

"I never expected I would go first. Was it hard after I left?"

"It was dark and confusing. Poor Leah. I don't know what my granddaughter would have done without your great-niece to love her and help her through it."

"Tory is stronger with Leah at her side, too."

Lori nodded. "They'll be fine." She smiled. "Did you have to wait long this time, sweetheart? I couldn't keep track of the days. The dementia stole that from me, but sometimes I thought it was actually a gift because it kept me from knowing how long I was without you."

"It doesn't matter how long. I would wait all of eternity for you."

Lori looked around. "So, this is heaven? No angels or choirs? No judgment of our sins?"

"Are you disappointed?"

"Heavens, no. I'm relieved."

They laughed together, and Willie stole another kiss.

"Apparently, we must have done something right. Our eternity will be spent in the place where we shared our happiest memory." She gestured toward her offerings under the gnarled old oak.

Lori's smile went from sweet to brilliant. "Oh, Willie. In all the years I've loved you, I'm glad you never changed."

Willie winked at Lori. "I brought a blanket and a jar of Papa's scuppernong wine."

Martha Miller is a Midwestern writer and a Lambda Literary Award finalist for *The Retirement Plan: a Crime Story*. She is the author of four other lesbian books and winner of, among several awards, an Illinois Arts Council Artists Fellowship. Her stories, reviews, and articles are widely published. She teaches writing part-time.

This story features characters from *The Retirement Plan*.

DILEMMA
MARTHA MILLER

Homicide Detective Morgan Holiday and mother-of-one Chelsea Brown had been seeing each other exclusively and sleeping together for over six months when Chelsea broached the subject of living together. Although Morgan wanted to live with Chelsea, there were reasons to go slow. First, she was living in her own home, actually the one she grew up in, and she and the bank had a big investment in it. Second, Chelsea had a kid and the kid was part of the deal. Sometimes when Morgan came home after a day of family time, she shut off her cell, had a big dish of ice cream, and went straight to bed—her own bed. Dominick wasn't a bad kid, as four-year-olds went, but Morgan found she needed some alone time now and then. How could she get that with all of them living under the same roof?

One night, Uncle Sandy was babysitting and Morgan and Chelsea were lying in Chelsea's bed in the stunning afterglow of sex when Chelsea rolled onto her side and propped her head up with a folded pillow. Inches from Morgan's ear, she put a finger into her mouth, getting it wet, and made soft circles around Morgan's nipple, first one and then the other. "If you lived here, we could do this every night."

"Mmm." Morgan threw her arm around the woman she loved and drew her into a deep, messy kiss.

Chelsea pulled away. "That's not an answer."

"You wanted an answer? I thought…well, never mind."

"Can we talk about it?"

"Now?"

"If not now, when?" Chelsea said.

Morgan felt the ice beneath her grow thin and considered her response carefully. Finally, she said, "When all my blood is in my head where it belongs. Sometime when we haven't literally just fucked our brains out." Untangling herself, Morgan threw her legs over her side of the bed and, with one toe, fished around for her underpants.

Chelsea was silent for a moment. "That's not fair. We're always fucking except when Dom is around, and we can't really discuss it when he's here."

Morgan crawled back into bed and knelt over Chelsea, kissing tiny circles on her belly.

Opening her legs, Chelsea gave Morgan's head a push. "You're changing the subject."

Morgan slid two fingers inside Chelsea and touched her clit with her tongue.

The subject was officially changed.

The next time they were alone, Chelsea kept her clothes on. They grilled steaks outside for just the two of them. Morgan basked in the easy intimacy. Chelsea knew just how Morgan liked her steak. Of course, a couple of restaurant cooks knew the same thing.

The late-afternoon sky was going gray as clouds, swollen with the rain that had been promised later that night, moved in. They took the meat and vegetables inside and sat dinner on the kitchen table. Chelsea lit a candle and they dished up the food.

They ate in silence. Morgan had had a tiring day at work—meeting with the county sheriff, briefing higher-ups, dealing with the media, and interviewing witnesses to another drive-by.

"You want some wine?" Chelsea asked.

Morgan shook her head. "I'm fine for now. Maybe later."

"Can we talk now?"

Morgan sighed. "I'm tired."

"Is talking so much work? Why do you keep putting me off? I'm starting to think you don't want to live here, that you're only in this for the sex."

Morgan put down her fork and knife. "You know that's not true. I'm conflicted about this. I'd have to sell my house. I can't make the payments there and pay my expenses here at the same time. Plus I work for the city, and they're thinking of making a law that city workers have to live inside the city limits."

"So you don't want to sell your house? Why not?"

Morgan shrugged. "Right now the market isn't great, and this is the place that you and your ex bought together. I'd have a hard time thinking of it as mine."

"Well, what a surprise—your house and your employer. I thought you'd have some problem with Dom, helping to raise him or something. Coming into a child's life is a big deal. Sometimes I see the relief in your eyes after an afternoon of doing his stuff."

"I'm fond of the kid," Morgan said. "He can be a handful, but he's not a reason."

Neither of them mentioned the dogs.

Chelsea's house was in the country, and people sometimes dumped dogs in the area. She took them in. Most of the time she had over a dozen dogs of different shapes and sizes. She had large wire kennels along the side of a huge garage. When she was home, she let them run in the yard. They were a good-natured pack of mutts—all spayed and neutered, all up on their shots. Chelsea's ex, Laura, was a veterinarian, and all of this came free of charge. Between them they found homes for many of the strays and, although the rare aggressive dog had to be put down, mostly the dogs lived good lives. Morgan loved the way they came running to greet her when she pulled in the driveway. In spite of the shared dogs, the ex made herself scarce, at least when Morgan was around.

Chelsea held up her hand. "Okay, stop. I understand and I won't mention it again."

As soon as Chelsea said that, Morgan wanted to move in. "Ever?"

"Never. When you decide the time is right, we'll talk again."

That had been too easy, and Morgan soon found out why. Late that night as she drove back into the city, the rain washed across the wearily sliding windshield wipers, and more rain beat down through the black beyond that. Headlights in the opposite lane reached out like burning fingers straight into her eyes. She slowed as a truck passed, completely obliterating her view of the road as it threw more water across her windshield.

If she moved in with Chelsea, there'd be no more middle-of-the-night drives home. She'd have to drive into the city for work, and at other times they could just turn out the light and pull up the blankets.

She was sure Chelsea was the one. She could see them growing old together. She could imagine sending Dom off to college and holidays with grandchildren. Recently she hadn't been able to see her life any other way.

Coming into town, she pulled off at a gas station and sat listening to the beating rain. She texted Chelsea: *Success in love is success in life. Let's buy a place together.*

The next morning, after what Morgan thought was a long wait, she got a text from Chelsea: *K.*

Later when they spoke on the phone, they decided to see what was available, big enough for the three of them, and in the city. They went to some open houses. Morgan was sure she'd be the one to drag her feet, but after looking at several places, Chelsea was the one who was hard to please. She had to consider school for Dom. That disqualified several of the less expensive places.

While they looked, Morgan made herself start going through her mother's things. When her mom died, Morgan had put her belongings in the smaller of the two bedrooms and closed the door, promising herself she'd get to them, and over the past year she'd tossed in other things she couldn't decide whether to put away or pitch.

But if she was going to sell the house, she'd have to go through everything.

After a particularly disappointing Sunday of open houses, Morgan cleared boxes off the bed and started sorting. She sifted through a box of old bills and receipts as the muscles in the back of her neck tightened. The house they'd seen earlier would have worked: a Cape Cod, two bedrooms on the main floor and two more upstairs under the slanted ceilings with dormered windows in the front. No garage, but they could build one. But the street was "too busy for Dom and the dogs."

When they'd first talked to Dom about the move, he'd asked, "Will we take the dogs?"

Chelsea said, "Maybe one or two, but not all. Laura will find new homes for them."

Morgan loved dogs, so that connection with the ex hadn't bothered her too much. Chelsea and Laura had split over Laura's infidelities, so Morgan, who'd only been with one other woman, easily made a promise of fidelity. Chelsea seemed sufficiently disconnected from Laura until now, but finding homes for that pack of dogs would be difficult, if not impossible.

Dom asked, "Will I have a room big enough so my friends can come over and play?"

"That's right," Chelsea said, "Morgan and I will share. But you get your own room, and it will be big."

That night as Morgan carried a large bag to the trash, she wondered if they'd ever be able to find the right house. It seemed like Chelsea didn't want to move. She lived down the lane from her parents, and the house and land had been in her family before she and the ex had purchased it. Maybe she felt disloyal selling to a stranger.

Monday morning on the way to work the call came. Morgan hit the Bluetooth and Chelsea's voice replaced Susan Boyle's. "Morgan," she said, "this isn't going to work."

"Okay," Morgan said uncertainly.

"It's just too complicated."

"As I recall," Morgan said, "you're the one that brought it up. You wanted to live together."

"That's when I thought you'd move in here with us," Chelsea replied.

Morgan remembered the weekend devoted to sorting out her mother's things, not easy, not something she'd have chosen to do for at least twenty years. But she'd done it for Chelsea. "Move in with us." Her tone was cutting, but she couldn't stop. "By us you mean you, Dom, the dogs, and your ex, right?"

"That's not fair."

Morgan said, "Sorry," then hit Disconnect.

Morgan pulled into a Starbucks and parked. She didn't want to break up, but she needed to calm down. She wished she hadn't mentioned the ex. It sounded petty. What if Chelsea turned back to Laura for comfort? Her fingers drummed on the steering wheel. Glancing at the clock, she saw that it was past time for the workday to begin. She considered calling in sick and driving out to see Chelsea, but quickly rejected the idea. Refusing to act like a bird that enjoyed the cage, she decided to let herself and Chelsea cool down. She put the car in gear and pulled back into traffic.

The day was a busy one. Morgan thought about their conversation several times. She ate lunch at her desk, wolfing down a microwaved burrito and root beer. With plenty of reports to be filed, she was the last one in the office. The sun was setting as she drove through McDonald's, ordered her dinner off the dollar menu, and drove home expecting a message from Chelsea. The only message was from the cable company wanting to sell her more channels. She was worried and disappointed. Okay, pissed. She wanted to call Chelsea but forced herself not to out of spite. By bedtime she was sure the ex was taking her spot. Maybe she'd never really had a spot.

That week November arrived with drizzle and depression. It seemed like it was always dreary and dark. Morgan's eyes felt like she had tucked brambles under each eyelid, as if she'd been stirring concrete with a straw. On Tuesday night she stopped at Tallulah's after work for a beer. When she stepped inside out of the wind, she found the place quiet. A card game was going on at a table back near the dance floor. The barmaid was a stranger. She was young and butch, with rosy cheeks, a nice smile, and one of those buzz haircuts that Morgan wished she had the nerve for but didn't. Another couple came in and the barmaid waited on them and then stayed to talk. They were all in their twenties and all had those goddamn haircuts. Morgan tossed a dollar on the bar, turned up the bottle and emptied it, then headed for the door. Behind her she heard the infants laughing.

Morgan wanted to call Chelsea, but after three days it would have been an embarrassment. She had her pride. Chelsea had started it, anyway. Anger became more about Chelsea not calling than about the move. How could something so stupid come between them? Morgan didn't want to move. They had a good thing. Or they *had* had a good thing. All this over a phone call, disembodied words attached to nothing solid. Sure, they'd only been together six months. Sure, they'd spent a lot of that time in bed. Orgasms were terrific, but they weren't the remedy for every injustice—at least Morgan didn't think so. She just wasn't sure where the injustice lay in this, but she was pretty sure that she had been wronged. Moving was a major change. Maybe Chelsea thought she'd been ready and just wasn't. Maybe she was alone in that bed they'd shared, crying because Morgan hadn't called. Well, good then.

❖

Late Friday afternoon as they headed back to the police station, Redick, Morgan's bald-headed ex-Marine partner, pulled their unmarked car off the road and turned to her. "What's up?"

"What do you mean?"

"Something is wrong. You've been a viper all week. I can't take it anymore."

Morgan glared at him. But he sat there waiting. Finally she said, "I'm fine."

"Is this a romantic problem?"

"None of your goddamn business."

"I guess you don't want to talk about it."

"What made you think that, Sherlock?"

Redick stared at her, his brows knit, letting the silence unwrap around them.

At last she said, "It's Chelsea."

Following a short bark of nervous laughter, Redick said, "Thought so."

"We don't seem to be speaking."

"Don't seem to be? You aren't sure?"

Morgan sighed. "I guess not." She waited out another silence, listening to her thoughts growl.

Then Redick said, "I read something that might apply here. I was in the dentist's office and there was this *Reader's Digest* and I picked it up and paged through it. In the jokes part, I read something like, 'When you meet the right person, you know right away, but when you meet the wrong person, it takes a year and a half.'"

Morgan felt a pinprick of a headache. "What's your point?"

Redick shrugged. "Is she the one?"

Morgan nodded slowly.

"You can't be a duck until you learn to quack."

"Huh?"

"Quit fucking around and call her."

"But I think I'm right."

"That's a dilemma for assholes," Redick said. "Most of the time it just don't matter. Life don't reward longevity or merit. There's no Silver Star for being right."

Before she could reply, they were interrupted by Redick's phone. He answered and spoke briefly and then pulled back into traffic.

"Ducks," Morgan said. "Is that *Reader's Digest* too?"

"Naw, I read it somewhere else, can't remember, but think about what you want, okay?"

Morgan thought about it. She was still thinking about it at nine thirty that night when she pulled into Tallulah's packed parking lot. She had on a yellow oxford shirt and a new pair of black jeans that hugged her hips just right. The bar was full, so she ordered a beer and carried it to the back. She recognized the two women who'd been in the bar earlier that week. Actually she recognized the buzz cuts. A third woman, who looked familiar, was with them. Her dark hair was about the same length. They were laughing. Morgan recognized the laughter and couldn't seem to stop herself from approaching the table. The women, turning to face her, were suddenly quiet.

"I don't talk to you for a week and you go get your head shaved?"

Chelsea ran her hand over her head and smiled. "You like it?"

Morgan said, "It looks hot."

"Thank you. I think." Chelsea pulled out a chair. "Are you alone? Want to join us?"

Even as she stepped toward the chair, Morgan said, "I was just leaving."

"Aw, come on." Chelsea turned to her friends. "This is Morgan, the one I was telling you about. Morgan, this is Laura and her partner Barb."

Morgan stared at Chelsea. She'd never seen Laura before, not even in a picture. "Laura, as in your ex Laura?"

Chelsea nodded.

Morgan took a significant swallow from her beer bottle and shook hands with the women in turn. A slow song started and the two seemed anxious to dance. Holding hands, Laura led Barb away. The dance floor was filling up as Laura pulled Barb into a sexy embrace. With a slow hip-grinding motion, they moved out of view.

Morgan's body tingled. She wanted to touch Chelsea, to press their breasts together, run her hands over her ass, and grind her hips. "Wanna dance?"

Chelsea smiled. "Don't we need to talk first?"

Morgan took Chelsea's hand and stood. "The song will end if we don't get out there." At the edge of the dance floor, Morgan pulled

Chelsea into a tender embrace and rested her chin on the bristly new haircut. She pressed her thighs together, afraid she might come right then and there.

Chelsea looked up at her, closed her eyes, and opened her mouth to a wet kiss. Finally pulling away, Chelsea said, "I've missed you."

Morgan shoved her knee between Chelsea's legs. "I've been crazy without you. I was wrong about everything."

Chelsea nibbled at her ear and hoarsely whispered, "It was Dom's school. My family. The dogs…"

"Of course, you're right. I was wrong."

"Could you stand to move out to the country with Dom and me?"

Morgan's crotch was damp. Sweat beaded on her forehead. "I don't think I could stand it if I didn't." Her tongue found its way into Chelsea's ear. She whispered, "We are going to work this out."

Chelsea pulled away. "When all the necessary blood is in our brains?"

"Right." Morgan blocked her progress. "Wait, I haven't had enough."

"The song's over. We're alone out here."

"Who cares? Another song will start in a minute." Morgan guided Chelsea to the nearest wall and pressed another long kiss on her lips.

"You girls want to get a room?"

Morgan glanced toward the voice. It was Laura, with Barb, swaying her hips to Rihanna's "Te Amo." Chelsea just smiled and put her arms around Morgan's shoulders to pull her back into the kiss.

"Well, there's nothing like a happy home," Laura said, and danced away into the gathering of sweaty lesbians.

Sheri Lewis Wohl grew up in picturesque northeast Washington state and always thought she'd move away. Never did. Now she happily writes surrounded by mountains, lakes, and rivers. When not working or writing stories, she trains for triathlons and is a member of a K9 Search & Rescue team.

This story features characters from *Burgundy Betrayal*.

WOLF NIGHT
SHERI LEWIS WOHL

Yellowstone River Valley, 1835

She did not scream as pain ripped through her body. Scorching hot and coming fast, it was as if an enemy's arrow had pierced her flesh. Still she made no sound. A chief did not let discomfort of the body distract her.

Another pain shook her. The soft intake of her breath was all she'd allow to pass her lips. Her wives knelt by her side, wiping the sweat from her brow, singing softly to the spirits. The child was coming.

Dark Moon placed a hand on Pine Leaf's swollen belly, her touch gentle and loving. "Not long," she whispered. "He will be here soon."

Since the moment she'd known the child grew inside her, Pine Leaf knew it was a son. Her visions had shown her his face and his future. He would be strong, leading her people with his back straight and his head held high. When their way of life was destroyed and her people nearly broken, he would carry her blood into the generations that survived and one day her descendants would stand tall once more.

Dimly, through the constant pain, she sensed danger coming closer. The spirits had been speaking to her, warning of what approached. Distant hooves pounded, sending vibrations through the ground at her back. Her life didn't matter. Her son's did.

A pain, deep and terrible, ripped through her and everything changed. Her son came into the world under the sky, dark and filled with stars. She turned her head to the wolves that sat on their haunches, their black eyes scanning the night as if they were standing guard.

Pine Leaf dropped her gaze to the black hair that covered her son's head and the features that mirrored her own. She saw none of the man who tried to call himself *husband*. The child at her breast was her son. Her legacy.

The howl of one of the wolves rose on the night air. Holding her son against her breast, she whispered his name. "Black Wolf."

Spokane, WA, present day

Cam Black Wolf sat in the chair next to the big fireplace with her feet on the stool watching the flames and feeling incredibly relaxed despite the topic of conversation.

"So," she looked over at Kara, who was stretched out on the sofa, her arms folded behind her head and her feet up on the arm, "how exactly do we want to do this?"

This was the wedding they were planning. Once the state of Washington passed the same-sex marriage law, it was a given, they were getting married. Or at least for her it was a given. In fact, she couldn't recall anything in life she'd looked forward to more, with the possible exception of spending the rest of it with the woman she was madly in love with. They already had the license. They already had the time and location. All that was left was deciding what to wear.

"I say we go combo style," Kara said casually.

"Combo style?"

"Yup, we do old-fashioned white dress for me—you know, all virginal-like." She winked at Cam. "And a beautiful elk tooth dress for you."

Giving it a little thought, Cam decided it was actually a pretty good idea. "I like it."

"Yeah, it will make my mom really happy. She always wanted to see me in a white wedding dress." Kara smiled and shrugged. "Of course, she sorta hoped I'd be marrying a guy, but this will make her just as happy."

Cam smiled back at her and nodded. Kara's mom was okay. Yeah, she probably hoped for a more traditional relationship for her only daughter, but she didn't let it slow her down. She was probably more excited about the wedding than either Kara or Cam.

She thought about the elk tooth dress Kara suggested and her smile grew. "I can wear Pine Leaf's dress, and I guarantee it will make my dad pass out."

"Pine Leaf?" Kara looked at her quizzically.

"You don't remember, do you?"

"I know you told me something about her before. She was some kind of kick-ass Crow chief, right?"

Cam nodded, thinking about her long-ago ancestor. Pine Leaf was so much more than a chief. She had been what they'd today call a trailblazer, breaking down all the barriers in her time and respected all the more because of it. Wearing dresses was definitely not Cam's style, but she'd be proud and honored to be married in Pine Leaf's.

"Yes, she was a chief. She was also a lesbian, though no one called her that in those days. She was simply referred to as two-spirited, someone who possessed the spirits of both male and female. She even had several wives."

Kara tilted her head and studied Cam. "Yeah, well, you're only getting one wife, so don't get any ideas. Hey, if she was a lesbian, how did she become your ancestor? In those days, there had to be a guy somewhere in the mix, you know what I'm sayin'?"

Cam knew exactly what Kara was getting at. Thinking of the stories she'd been told about the woman chief who shared her blood made her frown. "Yes, there was a man. By all accounts one obsessed with Pine Leaf. Her—not so much with him. He was such a pest she finally gave him an impossible test to prove he was worthy to marry to her and then sent him on his way. She never thought he could pull it off. Took him ten years to do it, but he did and then came back to claim her as his wife. Joke was on him, though. It only lasted a matter of weeks and then he disappeared. Nine months later my ancestor Black Wolf was born."

"What happened to baby daddy?"

Cam shook her head. "Don't know. Whatever went down, he took off and never came back."

Kara smiled, her green eyes lighting up. "I like her style."

❖

He dropped his bags on the living room floor and looked around. His needs weren't great, and thank goodness. The house was tiny, dirty, and cold. When his buddy Junior Petro offered him the place free of charge, he'd jumped at it. The location couldn't have been more perfect. Junior had neglected to mention it was a dump.

Then again, if all went as he planned, he'd only have to be here a few days. That's all he needed to accomplish his goal.

First things first, though; he couldn't even sit down in this place until it was clean. He left his bag on the floor and jumped back into his SUV. He'd seen a grocery store on the way in.

Three hours later, the small house was scrubbed clean. Except for the bedroom. He had no intention of ever coming into contact with what passed for a bed in there. He would throw his sleeping bag on the disinfected floor in front of the fireplace and sleep.

Now he could relax.

Now he could go about finding *her.*

Sitting at the table, he took an MP3 player from his pocket and pulled up the most recent file he'd downloaded. Reverend John Sizemore's voice filled the small room, his words of righteousness touching his heart. The reverend shared his wisdom on marriage, the sanctity of one man and one woman. Everything the reverend said calmed him and strengthened his resolve. He was doing the right thing. The only thing.

As the sermon went on, he spread a topographical map on the kitchen table and studied it closely, knowing that somewhere within the hills and mountains she waited. He would find her and he would save her. What she was about to do wasn't just wrong, it was a sin, and he couldn't allow her soul to be damned.

Twilight began to fall and the light dimmed. From his bag he pulled a lantern and switched it on. Electricity was another of the items Junior had neglected to mention. The house didn't have it. Not a problem. In fact, darkness was what he waited for. It was his time.

When the sun finally dipped behind the mountains and shadows engulfed the house, he snapped the lantern off. He stood and stripped, the air cool against his dark skin. The taut muscles of his stomach twitched with anticipation. His long, black hair hung loose against his back.

Naked, he stepped outside and tilted his head to the sky. Stars were sprinkled across the inky blackness, and a creamy moon glowed. He inhaled deeply and called the change.

❖

Cam hung up the phone, staring at the handset for a long moment. Her father's call was disturbing on a number of levels. Not just because it threw a wrench in their wedding plans but also because it was just plain wrong.

Out back on the patio, Kara sat in front of the gas fire pit with her feet propped up on an empty chair. The gate was open, giving them a perfect view of the dam where water poured clear and clean into the river. She looked beautiful in the moonlight, her red hair curling around her face and her eyes bright. Cam didn't think she'd ever tire of watching her.

"What's wrong?" Kara asked. "Not getting cold feet, are you?"

Cam laughed. "Hardly. No, my dad called. Right after we made the decision about the dresses, I called him and asked him to bring Pine Leaf's elk tooth dress to me." She pulled a chair close to the fire pit and sat beside Kara.

"He doesn't want you to wear it?"

"No, that's not it. He was thrilled just like I knew he would be. The problem is the dress is missing."

"I thought you said it was in the tribal museum."

"It was."

"Oh." Kara drew out the single word. "That can't be good."

Cam's thoughts exactly. On loan from her family, the dress had been part of an exhibit in the museum for years. The only two people who had authority to move the dress were Cam and her dad. So where was it? Better question—who moved it?

"No, it's not good at all. It should be in its case at the museum."

"Maybe they moved it for cleaning or they're changing the exhibits around?"

"Or maybe someone stole it. The dress is incredibly valuable even without the history behind it."

Kara put a hand on Cam's arm and then leaned over to kiss her. "It'll turn up," she said against her lips. "And if not, you can wear a pretty white wedding gown too."

Cam laughed, her eyes crinkling. "That'll be the day."

❖

In the daylight, the cottages on the ridge overlooking the dam were lined up like tidy soldiers. Each was a little different, but all were pieces of a bygone era meticulously restored and maintained. Hers was larger than most of the others and closest to the dam. With a wide front porch and a fenced backyard, it showed the unmistakable signs of life while the others appeared to be unoccupied.

Last night his run had brought him right here. Her scent had been strong and he'd had no trouble tracking her. He'd been confident she would be easily located. He knew her scent so well, and beyond that, their connection was strong. A few miles of separation was not enough to crack it, let alone break it.

The other one came out the front door, and through his high-powered binoculars, her short red hair glowed like a stoplight. His hand shook, blurring her face. How could *she*? God decreed one man and one woman, and beyond that, this woman was not one of them. It was wrong in every way.

He would make it all right and in the end, she would thank him. This had been decreed by God, and his heart was filled with the light of righteousness. Soon everything would be as it should. She would belong to him and they would begin their life together.

And the other one? He smiled as he thought about what he had planned for her.

❖

Kara handed Cam the phone. "You're gonna want to listen to this."

Cam frowned, put the phone to her ear, and listened to Jake Ford, Kara's supervisor in the Park Service. "Seriously?" she questioned when he finished.

"Yeah," Jake confirmed. "I had three calls last night from folks sighting a white wolf."

"There are no white wolves in this area. The only pack in the vicinity is up near Springdale, and they're tracking them pretty damned close."

"I know that and you know that, but apparently this albino wolf doesn't know that."

A chill crept down her spine. "Let me make some calls," she told him. "I'll let you know what I find."

She put the phone down and stared out the window. It couldn't be.

Kara's hand on her arm made her turn around. "What is it, Cam? All of sudden your face went white, and that's a pretty good feat for you. Is it the wolf sighting?"

Cam nodded. It was much more than that, though. "I have a bad feeling about this wolf."

"What's so special about this one besides its color?"

"It might not be a wolf."

Kara frowned. "You think we have another werewolf on our hands."

The werewolf that had killed innocents in the park a year earlier wasn't an issue any longer thanks to Kara and her powers. No, she wasn't worried about the return of a bloodthirsty werewolf. This was something much different and a whole lot scarier.

"No, I don't think that. I'm more concerned that it's another Crow shape shifter."

"Yeah, but you know all the shape shifters, so no problem, right?"

She shook her head slowly. "Big problem if it's who I'm afraid it is. Think crazy stalker crossed with violent shape shifter."

Kara whistled. "Oh shit."

❖

He waited and watched. The pattern of their daily life was what he was most interested in. Knowing what they did, how they moved, where they went—those were the keys to making it all happen.

The same capacity for endless patience was how he got here in the first place. No one really understood him or what he was trying to achieve. In the old days things were simpler, and he would be the one to bring those days back. Between his vision and her blood right, they would restore the nation to the glory it once had. Together, they would be unstoppable.

Everything had its order, and he was beginning to formulate his plan. The sun rose until it was directly overhead. His stomach growled. Still, he kept the binoculars trained on the house. The red-haired one came out again, carrying a mountain bike. She snapped on a helmet and rode up the hill that led to Riverside State Park.

He pulled the binoculars from his eyes and set them on the ground. His clothes followed. Though it was forbidden to change during daylight hours, he didn't care. He was rewriting the rules.

Calling the change, he ran down the hill and across the bridge. He paid no attention to the stares of the few drivers who crossed his path. They didn't matter.

❖

"Dad, are you sure?"

"I talked to the hospital personally. Then I called the sheriff. He's gone, and nobody knows where."

"How?" Her voice rose. "How in the hell did they lose him?"

"Million-dollar question, sweetheart. Sounds like he's been planning his escape for a quite a while. Pulled it off without a hitch."

"Somebody has to know something."

"You'd think so, wouldn't you? But apparently, he planned and carried it out all by himself. Didn't say a word to anyone."

"This is a disaster."

Her father's voice was dire. "This is more than a disaster, this is dangerous. He'll be coming for you."

"Yeah, I know." The dread that wrapped around her heart was dark and deep.

"I'm on my way and I'm bringing help."

Usually she'd tell him to stay put. She was a big, strong woman, capable of taking care of herself. The problem was this wasn't just about her. By association, Kara was neck deep too. She'd take his help.

She knew Dad was expecting a fight. He didn't get one. All she said to him was "Hurry."

After she put the phone down, Cam started to pace. The second she'd heard Jake's description of the white wolf, she'd had a sick feeling. She supposed that in the back of her mind she'd always harbored the thought that he might come back. They'd done everything they could to stop him and from all appearances were successful. The problem was he was smart and powerful.

And crazy.

The legal issues were handled. The medical issues were handled. The crazy issue? Not so much. Someone that smart and that disturbed wasn't easily stopped. Yes, he was confined in a maximum-security psychiatric ward, and for most people that would be enough. He wasn't most people.

When they were children, Philip was her best friend. While her father, as the only doctor on the reservation, healed their people, Philip's father took care of the ranch. The two kids were together every day.

She couldn't remember exactly when she noticed something was different about him. Maybe she'd always known, but because he was her best friend, she ignored it. So what if he was odd. He was the one who was always there for her and had her back. At least until she shared her most secret of secrets.

They were both eighteen, and she was more than ready to come out of the closet. She didn't have a single doubt that he would support her. Even now it astonished her how wrong she'd been. When she came out, it was as if it pushed him over some invisible cliff. What once was eccentric behavior morphed into something dark and dangerous.

His lack of support saddened her. She knew her truth would alienate some, she just didn't expect him to be one of them. And she really didn't foresee how it would change him.

The stalking started slowly. At first she didn't realize what he was doing. When her first real girlfriend was attacked by a stranger, who was never caught, they all thought it was a case of homophobia. Montana wasn't exactly a hotbed of gay tolerance.

When her next girlfriend's tires were slashed, she began to wonder if something more was going on. By the third attack at a discreet club in Missoula, she knew she was the common denominator.

Then the phone calls started. The threats. The following. The tribal police were the ones who tracked it back to Philip, and when they did, he snapped. She touched the small scar at the base of her neck and remembered the night he'd held a knife to her throat. He'd taunted the police. Kill him, he'd kill her, they'd be together for eternity.

He cut her, all right, just before he was Tasered. It was enough to take him down. No fewer than three psychologists evaluated him. He never went to trial. He'd been in lockup ever since. Plenty of meds. Plenty of doctors. No change. His form of crazy just didn't respond to help.

❖

It took him a while to find her. The girl did have a pair of legs on her. She powered that mountain bike through the park like a boat gliding on calm water. If only she'd had the good sense to live according to God's plan, she could have made some man a very good wife. Those legs wrapped around a guy would be incredible. But no, she had to defy nature, and now she'd pay the price.

Wasn't his fault. She was the one who made this choice. She should have known what she was doing was wrong. Men and women belonged together. Period. When they tried to defy what was right, there were consequences.

Keeping to the high brush, he kept her in his sights. He had to wait for just the right place. His paws barely hit the ground as he ran in near silence. She would never know what happened. A bit of a shame really. He'd have liked her to realize her sin was sending her into the arms of death.

Then again, what did it really matter? She'd be headed to hell, and that would certainly be enough to make her realize she'd damned herself. While his mission was to save Camille, he had no love for this woman who tried to damage his one and only. She had to die for her sins.

He watched as she pushed up a trail that traversed a ridge. He followed and paused only long enough to gaze down. It was perfect. Below, rocks jutted, sharp and numerous. God's plan in all its glory.

When she stopped, her legs straddling the bike, he was ready. She was gazing toward the river in the distance when he struck. He hit her full on and she rocketed off the ridge, bike and all. He pulled back, his paws scrambling for purchase. He didn't need to follow her off the ridge.

As he steadied, he stared down. She was motionless on the rocks, her bike partially on top of her. The scent of fresh blood caught on the air. He waited and watched until he was certain she wasn't going to move again and then he turned and ran.

❖

Cam was frantic. Kara hadn't come back to the cottage. Jake, down at the rangers' station, hadn't heard from her, and she wasn't answering her cell. Something was very, very wrong.

The quickest way to find her was to change, except that went against everything. She couldn't do it in broad daylight no matter how much she wanted to. Her time was the night, so for now, she'd have to go about finding Kara in the old-fashioned human way.

Like Kara, she had a high-end mountain bike. She grabbed it and started out. She didn't know the park like Kara did, but she was motivated, and that had to count for a lot.

By the time she got back to the house without finding any sign of Kara, darkness was beginning to fall. Now she wasn't just frantic, she was scared to death. If Philip had done something to Kara, Cam would find him and kill him.

The bike she threw to the ground had cost her an easy three grand, but she didn't hesitate. She dropped it as if was worth nothing. Compared to the life of the woman she loved, it was nothing.

It wasn't full-on dark and she didn't care. She stripped off her clothes right where she stood, readying herself to call the change. She didn't get a chance. Before she could even open her mouth, she heard a *zap* and then every muscle in her body started to spasm.

❖

This had gone better than he could have imagined. Camille was so focused on her little redhead that she didn't even hear him as he stepped around the corner of the cottage. By the time she heard the pop of the Taser, it was too late. She was all his.

He'd forgotten how strong she was. It took a little effort to get her into the car once he drove it around from its hiding place behind one of the other cottages. Her hands and feet zip-tied, she was effectively immobilized. She was still twitching as she lay across the backseat. He knew all too well how effective a Taser could be.

He ran a hand across her cheek. "Don't worry, love, it's almost over."

She was probably trying to say something, but it came out as a cacophony of garbled noises.

"Shh, don't try to thank me. It's going to be perfect now. Just like it was always meant to be. You and me, Camille-girl, you and me."

He was smiling as he pulled away from the cottage and turned onto Charles Road. Before he'd left the cabin earlier, he'd prepared everything. A fire was laid in the fireplace, his bedroll spread out before the hearth. Her dress was hanging on the door, waiting for her to slip into it. Before the sun rose, they'd be united in the eyes of God and their wonderful life together would begin.

She might be upset now. That would all change once the whole picture was revealed to her. He was protecting her, as he'd always tried to do. More importantly, he was protecting her soul. He was the only one with the power to save her from the evil ways that really weren't her at all.

At the cabin, he pulled her from the backseat and draped her over his shoulder. The tremors in her body were calming down. She would more than likely be resistant at first. He had a cure for that too.

Stupid doctors thought he was taking all that medication they put in the little white paper cups. No fucking way. His stockpile of meds was impressive.

He plopped Camille into the one nice chair and then went to his bag. Into the bottle of water he pulled out he dropped two white tablets, shaking the bottle until they dissolved. A tool for every job.

Her voice was shaky. "Philip, what have you done? Where's Kara?"

He smiled and came close. "No worries, Camille. Everything is going to be fine now." He held the bottle to her lips.

She shook her head violently. "*What* have you done?"

"Shh, just drink." She fought him and he grabbed her hair. "Drink."

Forcing her to hold still, he got a fair amount of the water down her throat even though an equal amount spilled down the front of her chest. It was enough. Give it a little time and she would be his in all ways.

❖

The damn water, she thought as the haze in her head cleared. Philip had forced water down her throat and then everything had gone black. Now the room was swimming back into focus.

A fire roared in the fireplace, making the dingy little cabin too warm. She tried to move, but her hands were still zip-tied together. It took her a few seconds to realize they were in front of her now. When he'd surprised her earlier, he'd secured her hands behind her back.

The second thing she noticed was her clothing. She'd actually been naked when he'd zapped her. Her gaze dropped to her feet. Moccasins were laced to her knees, the embellishments intricate and beautiful. So was the elk tooth dress that covered her body. The missing Pine Leaf dress.

"Philip, what are you doing?"

He moved into her line of vision and smiled. Like her, he was dressed as a traditional Crow. "Good, you're awake. Now we can begin."

"Begin what?" It was hard to think, the remnants of whatever he'd given her clouding her mind.

"Why, the wedding, of course."

"What the hell are you talking about?"

He leaned in and kissed her on the lips. "Cammie, you've always known we were meant to be together. You've had your little flings, your wild days. Now it's time to begin the rest of our lives. Together."

"I'm marrying Kara."

His face morphed into a mask of fury. "I *never* want to hear that name again. Do you understand me? Your time with that woman is over. We will never speak of it again."

The venom in his voice sent a shiver through her. Very quietly she asked, "What did you do, Philip?"

He smiled, a ghost of the boy she thought of like a brother showing in his face. "Let's just say I gave her a little shove in the right direction."

Cam closed her eyes and willed her mind to work. Somewhere in the back of her mind, she heard a ticking clock. Time was running out.

"I'm not going to marry you."

He shrugged. "Of course you are. God put you on this earth for me."

"God has nothing to do with this."

His smile made her sick. "One man." He pointed an index finger to his chest before turning it in her direction. "One woman."

One crazy, she thought. Her mind was clearing, and as it did, she could only see one way to escape. Closing her eyes, she concentrated with everything she had. *I'm coming, Kara.*

Then she called the change.

❖

No. No. No.

He saw her start to change and was desperate to make it stop. They had to say their vows. Had to be married in the eyes of God. Nothing could stand in their way.

The change was faster than he thought possible given the amount of medication he'd forced into her. How had she moved past the debilitating effects? He didn't have time to think it through. The only chance he had to salvage this night of their joining was to change himself. He didn't bother to take off his ceremonial garments. He didn't have time.

As Camille had done, he called the change, shaking off the human clothes as the wolf emerged. He'd thought she would bolt for the door the moment she changed, but she didn't. Instead, fearless and strong, the large black wolf with the golden eyes stared at him, fangs bared.

She was braced for battle.

His heart was sad as he gave her what she wanted. He'd foreseen their future together as man and wife. The game had changed. He'd not spend his life loving her. His only option now was to spend his life mourning her.

His howl split the night as he launched.

❖

A fury that roared through her body came out in a splitting howl. The sight of the white wolf lunging toward her only increased her emotions. He'd killed Kara, and for that he would die. She would rip his throat out.

As she readied for his attack, she was vaguely aware of a sound behind her and the rush of cool air that suddenly filled the room. Her teeth were bared, saliva dripping from her lips as his body hit hers with a giant thud. She sank her teeth into his fur, connecting with the flesh below.

The gunshot that split the night barely registered as she shook his body back and forth, the white of his fur flashing before her eyes. Slowly, it struck her that he wasn't fighting, and as she held on, the fur began to recede.

Releasing her grip, she dropped him to the floor. As she watched, the white wolf began to change until before her paws lay only a man, a hole in his chest. His eyes were staring sightlessly up at the ceiling.

She howled and then turned to the door.

"Come back, Cam."

The wolf in her wanted to tear the human apart. The human in her recognized her father. In moments, she was back and sobbing. "He killed Kara."

He held her and stroked her hair. "No, baby, Kara's fine. Jake and his crew found her unconscious at the base of one of the ridges. She's got a concussion and one nasty cut on the side of her head, but she's going to be okay."

"Really?" Could it be true?

"I promise."

Relief flooded through her as Cam wrapped up in the coat her father handed her. "How did you know where to find me?"

Her father rolled his eyes. "That dumbass Junior Petro. Process of elimination. Junior was the only one besides you that Philip would ever contact. He was drunk when we found him, and it only took about two minutes to get him to spill his guts. Came armed with silver bullets."

"It's over, then? Really over?"

He kissed the top of her head. "It's really over. Now let's get you to the hospital. We'll check you out and then you can go check on your woman."

❖

The night couldn't have been more beautiful if they'd custom-ordered it. The moon was golden, the sky sparkled with stars, and all their friends were there. Cam's father, Kara's adoptive parents and her biological sisters, everyone from the Spiritus Group: Riah and Adriana, Colin and Ivy, Tory and Naomi. It was a perfect night for a wedding.

At first, she'd thought Pine Leaf's dress was ruined after her change. Her father had picked up all the elk teeth, the moccasins, everything, and given it to one of the women back in Montana. She'd restored it and now Cam stood proudly wearing her ancestor's dress on the balcony of Riah's estate. With her hair braided and the choker that had also been Pine Leaf's around her neck, she was ready to commit the rest of her life to Kara.

When Kara came out of the doors on her father's arm, Cam's eyes filled with tears. Kara was always beautiful to her, but tonight, she was radiant. The dress she wore was long and white and gorgeous.

This was all a dream come true, one she never really believed would happen for her, and yet it was. She was going to marry the woman she loved. For real.

Five minutes later, her heart soared as she said those two simple words that meant so much: "I do."

Meghan O'Brien is the author of six novels published by Bold Strokes Books, including *Infinite Loop*, *The Three*, *Thirteen Hours*, *Battle Scars*, *Wild*, and *The Night Off*. She has written multiple erotic and romantic short lesbian fiction stories, which have appeared in numerous Erotic Interludes and Romantic Interludes anthologies, also published by Bold Strokes.

This story features characters from *The Night Off*.

THE FANTASY EXCHANGE
MEGHAN O'BRIEN

Walking into the sex club downtown where Nat had once taken the occasional client, Emily was certain the decadent display in front of her was something she would never forget. Men and women were parked at tables, in booths, and on couches all over the club watching as a bound woman was flogged onstage.

Nat must have seen her wide-eyed surprise at the show, because she leaned in close and whispered, "Maybe next time?"

Tonight's fantasy centered on exhibitionism, but nothing on the scale of being put on display for a crowd. Yet despite her trepidation about the idea of being marched onto center stage to withstand whatever punishment Nat might devise, a pleasant shiver ran up her spine when she imagined how the scene might unfold. "Maybe."

Nat kissed her cheek. "Come on, darling. Let's find a seat."

She led them to a booth set far back from the stage, close to the bar. Emily sat down first, grateful when Nat asked if she wanted a drink. "Please. But just one."

Nat kissed the top of her head. "I'll be right back."

Emily watched Nat walk away with her heart full of emotion. In a way, she hadn't lived until she met Nat. Only a year together and absolutely everything about her life was different. Her baby sister was thriving in college while Emily enjoyed professional success without working herself to death, and the kindest, sexiest woman in this patch of this universe made her feel cherished every single day.

Their relationship truly was something to celebrate. Emily grinned stupidly, which seemed to attract the attention of a dark-skinned butch leaning against the bar. The butch, who wore her hair slightly longer than Nat, raised an eyebrow and offered a sultry smile. Blushing, Emily looked back to the stage, where the flogging had finally come to an end. The woman secured to the metal frame heaved and shuddered as a feminine blonde set aside her flogger and picked up a harness and strap-on.

Shocked and more than a little thrilled by what was about to happen right in front of her, Emily glanced in Nat's direction and caught her gaze. Her partner leaned on the bar only a foot away from the flirtatious butch, and both of them watched Emily with lust-filled eyes. Nat tipped her head toward the woman beside her, then lifted her eyebrow.

Emily nodded and looked away quickly. A year of exploring her sexuality and playing out private fantasies with a lover she trusted had expanded her boundaries beyond what she'd ever dreamed possible. Yet tonight she was going to put herself out there like she never had before. The thought of fulfilling Nat's fantasy—one she'd known about since the very beginning of their relationship—excited her to the point she couldn't breathe. But to add her own fantasy of being watched into the mix?

She'd trusted Nat to guide her through challenging sexual scenarios in the past, and her trust never wavered. One utterance of their safe word—*unicorn*—and their play would end. She would be shielded from the eyes of strangers. Ultimately, she was in control.

Nat returned to the table and set a drink in front of her, then slipped into the booth on her other side. Aware that the cocky butch at the bar still had an unrestricted view of her, Emily wasn't disappointed to find that the stranger's scrutiny hadn't ceased.

"She enjoys looking at you." Nat waited until Emily met her eyes, then took a drink of her beer. "Can't exactly blame her."

Face heating, Emily said, "It doesn't bother you?"

Nat chuckled. "No. You're mine." She set down her beer and scooted closer to Emily. Seizing her chin in a tender but firm grasp, she said, "Tell me."

"I'm yours." When the intensity of the emotion that passed between them overwhelmed her, she lowered her eyes to stare at her lap. At Nat's request, she'd worn a simple, flowing red dress. The material was soft and silky, and the fact she'd forgone stockings and wore only a lacy red bra and panties made her feel free, uninhibited, and sexy as hell. She was equal parts nervous and aroused, scared to see where tonight would go even as she yearned for Nat to take her there.

Nat leaned in. "Do you like what you see onstage?"

Without pulling out of Nat's grip, Emily used her peripheral vision to glimpse the show that continued for the enthusiastic crowd. The blond domme stood behind her sub, one hand on her shoulder and the other on her hip. She thrust inside the restrained woman with one powerful motion, drawing a muffled scream from behind the ball gag in her slave's mouth. Emily shuddered and looked at Nat, who gave her a knowing smirk.

"Yes," Emily said simply.

"Are you wet?"

She stared into Nat's eyes without blinking. "Everything about being here with you tonight is making me wet."

"Open your legs." Nat kissed her bottom lip before drawing away with a sharp nip. "Let me check."

Wondering whether the woman at the bar was still watching, Emily parted her legs. Nat released her chin and slipped her hand beneath her skirt. Emily gasped as Nat drew her finger along her panties, tracing a line over slick, sensitive labia and teasing her swollen clit. Barely breathing, Emily sat statue still and savored the possessive caress.

Nat grinned. "I guess you are." She removed her hand and nodded at the bar. "Your new friend can't take her eyes off you."

"Did she see that?"

Nat stared at something over Emily's shoulder. "She did."

Emily's cheeks were aflame. "Oh."

"Don't play innocent. You love it." Lowering her voice to a bare whisper, Nat spoke directly into her ear. "Why don't you pull up your dress and show your new friend what belongs to me?"

It had been a long time since one of Nat's commands filled her with such exquisite embarrassment. Here they were—the moment of truth. If she couldn't obey now, the success of their entire evening would be thrown into question. Yet as humiliating as it was to expose herself for a stranger in a public place, this was exactly the type of scenario she'd always fantasized about.

She reached for the hem of her dress, but Nat stopped her. "Look at her when you do it."

Emily took a deep breath and turned in her seat. She made eye contact with the woman at the bar, who stared intently from beneath hooded lids. Nat curled an arm around her middle and tugged her closer, then cupped her breast lovingly. Kissing Emily's earlobe, she murmured, "Lift your skirt and show her your wet panties, darling."

Only with Nat did she feel safe enough to do something so daring. Amazed at how far a shy accountant could come in just a year, Emily slid the hem of her skirt up her thighs until her panties were exposed. She could practically see the butch's visceral reaction to the sight—nostrils flared, knuckles white as she gripped the edge of the bar.

"Don't stop there." Nat kissed her neck. "Pull them to the side and give her a good, long look."

Even though she knew that there was limited visibility inside the dim club, Emily's breathing grew ragged at the thought of revealing herself so blatantly. Already she could see that she'd caught the attention of a man farther down the bar who watched the space between her legs with an expression of poorly concealed anticipation. Strangely, the idea of having a mixed-gender audience wasn't completely off-putting.

Nat trailed a string of gentle kisses along her jaw. "Are you going to obey, or do I have to punish you?"

Emily knew better than to answer *both*. Emboldened by the sound of the fucking onstage, she grasped the crotch of her panties and tugged them over, exposing her aroused sex to the cool air. She stared directly at the dark-skinned butch, who took a long pull of her beer without allowing her eyes to stray.

"Don't look away from her." Nat dropped her hand from Emily's breast to her pussy, then sank one long finger deep inside.

Surprised by how quickly Nat was moving things along—but oh, so very grateful—Emily arched her back and moaned. The butch set her bottle down and licked her lips. She seemed to make eye contact with Nat for a moment, then boldly returned to watching Emily get fingered.

"Does this satisfy your desire to be watched, my darling?" Nat withdrew, using her fingers to spread Emily's labia open lewdly. "It's a shame the lighting is so bad in here. Imagine if I had you trussed up in front of her. I could show off every inch of your beautiful body."

Emily's pulse pounded at the promise in Nat's words. She knew Nat's fantasy, and the thought of allowing the stranger who watched her so hungrily bear witness as she was pushed to her limits was downright intoxicating. "Yes, mistress," she said, shifting more fully into her role. "I'd like that."

"I know you would." Nat sank back into her with two fingers, spreading them to stretch her to a point just shy of discomfort. "Do you think she has any idea about what a pain-loving little slut you are?"

"I don't know." Emily inhaled, ready to keep speaking, but Nat cut her off by pulling out and delivering a sharp slap against her puffy labia.

"Let's show her," Nat murmured, and slapped her again.

Emily cried out in surprise as a delicious thrill of pain shot through her lower body. She forced her eyes open with effort, aroused by the sight of her admirer now fisting her hands at her sides, her drink wholly forgotten.

But then, just as suddenly as everything started, it stopped. Nat pulled her panties back into place, tugged down the hem of her skirt, and ended the show. Emily felt nearly as bereft as the stranger looked. Turning slightly, she focused on Nat's chin. "Mistress?"

Nat gently but firmly pushed Emily away. "Go invite your friend to join us in a private room. Ask her if she wants to watch me use you. Make sure she knows she's just the audience."

"Yes, mistress." Emily could barely stand. It took every ounce of her concentration to walk the twenty feet to the bar, then all her courage to speak to the handsome stranger who greeted her approach with a cool grin.

Luckily, the stranger broke the ice. "Don't tell me she got you off already?"

Emily managed a shaky laugh. "Unfortunately, no."

The butch offered Nat a friendly, long-distance nod. "Soon, I'm sure."

"Depends on my mistress's mood." Emily leaned against the bar, grateful for the support. "And my behavior."

"I see." Exhaling, the butch grabbed her beer and took a swig. "Well, tell your mistress thank you for letting me have a peek."

Emily smiled. Thank goodness for perfect openings. "Actually, she wanted me to ask you something."

The bottle of beer went back on the bar, once again forgotten. "Did she?" The butch stepped closer, but stopped when Emily took a half step back. "What's that?"

Bracing herself for the possibility of rejection, Emily said, "Do you want to join us in a private room? My mistress would like you to watch her use me."

"Use you, huh?" The butch's throat tightened and she flicked her gaze back to Nat. If she was uncertain about the proposal, she didn't show it. "I can do that."

"Great." Emily relaxed, pleased the fantasy exchange was so thrillingly on track. "As long as you're okay spending the next hour or two as a spectator."

The butch laughed. "I'm very all right." She dropped her gaze to Emily's cleavage and leered. "I've been undressing you with my eyes since you walked in. I can't wait to see the real thing."

"Okay, then." Shyly, Emily said, "What's your name?"

"Billie." She offered her hand. "It's a pleasure to meet you…"

"Emily." She shook Billie's hand and gestured at the table. "Shall we?"

Billie followed close behind. "Please."

Nat slid out of the booth and greeted Billie with a firm handshake. "Nat."

"Billie. Thanks for the invitation."

"Thank *you* for giving my girl an audience." Nat wrapped an arm around Emily's waist. "Do you like what I've shown you so far?"

"She's gorgeous." Billie kept her eyes strictly on Nat, almost as though Emily wasn't there. "Very nice."

"But you'd like a better look?"

Billie matched Nat's playful grin. "I'd love a better look."

"Good." Nat took Emily's hand and led her away from the table, Billie bringing up the rear. "Our room's in the back."

Emily's stomach leapt into her throat as they walked across the noisy club. The throbbing music only partially covered the sound of the woman still being mercilessly fucked onstage. Around them were people in various states of undress and all manner of sexual positions and configurations. When was the last time she'd felt this bashful about anything sexual? Nat had helped her experience so much since they'd been together. To have Nat once more take her somewhere new— exactly one year to the night when she'd tested Emily's sexual limits for the first time—was so perfectly, utterly right.

Their room was at the top of a staircase in the back corner of the club, behind a door that locked from the inside. Nat ushered them in and secured the dead bolt, leaving Emily to gape at the equipment that had been laid out on a long steel table. Thin black rope, a pair of shears, a harness and dildo, a large wand vibrator, a paddle, a riding crop, lube…clearly Nat had put plenty of thought into this encounter. Like she always did.

There was a couch and a mini-refrigerator on one side of the room, and on the other, a looming metal frame. A simple high-backed chair sat in the middle, hinting at possibilities that made Emily's inner thighs slick.

Emily turned to Nat and found dark, hard eyes staring back. She dropped her gaze immediately, not allowing her focus to stray from Nat's chin. Submission was her only objective now that the scene had begun.

"Take a seat, Billie." Nat stepped close to Emily, unwavering in her scrutiny. She ran a finger up Emily's arm, then down into her cleavage. "You, get out of this dress. Show Billie how pretty you are."

Emily took a chance and lifted her face so she could check in. This was the first time they'd included another person in their play. Nat seemed relaxed, in control, and very turned on. Somehow she managed to offer unspoken reassurance without dropping her stoic mask, infusing Emily with the confidence to grab hold of the zipper on the side of her dress.

Nat clucked her tongue. "Turn around and face Billie. She can't keep her eyes off your tits, so let's not tease her."

Emily's cheeks warmed at the naked hunger on Billie's face. Perched on the very edge of the couch, she seemed eager for Emily to comply. Smirking, Billie said, "No, let's not."

Nat delivered a hard smack to Emily's ass, lifting her skirt high up on her thighs with her hand. "Go on. Don't test my patience."

Emily's breathing hitched. Billie must have noticed her reaction because she bared her teeth in a predatory smile. "Does this one like to break the rules?"

Nat chuckled. "Slut is actually an obedient girl, most of the time. That doesn't mean she doesn't enjoy a good, hard spanking, though."

Not quite ready for that yet, Emily went ahead and unzipped her dress. She couldn't hold Billie's gaze as she stepped out of the silky red material and kicked it aside. Nat's strong hand gripped her neck before she moved down to pinch Emily's nipples through her bra. "This is the best part. The anticipation. Am I right, Billie?"

Billie was so rapt on the action that she didn't answer. Nat was completely in her element. Billie was under her sway just as surely as Emily was. That meant Nat controlled everyone's pleasure. Emily knew her well enough to realize that this aspect of their collaborative fantasy was pitch perfect in every way.

Billie nodded dumbly. "I don't know. I sense that the best is yet to come."

Nat snickered. "You've probably got me there." She stepped in front of Emily and fixed her with a reproachful look. "Why'd you stop?"

"I—"

"Let me help." Nat grasped the cups of her lacy red bra and pulled them down, causing her breasts to spill out. Then she stepped away, leaving Emily in full view of her audience.

Blushing, Emily stood with her hands laced behind her back. Fixing her bra would be a serious misstep. "May I continue undressing, mistress?"

"What do you say, Billie?" Nat slipped a hand into the back of Emily's panties and squeezed one cheek, then the other. "Should she continue?"

Billie reclined against the couch cushions. "Yes."

Nat grabbed a bit of flesh and pinched. "You heard her. Keep going."

Careful not to betray any hesitation, Emily reached behind her back and unclasped her bra. She tossed it aside and lowered her panties to her ankles. Nat grabbed her shoulder as she bent over, keeping her on her feet while she administered two hard smacks. Whimpering, Emily straightened and kicked her panties out of the way.

That accomplished, Emily realized how very naked she was. Billie sat motionless, hand on her stomach, seemingly content to run her hungry gaze from Emily's breasts to her pussy and back again. "Does her pussy taste as good as she looks?"

Nat tapped the inside of Emily's thigh. Emily set one foot to the side, then bit her lip when Nat dragged fingers through her wetness. Nat crossed the room and offered them to Billie. "Say please."

Billie's nostrils flared, her throat tensed. Emily sensed that she was used to being dominant. "Please."

Clearly pleased, Nat said, "Try her."

Billie touched her tongue to Nat's shiny fingertips, then captured them between her lips. The contrast between Nat's light skin and Billie's chocolate brown triggered clenching arousal that threatened to take Emily too close to the edge, much too quickly. As though sensing her dilemma, Nat returned to stand behind her.

"Well?" Emily could hear the smirk in Nat's voice. "Does it?"

Billie nodded and sank back into the couch cushions. "Yes."

Nat patted Emily on the bottom. "Be a good slut and get Billie a drink from the fridge. She looks like she needs one."

Emily knew exactly what Nat was doing. Not only would this task delay the festivities, thus heightening Emily's anticipation, but also, following domestic commands while nude was demeaning in the extreme. Nat was well aware of the effect this would have on her. With a quiet "Yes, mistress," Emily went to the fridge, focused only on her destination, and didn't allow herself to look at the other women in the room.

"Isn't she magnificent?" Nat said when Emily bent to pull a bottle of water from the mini-refrigerator. "I acquired her last year." Softening her voice, she said, "And I intend to keep her forever."

"Smart," Billie said. She seemed to drink in the sight of Emily's bare curves as she approached. "She looks like a keeper."

"You have no idea." Nat caught her arm as Emily returned to stand at her side. "Let me show you." Tugging Emily along, she went to the high-backed chair and sat down. "Across my lap, slut."

Over-the-knee spankings were high up the list of Emily's favorite sexual acts. Yet this was also what made her feel the most vulnerable. Even knowing that they were in like-minded company, Emily battled a moment of doubt about letting Billie see her so ready and willing to accept a painful punishment.

Nat didn't allow her a chance to refuse. She yanked Emily down and wrestled her into position over her knees. Emily planted her hands on the floor in an attempt to regain leverage, but Nat kept her effectively pinned in place and helpless without seeming to try.

"What's our safe word?" Nat said aloud for Billie's benefit.

"Unicorn." Emily tried not to smile when Billie smirked.

Smack. "Is this funny?" Nat barked.

"No!" Emily cried out, startled by the suddenness and strength of the first blow. *Smack.* On instinct, she reached back with one hand and tried to shield her ass until she could gather her resolve to take another blow. Unfortunately, she only managed to throw herself off balance, which Nat made worse by catching her hand and holding it loosely against her lower back.

"What are you doing?" Nat's voice radiated displeasure. "Don't block me."

"I'm sorry, mistress." Emily gently withdrew her hand from Nat's, moving it back to its place on the floor. "It won't happen again."

"Damn right it won't." Resting a hand on her already stinging ass, Nat rubbed the skin gently. "Billie, get over here and grab hold of her hands for me."

Billie didn't waste any time, clearly excited to be involved. She sat cross-legged on the floor in front of Emily and took one of Emily's hands in each of hers and held them tightly on her knees. "Like this?"

Nat's next blow was slightly softer but Emily still struggled, and Billie was able to hold her down easily. "Perfect," Nat said, and hit her again. Alternating from cheek to cheek, she established a steady, relentless rhythm that built on the stinging discomfort of the first blows in an excruciatingly gradual way.

Emily bit her lip hard at what felt like the hundredth lash, spreading her legs far apart, desperate for pleasure to ease the pain. Nat continued to deliver hard slaps low on her bottom, allowing her fingers to smack wetly against Emily's labia. Groaning, Emily stared into Billie's brown eyes as she willed herself to make it through one of the most prolonged spankings Nat had ever administered.

Finally, the spanking ceased. The tears started as soon as Emily took her first uninhibited breath. With an expression of sweet concern, Billie looked up at Nat, who chose that moment to very slowly slide one finger deep into Emily's pussy. Emily moaned, drawing Billie's attention back to her face.

Nat pulled all the way out, then thrust back in. "Tell Billie what I'm doing, slut."

Inexplicably shy about having Billie right there while Nat fingered her, Emily mumbled, "My mistress is fucking me with her finger."

"What am I fucking?" Nat asked lightly.

Afraid that she knew exactly what Nat was fishing for, Emily chose a safer answer. "My pussy, mistress."

Nat withdrew and swiftly took hold of Emily's labia in a careful but demanding grip. "You know what this is called, slut. Use the correct word."

One year later and this still had the power to make her blush— especially with Billie still holding her hands. Afraid to incite Nat's disapproval if she hesitated, Emily blurted, "She's fucking my cunt."

Nat released her labia and gave her a light slap that sent electric sparks of sensation shooting through her lower body. "Is that what I'm doing now?"

Emily shook her head frantically and met the next, slightly harder smack with a determined groan. "No, mistress. You're slapping my cunt."

"Why?"

"Because I'm a dirty bitch who likes it."

Billie's eyes had gone feral and hungry. "You are a dirty bitch, aren't you?" she murmured, stroking her thumbs over the backs of Emily's hands. "You can't get enough of this."

Emily didn't answer. She didn't need a correction to know that speaking to Billie without permission was a bad idea. Unnerved by Billie's proximity, Emily lowered her head and stared at the ground— only to be promptly pulled up by her hair.

"Don't stop looking at her," Nat husked. She slapped Emily's sex lightly, setting up a driving rhythm that managed to push her close to release within minutes. Chest heaving, Emily focused on keeping eye contact with Billie and not succumbing to orgasm.

Nat stopped slapping and instead slipped her hand wetly over Emily's mound, rubbing her soft, slick flesh with her palm. Emily's hips jerked into Nat, her body rebelling against her cautious mind. Nat stopped abruptly, but she left her fingers curled lightly around Emily's wet sex. "Billie, on the table is a riding crop and a paddle. Choose whichever you want for her last ten licks."

Emily swallowed. She waited to hear what Billie would choose. Rather than speak, Billie released Emily's hands and walked away. Seconds later, Nat brought down the leather paddle on her left buttock.

"Count them off," she ordered.

"One." Emily was almost grateful when Billie sat and took her hands again. Being held in place made it easier to accept the pain and push through it. When Nat hit her again, she held up her head and smiled at Billie. "Two."

She counted off all ten blows, not shedding tears until number nine, and then only a few. When Nat was done, she handed Billie the paddle, which Billie returned to the table. Emily remained prone over Nat's thighs, unsure what to expect next.

Nat rubbed soothing circles over one cheek, then the other. "You deserve a reward for taking that so well. Do you want to come?"

"If that's what you desire, mistress." Emily took pride in how well-versed in submission she'd become. These days, she usually knew exactly how to answer Nat's questions. "Please use my body however you see fit."

"Good girl." Nat rubbed tight circles over Emily's painfully swollen clit. "Now stand up."

It was a wonder she was able to comply. Her legs had turned to rubber and her entire body shook. Once she managed to get to her feet, she laced her fingers behind her back and stared at the floor. She loved how the subservient pose made her feel—not to mention how *commanding* it made Nat seem.

"Billie, bring me the rope and the shears. It's time to give my little slut the pleasure she deserves."

Emily watched dry-mouthed as Billie gathered the supplies. They'd played with restraints in the past and Emily had absolutely loved it. Really, she loved *everything* that Nat imagined for their encounters, but the one element of Nat's fantasy that would challenge her was being forced to orgasm over and over. Even more than a painful spanking, it required serious mind over matter for her to withstand pleasure overload.

Nat took the rope from Billie and turned to Emily. "Kneel."

Grateful not to have to support her trembling weight, Emily sank to the floor. She bowed her head in classic slavegirl submission and waited.

Nat knelt behind her. "Arms behind your back."

Emily obeyed, swallowing a little nervously as Nat passed the rope around her upper body—once, twice—while tying it off under her arms. She stared down at her bare breasts, now framed by the black rope. The sight made her so wet that she stopped paying attention to the expert binding of her hands. Lifting her eyes, she found Billie standing to the side, looking just as turned on as she felt.

Nat tightened a knot. "Take a seat, Billie. Enjoy the show." Billie sat as Nat made a cut with the shears. "Is that comfortable, slut?"

Emily tested the rope, which didn't strain her unduly. Luckily, Nat had chosen to tie her in a position she could hold for a while. "Yes, mistress."

"Good. Now legs." Nat cut two lengths of rope. "Sit so your knees are bent and your legs are fully tucked under you. I'm going to tie you just above the ankle and just below the knee."

"Frogtie," Billie said, reclining on the couch cushions. "Nice choice."

"It's one of my favorites." Once again, Nat looped and tied off the rope as Emily sat motionless. "So she can still spread her slutty legs for me." Nat paused to fondle Emily's sex. "Easy access to my favorite toy." Drawing away with a slap, she finished the first leg and moved to the second. "Slut, when's the last time you made yourself come?"

The out-of-the-blue question caught Emily totally off guard. "Um…"

Nat gave her another sharp slap, setting off a riot of sensation that made her moan. "That's not an answer."

"Yesterday morning, mistress." "Unauthorized masturbation" was a frequent excuse for her punishments in bed, so she wasn't shocked that Nat would ask. "I'm sorry."

"You sure do get horny a lot, you nasty bitch."

Emily's entire body burned with embarrassment. "Yes, mistress."

"What did you use? Your hand?" Finally done tying her into a position that left her unable to stand but free to open her legs and be placed in a variety of poses, Nat slipped on her harness and dildo, then turned to face her. "Did you use a vibrator?"

Emily couldn't take her eyes off the wand vibrator that was suddenly in Nat's hand. They'd never used one before. She didn't use vibrators much at all. "No, mistress. I used my hand."

Nat knelt once again at her side. She powered on the wand, which buzzed menacingly. "Spread your legs."

Emily set her knees apart on the floor, careful to keep upright without the use of her arms for balance. She definitely felt clumsy, and very, very helpless. "Yes, mistress."

Nat pinned her with a stern look. "Hold this position."

Swallowing, Emily whispered, "Yes, mistress."

The first touch of the vibrator to her clit was pure, glorious bliss. *Finally*, she was on her way to the destination she'd craved all night. The sensation was intense and deeply satisfying, making it impossible not to rock her hips against the wand.

It only took a couple minutes for the powerful vibration to bring her to the edge. Her thighs quaked, and she took deep breaths to relax. The rope made it extremely difficult to pull away, so the best thing to do was just let it happen. She had to accept that she wasn't in control. And that it was okay, because Nat always kept her safe.

"Mistress, may I come?" Emily curled her toes, staving off her climax. "Please, mistress, please, please, *please*."

"Do it," Nat said lazily.

Emily threw back her head and yelled hoarsely as waves of pleasure rolled through her body. The sensation built and built and built until she couldn't stand it anymore, but there was no escape. She tried to close her legs, but Nat was right there to force her thighs back open with one strong hand while she rubbed the vibrator over her with the other.

Desperate to distract herself from the painful ecstasy that sliced through her body, Emily gazed wildly around the room until her attention landed on Billie lying back on the couch. Billie's hand moved in her jeans and her chest rose and fell rapidly. Somehow the sight of Billie taking pleasure from her delicious torture made it easier to withstand.

Nat pulled the vibrator away minutes later, when sweat ran in rivulets down Emily's chest and back. She struggled to regain her breath, then whimpered when Nat swiftly repositioned her so that her chest and shoulders touched the floor and she balanced on her knees. It was an awkward but reasonably comfortable position that rendered her completely helpless. Her juices literally dripped from her, coating her thighs.

The vibrator touched her clit again. "What do you want?"

Emily yelled in pleasure-pain. "To please you, mistress!"

"Do you want to come?"

She was almost positive that she'd been coming for an eternity by now. "I am, mistress."

Nat slapped her already sore bottom. "Keep going, slut. Isn't this what you wanted?"

"Yes, mistress," Emily choked out. Her legs shook so hard that she didn't know how much longer she could hold position. She wanted to collapse on the floor. "Please, mistress."

"Please what?" Nat rubbed her with the buzzing wand. "Please make you come?"

"No, mistress."

Smack! "No?" Nat said in a dangerous voice.

Emily said the only thing her exhausted brain could manage. "Yes, mistress."

"What is it, then?" Nat removed the vibrator and Emily sobbed in relief. "Yes or no?"

Determined not to break position or her perfect submission, Emily said, "Whatever you desire, mistress. I'm yours."

The buzz of the vibrator ceased. Emily relaxed, then inhaled sharply when Nat spread her open and entered her with her long, thick cock. Nat grabbed hold of her feet, which were nearly level with her thighs, and used them for leverage to very slowly fuck her.

"Your cunt is dripping," Nat said in a sultry voice. "I've never seen a slut so ready to be fucked." She gathered up a bit of the wetness with her finger and gingerly worked it into Emily's anus. "You ever seen such a nasty slut in your life, Billie?"

Sounding out of breath, Billie said, "Never."

"You close, Billie?" Nat moved her free hand to Emily's hip. "Think about how fucking hot her cunt feels wrapped around me. Think about how sore she'll be tomorrow."

A soft cry of pleasure sounded from above her. Nat withdrew from her ass so she could grip Emily's hips and thrust faster. Emily tightened her hands into fists and rode out the convulsions Nat triggered. She lifted her ass higher and rocked back into Nat, desperate to hear her lover's release.

When it came, Nat moaned and pounded into her a few more times, then bent over her back and gathered her into a loving embrace. "Happy anniversary, Emily," she whispered under her breath. "I love you."

"I love you, too." All of a sudden she was desperate to get out of her restraints and into Nat's arms.

Across the room, she heard the door click shut. Nat carefully withdrew from her pussy and eased her up into a kneeling position. As Nat went to work untying rope, Emily said, "Guess she realized it was about to get mushy."

"Nobody wants to see *that*," Nat teased. She freed Emily's legs, waiting for her to stretch them out before starting on her arms.

Emily glanced around the room again, then frowned at the looming metal frame. "What was that for?"

Nat chuckled. "Mostly to freak you out. Also, it was already in the room and they didn't want to move it."

"Oh." Pleased when her arms were finally released from their prison, Emily rubbed her wrists to ease the slight soreness.

Nat took over the rubbing, her hands now as gentle as if she were handling a tiny kitten. "Maybe next time?"

Emily was pretty sure there was nothing she couldn't handle with Nat by her side. "*Definitely* next time."

Andrea Bramhall lives in Norfolk, UK, with her partner and their two collies. Summer finds her running their campsite, and winter writing the stories she dreams up. Her first novel, *Ladyfish*, was awarded an Alice B. Lavender Certificate in 2013. Friend her at facebook.com/Andreabramhall, tweet her @Andreabramhall, or find her at www.andreabramhall.co.uk.

This story features characters from *Clean Slate*.

CAPTURED ON CANVAS
ANDREA BRAMHALL

Erin pulled the ice-blue shawl tight about her shoulders as she stepped out of the car and took Morgan's hand. She smiled and let herself enjoy the sight of Morgan in her black tailored pantsuit and violet-colored shirt, and the excited flush that covered her cheeks as she bowed toward Erin.

"My lady." The playful grin on Morgan's face caused the fine lines beside her coal-dark eyes to crinkle as they danced with amusement under the light of the full winter moon. "Would you allow me the pleasure of escorting you to this evening's event?"

Erin laughed gently and tucked her hand into the crook of Morgan's elbow. "So gallant."

"You look stunning, Erin."

Erin automatically ran her hand over her stomach, smoothing out any wrinkles from her silk dress. The blue of the backless halter-style dress matched her eyes and contrasted with her thick dark hair, piled high on her head, wispy tendrils tickling the nape of her neck. She felt beautiful, and the heat in Morgan's gaze felt like flames licking at her skin. She shivered and hoped she could blame her body's reaction on the chilly January air, but they both knew the snow on the ground and the promise of more lingering in the air was not the real reason for her response.

She swallowed and whispered, "Thank you. So do you."

"Are we ready for this?"

"Nervous?" Erin raised an eyebrow as Morgan shrugged sheepishly.

"Very."

Erin wasn't surprised. Morgan had been working toward this evening for several months. It was the culmination of hours of sketching, painting, mixing colors, remixing colors, blending pastel crayons to create just the right texture. The frustrated days she'd spent hunched over canvas, paper, and swaths of silk as she created her exhibition, all of it leading to this night. Morgan's exhibition—her first exhibition, and Erin was equally nervous and excited.

She hadn't seen a single piece that Morgan had created for the show. Every request to view her work had met with the same response: "I want it to be a surprise for you too." And Erin had respected that, even though the secrecy was killing her. Now they were both here, ready to witness Morgan's creations and the reactions to them, and Erin was terrified that she wouldn't be able to do justice to her wife's work. That her analytical brain would not be able to let go and feel what Morgan wanted her to. She worried that she would be unable to see beyond the paint to the woman wielding the brush.

Erin tried to suppress the ripple of fear that ran up her spine and made her shudder.

"God, I'm an idiot. You must be freezing out here. You should have put on a coat." Morgan led her up the stone steps to the ornately carved doors and the marble foyer of the gallery and guided Erin inside.

"I put one in the car in case it gets colder later. I'll be fine inside." She smiled and waited while Morgan checked her coat and Erin's shawl before tucking the small ticket into her purse.

"Can I get you some champagne?"

Erin laughed. "Pushing the boat out tonight?"

"Well, it is a special occasion."

"Oh yes, someone's fortieth birthday, isn't it?" She winked playfully as Morgan scowled. Erin agreed with Robyn—Morgan's new agent—that launching her first exhibition on such a milestone birthday would create an extra buzz about the event. Morgan was still to be convinced.

"I don't know where you heard that, but it's all a bunch of crap for the press. I'm trying to impress someone."

"Really?"

Morgan nodded. "Someone very important." She lifted Erin's hand to her lips and brushed a kiss across her knuckles. "Champagne?"

"Please." Erin smiled, admiring the way the fabric pulled tight across Morgan's arse as she walked to the bar. Moving into the gallery, she idly picked up a leaflet, turning the pages without looking at them.

"Anything interesting?" Morgan held a champagne flute out to her. Erin shook her head as she took the glass and sipped at the effervescent liquid. The dry acidic flavor balanced the fruity citrus notes and the gentle aroma of honeysuckle and candied orange peel.

"I wasn't really reading it." She tossed the flier back on to the table and leaned a little closer in to Morgan.

"I don't want to, but I have to talk to a couple of dealers, baby. Robyn thinks they could be interested in putting some of my pieces in their gallery in London. Do you want to come with me or take a look around?"

Erin followed Morgan's hand and spotted the two older gentlemen dressed in suits, one wearing a bow tie and the other a rather garish pink-and-yellow striped tie. She didn't relish the idea of making small talk before she had the chance to view Morgan's work. "You go on. I'll amuse myself for a little while."

"You sure?"

"Positive."

Erin took another sip of her drink and watched her walk away before she glanced at the first piece. It was a huge canvas, six feet high and four feet wide, and the image made her breath catch in her throat. A naked woman knelt with her back to the viewer, her feet tucked under her bottom and her hands lost in the masses of treacle-dark hair she was holding high on her head, exposing the entire length of her back. The valleys and rises of the woman's body were captured with exquisite detail, down to the tiny beauty mark on the sole of her right foot. Every brush stroke had been placed with reverence, deliberation, and a sensuality that vibrated off the page, stole Erin's breath, and made her tingle as though the brush had stroked her skin.

"It's exquisite, is it not?"

Erin turned to her left and smiled briefly at the man beside her. "It is very good."

"Good? Oh, my dear, you are looking at it incorrectly. This piece is not about good or bad. It is about passion. The power of the flesh. This guy really knows women." He reached toward the painting, pointing but never touching. "Look at the slow sweeping strokes down the spine, over the ribs, around the curve of her buttocks." He crossed one arm over his chest, rested his elbow in his hand, and stroked his chin. "The artist hasn't just painted this woman. He's made love to her with each pass of the brush."

Erin didn't comment on his assumptions as to Morgan's sex as she stared at the painting again and let her gaze travel down the long length of the woman's back—her back. The man was right. She could feel Morgan making love to her as she had created this piece. And knowing that released a wave of desire in Erin that burned fiercely, as did her mounting anger. She felt the sting of betrayal as she stared at her own body laid bare before the strangers milling through the space. She felt the growing need to cover each canvas to hide her own skin and to retrieve her shawl and hide beneath it. She could feel everyone in the gallery staring at her, their gazes drifting from one section of her body to another, flesh or canvas, it didn't matter. It was all her. And every look felt like a touch.

She walked through the gallery on weakened legs, sipping her champagne and hoping the next piece wouldn't affect her quite so strongly.

The sight of her slumbering body with her arm resting above her head, obscuring her face, made her cheeks burn with embarrassment. She realized no one would recognize her from the angle, but she felt exposed and angry with Morgan for putting her body on display in such a way. Something Morgan had assured her she would never do, that she didn't want to share any part of their intimate life with anyone else.

"Such love." The voice of the woman beside Erin was barely a whisper, and she turned in time to see her wipe a tear from the corner of her eye.

She sipped her drink, trying to keep her fingers relaxed around the delicate stem to save it falling victim to her bubbling rage. "You think so?"

The woman nodded without taking her eyes away from the picture. "The artist clearly worships this woman. The painting alone shows that, even without the title."

"You don't think it shows a lack of respect for the woman in the picture?"

"Not at all. Her face isn't shown. Her identity is kept private. The artist is showing her feelings, opening herself up, wearing her heart on her sleeve, but she isn't exposing her lover."

"Not exposing her lover?" Erin glared at the woman, incredulous that she could be so blind. "She's painted her naked body, how can you say she hasn't exposed her?"

"The artist has exposed herself. The woman in the picture doesn't."

"She's the one who's naked—"

"Her flesh, yes. But her soul is not." The woman pointed at the arm covering Erin's painted visage. "There is no face to show her expression or her feelings toward the painter. Instead this Morgan Masters has shown us exactly how she feels about the woman she is painting, how she adores and cherishes her. She gives away nothing about the woman in the pictures. Even down to the title. No clue about who the model is, what she is to Morgan, nothing. She is a mystery. But the title tells us even more about how the painter feels."

Erin glanced at the card mounted next to the painting. *Nothing is more beautiful than you wearing only the moonlight and my kisses.* Erin gasped and turned back toward the first piece, searching for its title. *If I were blind, within my heart I could still see the beauty that is you.* Tears welled in Erin's eyes and she looked at each new painting with a different view. Looking not at what Morgan was showing *of* her but what she was expressing *to* her.

She slowly let the sensuality and romance of each piece infiltrate her soul. She leaned in closer, needing to see more, and every detail caused her heart to beat a little faster, her palms to moisten a little more, and her vision to narrow until all she could see was the painting. She stroked her neck as she examined the short brushstrokes that had been used to mix the pigments until the skin tone was perfect; each tiny sweep felt like a kiss upon her skin.

The final piece in the exhibition was a canvas eight feet long and three feet high—a swirling vortex of blue, white, black, violet, indigo, and tiny flecks of gold that sucked her into the piece and held her hostage.

"Your eyes aren't just beautiful, they are the gateway to a world that I want to be a part of." Morgan whispered the title against Erin's ear, her breath raising goose bumps down Erin's neck, caressing her, teasing her. "Always."

Erin leaned back against Morgan's chest, the starchy cotton rough against her oversensitized back, and her nipples hardened.

"Do you like it?"

"It's beautiful." She turned her head and smiled at the faint blush that stole over Morgan's cheeks. "They're all beautiful."

"I was afraid you might be angry with me."

"I was. I felt exposed."

"That's not what—"

"I know." Gently, she kissed the corner of Morgan's lips and laughed. "I realized that when I talked to a woman over at the second picture."

"Do I want to know what you talked about?"

Erin shook her head. "It doesn't matter now. But she helped me to see that it wasn't your model who you were exposing up there."

"No. It was meant to be myself."

"Yes, I see that."

"There's one thing else I'd like you to see."

Erin waited, anticipation rising. Morgan handed her a glossy program and smiled sweetly.

"I wanted to call the show *Erin*, but I thought that would probably be a little bit obvious as to who my muse and my model is."

"Yes, I was going to ask you about that. I never posed for you."

"You don't have to." Morgan led her away from the huge painting of Erin's eyes. "I know every inch of your body, Erin. Every freckle and beauty spot." She trailed her finger over Erin's shoulder and down her arm. "I know every angle, plane, and curve of your body better than I know my own."

Erin pulled in a deep breath, trying to maintain her focus, but the air was heavy with the scent of Morgan's cologne. Cinnamon, citrus, and a hint of sandalwood played at the edge of her senses and drove her passion higher.

Morgan laughed. "If you keep looking at me like that, everyone's going to know who my model is, baby."

Erin looked down at the program and tried to focus enough to read the cover of the booklet: *Beauty is in the heart of the beholder.* She frowned. "Shouldn't it be 'in the eye of the beholder'?"

"Nope. This is a quote from H. G. Wells. One I like better."

"Why?"

"Many reasons. As an artist, so much emphasis is placed on the aesthetical beauty, and the same is true in society, in the media, and pretty much everywhere we look. But to me the fact that you are a beautiful woman isn't what makes you so beautiful to me. It really doesn't matter. You would be beautiful to me no matter how you looked. In my heart you are the most beautiful woman I have ever or will ever see. Because I love you. And true beauty is seen with the heart, not the eye." She placed a gentle kiss behind Erin's ear and whispered, "And my heart sees only you."

Erin gasped as her heart thundered in her chest. "How much longer do you need to stay?"

"This is my opening night, baby. I can't leave."

Erin closed her eyes, knowing Morgan was right, but her body and her heart ached for her lover's touch. "I've looked at every painting you have out there. Every brushstroke was put on that paper like you were painting it on my skin." Morgan wrapped an arm about her waist and rested her chin on Erin's shoulder. "Every time someone points to a section, it draws my attention and I feel…" Her voice cracked as she covered Morgan's hands with her own. "I feel like you've been touching me all night long."

"I know." Morgan shifted and placed a row of kisses along her shoulder. "Every time I looked at you I could see how flushed your skin was. How hard your nipples were, how your chest heaved when you breathed." Morgan led her out of the main room and across the marble foyer.

Erin's heels clicked on the hard stone floor and echoed up to the vaulted ceilings. She didn't register where they were going until Morgan closed the door behind them and sealed them in the dark room.

"I need to kiss you," Morgan said.

Erin tilted her face up, offering herself without question. Morgan's lips were soft but insistent, her tongue a teasing probe flicking across Erin's lips before seeking entrance to her mouth. She groaned in satisfaction when Morgan finally claimed her mouth, pressed her back against a wall, and cupped her face in her hands. Erin pulled Morgan's shirt from her pants and ran her fingernails the length of Morgan's back, loving the way she arched into her touch. She pushed her jacket off her shoulders, not caring where it landed, and threaded her fingers through Morgan's shaggy dark hair.

Morgan wrenched her mouth from Erin's and grinned when she moaned at the loss of contact. "Your dress will get all wrinkled if we don't stop."

"I don't care." Erin tried to pull Morgan's head back for another kiss.

"You will when we have to go back out there and face them all."

Erin knew she was right, but she still couldn't bring herself to care. She ached to explore every inch of Morgan's body just as her skin craved Morgan's hands and lips. Disappointment cut through her when Morgan eased her body away, and she closed her eyes in a weak attempt at controlling the desire that was raging through her.

"Turn around." Morgan whispered the words in the dark room.

Erin swallowed, her throat suddenly dry at the commanding tone in Morgan's voice. Her knees almost buckled as she turned within the circle of Morgan's arms. Morgan ran a fingertip down the length of each arm, grasped her wrists and placed her hands against the wall on either side of her head. She pressed a tender kiss against Erin's cheek.

"Don't move them."

Erin gasped as Morgan nipped at her earlobe and released the catch behind her neck.

"Someone might come in."

"Someone might." Morgan's hands froze, but her lips nibbled the edge of Erin's ear. "Do you want me to stop?" Her tongue was hot, flicking at her earlobe.

Did she? Her heart beat a riotous tattoo in her chest resonating in her ears; her skin tingled and pulsed everywhere Morgan had touched, and ached to be touched everywhere she hadn't. Her mouth watered, needing to taste Morgan's skin, her lips, her desire, and she knew there was no way she could stop now. "No."

Morgan trailed kisses down her back as she lowered the dress and helped Erin step out of it. The wall was cold against Erin's naked breasts as she leaned against it in only her panties.

"So beautiful."

"It's too dark to see, Morgan."

"I can see you." Morgan's lips found the back of her knee, her fingers running up the outsides of her thighs as she kissed, licked, and nipped her way back up Erin's body. "I can always see you."

Morgan covered her hands and entwined their fingers, slowly

lowering them to Erin's body. "Touch yourself. Slowly." She bit lightly at the junction of Erin's neck and shoulder. "Show me how you want me to love you tonight." She eased them away from the wall far enough for Erin to be able to move freely. "Show me how you want me to take you."

Erin groaned and bit her lips as she changed the position of their hands, putting Morgan's directly on her skin and twining their fingers again. She led Morgan's hands in a slow dance over her belly, up her sides, around the outsides of her breasts, and across her chest. Her nipples hardened at the inadvertent contact of Morgan's forearms, and she couldn't wait any longer. Her nipples turned stone hard under their fingers, and she tried to press her breasts farther into their joined hands even as she longed for the teasing to continue. She felt Morgan smile against her neck.

"You can't make up your mind, can you, baby?" Morgan pinched both nipples simultaneously and Erin felt it in her clit. She thrust her hips forward, desperate for some sort of pressure between her legs, but there was nothing but air. "You can't decide if you want to come yet or not." Morgan pinched again and Erin's sex throbbed in time with her heartbeat, her clit heavy and hard.

"Please." Erin tried to push Morgan's hands down her belly. "Please, baby." A plea, a prayer, a benediction, Erin didn't know and she didn't care if it resulted in her release.

"Not yet."

Erin felt the last of her reason desert her as Morgan turned her back against the wall and dropped to her knees. She pressed her face against the lace panties and hooked her fingers around the thin band of elastic. "Very pretty, baby, but they have to go."

She felt wanton in a way that only turned her on more, standing before her lover in nothing but her high heels and lace stockings. Her thighs trembled as she glanced down.

"I wish I could see your eyes right now." Erin reached forward and cupped Morgan's face. "I know what you're thinking when I can see your eyes." She heard the brush of hands running over plaster, then a single bulb overhead lit up the small storeroom. She squinted until her eyes adjusted to the new light. Morgan knelt in front of her, staring up at her.

"And what am I thinking?"

"The same thing I am. I love you." Erin leaned forward and kissed her while Morgan caressed the backs of her thighs. She straightened up, needing the support of the wall at her back. Morgan raked her fingers through the thatch of dark hair at the apex of her thighs. "Open up for me, baby."

Erin opened her legs and closed her eyes.

"No you don't. You said you wanted to see, so you keep looking at me."

Desire shot straight to her groin at the order breathed against her belly. This Morgan who took her, claimed her, commanded her, and did it all with such love and devotion that it only made her feel more cherished and adored felt so new.

She watched Morgan guide her hands between her legs.

"Show me," Morgan said, her gaze locked on Erin's hands as she stroked her slick, swollen lips and sighed at the heavenly pressure.

Her clit was hard between the tips of her fingers, and her desire flowed like silk as she dipped her middle finger lower and swirled her wetness over and around the hood. Morgan shifted, her lips parted, and her skin flushed. Morgan's pulse throbbed at her temple and another rush of wetness coated her thighs. Seeing Morgan react to her was the greatest aphrodisiac, making her feel powerful even at her most vulnerable of moments, when she was naked, undone, and gasping for air.

Erin used one hand to spread herself open, showing Morgan her most intimate self, before she pushed one finger inside, reveling as they moaned in unison. Morgan's fingers twitched into fists resting on her thighs, and Erin knew she was aching to reach out and touch her.

"Tell me." Morgan's voice was hoarse and cracking, heavy with desire. "Tell me how it feels. What it feels like to be inside you right now, with me watching."

Dizzy, Erin slid her finger slowly in and out of her own giving flesh, and words failed her. She wanted Morgan's hands on her, in her, her mouth taking her.

"Tell me."

"Hot."

"Your pussy feels hot?"

Erin's knees shook as she slipped a second finger inside. "Yes, but I meant you watching." Erin's voice sounded strange to her own ears.

Morgan grinned up at her. "It's so hot watching you like this, baby." Morgan leaned closer. "What else?" She was so close that her breath caressed Erin's slick flesh. Her hips bucked and pumped and Morgan pulled Erin's hands away. "No. Not yet."

Erin growled deep in her throat. "Morgan, no. I need—"

"I know what you need." Morgan's movement was fast and fluid, and Erin barely had time to register Morgan's pants falling to the floor before she was lifted up. She wrapped her legs around Morgan's waist, and the exquisite sensation of being filled consumed her. She twisted her fingers into Morgan's hair and held her head as they kissed. She clung to Morgan while each thrust drove her higher, closer, deeper, and the need for release burned through her.

Morgan whispered into their kiss, "Come for me." She thrust deeply, one final time. "Come with me."

Erin could do nothing but obey. Her muscles contracted and pleasure surged through her body, every heartbeat driving it deeper, every movement firing her ravaged nerves over the abyss.

When she finally returned to her body, Morgan was peppering her damp skin with kisses. "You okay?"

Erin laughed quietly. "Erm, yeah. You?"

"Definitely." They kissed, and slowly Morgan helped Erin back into her dress before she peeked round the door to ensure it was clear.

Erin wrapped her hand around Morgan's biceps as she led them back to the exhibition and nodded to a few people as they entered the room.

Erin's gaze fell again onto the painting of her from behind. She smiled, knowing Morgan was right. That beauty truly is in the *heart* of the beholder.

Maggie Morton lives in Northern California with her partner and their two cats. She is the winner of an Alice B. Awards 2013 Lavender Certificate for her first novel, the lesbian erotic romance *Dreaming of Her*. Her second novel, of the same genre, is *Under Her Spell*.

This story features characters from *Dreaming of Her*.

LOVE AND RAINBOWS
MAGGIE MORTON

Lilith woke up with a gasp and almost cried out. Next to her, Isa began to stir from sleep to wakefulness. While Lilith tried to catch her breath, Isa slowly sat up, arching her back a little as she yawned. At any other time, that subtle, sensual movement of her girlfriend's body would have made Lilith want to devour her, head to toe, and do all the things she'd found she liked to do just as much outside of the dream world as she had liked to do in it.

"What…mmm…what is it, sweetie?" Isa asked, wiping some of the sleep from her eyes. The pale morning light lit her up in the loveliest way, her hair a tumble of glossy, dark curls. Its wildness called out to Lilith, making her just want to grab it and…and then she thought that perhaps sex would be a good idea after all, as a glance at her lover's body showed that the cold morning air had made her nipples erect. They were incredibly tempting whenever they became that way, and as they continued to harden, her memories of the nightmare that had woken her began to fade. She leaned in to kiss her bad dreams away.

"Mmm," Isa said again, this time with her lips against Lilith's mouth. She pushed back from her after a few moments, though, placing her hand gently on Lilith's chest in the slight crevice between her breasts. "Another bad dream, huh?"

"Yes." Lilith looked down at the space on the bed between them, sliding her fingers against the crumpled sheets. "It was Shae again, telling me that something would go wrong on our day of commitment to one another…that she would make sure of it. We were in a dark hall, and she was staring down at me, floating midair and chained in place. So it's not as if she could harm me like that, but still…"

"But still, you want to wipe all those silly bad dreams out of your mind. And you think making love to me would be a good way to do it?" Isa looked mischievous now, as if she also thought it was a good idea.

"What better way do you know to wipe bad dreams from one's head?" Lilith grinned up at her shyly, but Isa's look revealed she knew better—there was nothing shy about Lilith when she wanted sex with her partner, and there never had been.

"Well, I think Dr. Isa prescribes a nice fuck."

"Oh, do you?" Lilith kissed her lover once again. Kissing Isa had never gotten old in the year she'd been living in the human world, and she'd found she much preferred touching her now-girlfriend in person rather than merely in her dreams. Yes, she thought, as she slipped Isa's nightgown off her shoulder and began to kiss her way down Isa's neck to where her breasts parted...yes, this was so very much better than it had been in Isa's dreams. Lilith laid kiss after kiss across her breasts, and then she found her way to Isa's nipple and began to suck.

Isa stroked Lilith's hair as she leaned back, clearly enjoying herself as Lilith sucked on her nipple and danced her fingers across to the other one and twisted it between finger and thumb. They'd been playing around with getting rougher with each other lately, and Isa showed no signs of surprise when Lilith pinched one nipple and placed her teeth against the other, biting down harder and harder as her fingers worked away on the other side. She pinched and bit even harder until Isa yelped in pain.

"Too much?" Lilith pulled her mouth away—she didn't like the idea of it being "too much," not at all, and her voice showed it. But of course, she didn't want to cause Isa more pain than she could take, either.

"No, it's just perfect," came the answer.

"Wonderful...shall I continue?"

"I just couldn't help making a sound. But please, don't stop!" Isa grinned a crooked, sexy grin and clasped Lilith's head, guiding it roughly back to her breast, where, for the time being, Lilith decided it rightfully belonged.

She continued sucking and biting and twisting and pinching, Isa's delightful gasps and moans and stuttered words urging on her hardworking lips and fingers. But this was not the main act, and she wanted Isa to come. She reached onto their large bedside table, where a well-loved dark-blue dildo sat, just begging to be used. She lifted it up and waggled it back and forth in front of Isa, whose eyes tracked its every movement—hungrily.

"Are you wet enough for this yet?" Lilith asked. In answer, Isa took Lilith's hand in hers and guided it underneath her nightgown's skirt to her very aroused cunt. "I'll take that as a 'yes,' then, darling."

"You know, I still love it when you call me that. *Really* love it. And I always will. I'm really looking forward to this Saturday."

Saturday. One day away, when their commitment ceremony was supposed to happen. And quick as that Lilith was back to thinking about her nightmare. Hoping to draw her mind away from it, she placed the tip of the dildo against Isa's clit and jiggled it back and forth a little.

"Fuck!" Isa bit her lip, a look of concentration and need painted across her beautiful, tensed features.

"You like that, don't you?"

"Oh, I really do. Yes, I do!"

Isa gasped as Lilith drove the dildo inside her, each bit of its length entering her with ease. It always did because beyond their love for one another, there was also immense heat. Lilith still possessed every single bit of her prowess as a seductress, and she could still make all of Isa's dreams come to life. Or at least, all of her fantasies.

Lilith leaned down, pushing Isa onto her back, and pushed up the silk skirt of her nightgown. She tilted the dildo to hit Isa's G-spot and let her mouth join in on the fun, closing her lips over Isa's wet cunt and clit. She continued to fuck Isa with the dildo as she fucked her with her mouth, and it wasn't too long until Isa began to tense even more, her cunt gripping the dildo until Lilith could hardly thrust it in and out. But she knew all of this was a sign for her to keep going, and she continued to shove the slicked-up dildo into Isa's cunt as her mouth and tongue worked away at her. Abruptly a delicious string of swear words and cries and Isa's shaking legs and torso signaled to Lilith that she had succeeded, and rather well at that.

When they stripped off their nightgowns to shower, the clock showed it was a quarter to eight. Neither woman had to rise especially early, considering the riches they'd stored in a large, locked box in the local bank—their gifts from the Dreammakers to thank them for saving Isa's city from the nightmare creature. Lilith didn't think about him much anymore, but now she had a new nightmare creature of sorts, and while she tried to scrub the dream out of her head as she washed her hair, it just didn't seem to want to go away.

She had no way to contact the Dreammakers now that her powers were all gone, and so she just had to hope it was a normal bad dream and not one brought to her by Shae herself. Shae, who shouldn't have been able to bring her bad dreams, since Dreammakers who turned to the dark side were always stripped of their powers and kept in a prison on the Nightmaremakers' land. Who better to watch over Shae than those who knew her best, after all?

Lilith had been certain that the evil Nightmaremaker was powerless now, so the dreams were probably just…cold feet? No, she didn't think she had those…more like happy ones, ones that wanted to dance whenever she thought about the ceremony to occur that Saturday. She decided it was worth dancing over, and she did a little jig in the shower. Isa laughed and kissed her on the cheek, and the last bits of the nightmare were washed down the drain.

Over a breakfast of waffles and fruit, Isa typed away on her laptop, making sure the last few tables had been organized in the hall they'd rented. It wasn't a huge group, but about fifty people would be attending, so it wasn't going to be tiny, either.

Isa's dad still hadn't responded to her email inviting him, but she'd tried not to expect him to. Months ago, when Isa had told him about her relationship with Lilith, he'd just hung up the phone. She hadn't heard from him since, and the emails she'd sent went unanswered.

After breakfast that morning, Isa went out to pick up her dress from the tailor's. They'd both bought vintage gowns at their favorite consignment shop, and while Isa knew that Lilith's gown was white, just like hers, she had no idea what it looked like, as Lilith had insisted they not see each other in their dresses before the ceremony occurred.

"Isn't that a silly straight people thing?" Isa had asked her. Lilith had started having her nightmares by then, though, and she didn't want the slightest chance of a jinx that could ruin their most important day.

Well, actually, it was their second most important day. The first was the morning that Lilith had been sent to earth, Lilith thought, as she left their apartment to go for a walk. The day was sunny and warm, the sun's heat a delight upon Lilith's bare arms and legs. She hoped that Saturday's weather would be just as nice. They were having the ceremony outdoors in the local botanical garden's largest grass field, its lush green turf surrounded by beautiful, sweet-smelling roses. Lilith knew they smelled sweet because she'd insisted that she and Isa smell each and every one of them while they were at the gardens, and Isa had taken her hand and agreed to with a smile and a laugh.

There were roses right outside their apartment building, and Lilith stopped to smell those as well, her thoughts still on the special event to come. As she reached the front door of the café, she made a decision: she would *not* allow those stupid nightmares to ruin the rest of her day—or that Saturday, either!

Later that afternoon, she and Isa picked up the cake, tiered and chocolate with pink-and-white icing. Lilith had put on a little weight in the human world, but Isa had assured her she still looked terrific, her reassuring words followed by a very aerobic romp on the kitchen floor. Lilith was thankful for the extra padding then, because hardwood floors and naked bodies weren't that good a pairing.

Over dinner, Lilith told Isa she was through with having her bad dreams cause her any trouble, and she didn't want them to cause any more worries for Isa, either. Later that night, Lilith drifted as they cuddled in front of the TV and eventually fell asleep against Isa's shoulder. As she dreamed, she was back in the same room—the one with Shae hanging from the wall. Shae voiced her usual threats, but this time they fell on uncaring ears.

"I don't care what you have to say," Lilith told the evil woman, "I won't let you ruin the ceremony."

"Oh, *I* won't be the one who ruins it. No, it will be someone else. I've sent him dreams to tell him what to do on your 'big day.'" Those last words came out in a voice full of bitterness and spite.

"I don't care," Lilith told her again, crossing her arms and staring up at her with equal parts pride and defiance. "Nothing can ruin it because Isa will be there, and she's all I need to have the day be perfect and wonderful."

"You'll see…"

The dream shimmered for a moment, as if it were a mirage, and Lilith heard the words, "No, Lilith, I won't let it happen—I promise. I will fix everything." They were spoken by a very familiar voice.

"Aileen? How…is that really you?"

And then Lilith woke up. Had that been her friend Aileen, her fellow Dreammaker in the human world? Did that mean the dream was real? If it did, there was much that had to be explained.

The phone began to ring, and Isa hurried to answer. "Hello?"

Lilith couldn't make out the voice on the other end, but could tell it was a man. Whoever it was, his call had surprised Isa a fair bit. Her brow furrowed as she listened to what the person on the other end was saying.

"You're coming? Really?" Isa mouthed the words "my dad" to Lilith. "Okay, we'll see you there…what change—I mean, never mind, I'm just really happy that you're coming. You have no idea how happy I am. Really." She paused for a few minutes, then grinned at Lilith, giving her a thumbs-up. "A dream? Oh yeah, I totally know how much those can affect your life."

She said good-bye and hung up the phone. "I just…I can't believe it! He told me that he'd changed his mind about us…he'd been having nightmares for weeks, telling him to come here and ruin our ceremony, bring a Bible and tell us how evil we were and all…and then, just a few minutes ago, he had another one, with a woman named Aileen in it. That name sound familiar?"

Lilith nodded instantly. "Yes, of course! I just had a dream as well. Call Aileen and Iriana, and tell them we simply must see them. But in private. We'll bring them apple pie from the diner to make up for the interruption. Our dear ex-Dreammaker friend has a lot of explaining to do, my darling!"

They picked up pies at Minnie's and arrived at their friend's loft a little after ten. Lilith practically dragged Isa by her hand as they hurried to the door. She didn't wait a single second once there, knocking on the door and tapping her foot on the floor, looking like the very picture of impatience.

"Yes?" came a voice behind the door a few moments later. Aileen's.

"You know who it is, so just open the door!" Lilith heard a laugh coming from behind it as soon as she said this.

The door swung open, and there stood a sleepy-looking Aileen, dressed in a set of purple satin pajamas, her graying red hair sleep-tousled. She appeared to only have just woken up, and maybe she had. There were no mirrors to travel through in this world, and perhaps entering people's dreams required more as a result. Something else to add to her growing list of questions for her friend.

"Do come in." Aileen sniffed a few times as the two younger women entered the apartment. "Is that apple pie I smell? I must still be dreaming because I was just thinking of Minnie's pies before you arrived, and that's just too crazy a coincidence."

"Not as crazy as dreaming about you and then hearing about some woman with your name being in someone *else's* dreams!" Lilith eyed her friend up and down. It wasn't malicious, what Aileen most likely had done, not at all, but it was still...it was still... "How on earth did you do what you did?"

Aileen led them over to the room's new, non-paint-spattered couch and took the pie from Lilith. "Honey, hurry up! They've brought pie!"

"Wonderful!" Iriana appeared at the far end of the room. "I'll get out plates and utensils. Aileen, go right on ahead without me. You know more than I do, anyway." The pie was passed to Iriana, who looked as elegant as always in a long, silk nightgown that matched her girlfriend's PJ's, to take to the kitchen.

"Well?" Lilith just couldn't wait any longer. "How did you wind up in my dreams? And in Isa's dad's dreams? And all without a mirror?"

"What do you think, sweetheart?" Aileen called over her shoulder. "Should I tell them? Or just keep it a mystery?"

"I vote for you telling us," Isa said, raising up an open hand and waving at Aileen. "I don't even know as much as Lilith knows, after all!"

"I suppose I don't have much of a choice, then. Well, where to begin..." Aileen pulled the wicker rocking chair closer to the couch where Isa and Lilith sat. "Of course, I should begin with the dream I had two nights ago. I was certain it couldn't possibly have been real, as just like you, Lilith, I was certain I no longer had any connection to the dream world, or the world that used to be ours. But in the dream, Amaya came to me and said she was bestowing me with some of her power in order to save your ceremony. Apparently, one of Shae's old friends had snuck some magic into the food brought to her each day, and Amaya had discovered this when she happened to peek into Lilith's dreams."

"My dreams?" Lilith gasped. "What was she doing in *my* dreams?"

"Amaya was checking in on you two just to make sure the nightmare creature was gone for good. But of course, that was when she saw Shae. To make a long story short, Shae had also been coming to Isa's father, Warren, in his sleep, trying to force him to come to your commitment ceremony and ruin it. I was sent a bit of power through my dream of Amaya, and I used it to enter your dream and Warren's dreams. I tried to convince him what a mistake ruining your ceremony would be. Turns out I did a little too good a job."

Iriana now brought over her favorite tray, the one which Aileen had brought her in her dreams many years ago. On top were four lapis-colored plates, the pie, and four forks. She doled out generous slices of pie as Aileen continued to tell her story.

"Now," Aileen said, around a large mouthful of pie, "he wants to come to the wedding to see his daughter for the first time in years and to make amends with her. I hope that won't be a problem for you, Isa."

"Not...not at all." Isa took Aileen's hand and laid a quick kiss upon its top.

"Hope that didn't make you jealous, dear?" Aileen teased Iriana with a nudge against her arm.

"Not at all. I know the dear girl is just happy."

"Overjoyed, more like!"

Lilith thought Isa might start bouncing in her seat. Not a bad thing!

"You see," Lilith said, placing her plate on the table and wrapping her arms around Isa, "she's been trying to contact him for years, trying to get him to let her back into his life. I didn't know...I didn't know it would be possible for him to change his mind. You must have quite impressive powers of persuasion, Aileen."

"All it took was a few choice words—reminders of his wife and what she would have wanted for him and his daughter. I don't know if I can promise a complete turnaround of his ways, Isa, just so you're warned, but I know he will be glad to see you and will at least be civil."

Isa ate her last bite of pie and stood, pulling Lilith up from the couch along with her. "I hate to eat and run, ladies, but we have very important plans in just a few hours, and we both need our beauty sleep."

"Oh, you have no use for such a silly thing." Lilith kissed her for a few seconds. "You are far, far too beautiful already."

Once they got home, they hurried into bed, but Isa clearly had no plans to go to sleep quite yet. As she was spooning Lilith, she pulled back Lilith's garnet-red hair and began to suck on her ear, biting down a little when Lilith tensed.

"Not ready for bed yet, my darling?" Lilith let her voice show she wouldn't be opposed to some playtime before they slept.

"Remember," Isa whispered into her ear, "you said I don't need any beauty sleep."

Lilith laughed at that. "And after all," she said, turning to face Isa, "you're always the most beautiful when I'm making love to you."

"You really think so?" Isa looked shy for a moment, but then the moment passed, and she kissed Lilith firmly on the neck, sucking away a little as she did.

"No pre-wedding hickeys, if you please!" Lilith yelped as Isa smacked her on the ass.

"No more talking, just sex," Isa mumbled against her collarbone, sinking her teeth in only seconds later.

Lilith discovered she could gasp in pain and smile at the exact same time. She continued to smile as Isa got out their brand new-nipple clamps, and smiled even wider when Isa said, "I think it's okay to leave marks where your dress will cover them, don't you?"

As the first clamp was attached, Lilith gasped, and then again when the second one was clamped onto her other nipple, and then a third time when Isa gave them a little yank.

"Just making sure they're firmly attached," Isa said. "We can't have them coming off while I fuck you."

They stayed attached as Isa donned their strap-on with the dildo they'd used that morning. The clamps stayed attached when Isa began to insert the dildo; they stayed attached as Isa began to fuck Lilith… and they stayed attached as Lilith came, again and again, her cheeks glowing pink and her lips blood red as she arched her back for the fourth time in a row.

The next morning, they parted, having planned to arrive at the ceremony separately. The minutes before the ceremony practically flew by, at least for Lilith. She hoped that Isa was as excited as she was.

When she watched her partner, her long, ivory gown swishing back and forth in the gentle breeze, approach the rose-covered arbor where she stood waiting, the look on Isa's face made it clear that yes, she was as excited as Lilith—oh, was she ever! Lilith had only seen her that happy one other time—when they'd both woken up in the human world those many months ago. As she took Isa's hand, her whole being brimmed over with love for this gorgeous woman.

And then she heard a male voice yell out, "Wahoo!" Turning, she caught sight of a man wearing a rainbow-covered tie sitting back down. She recognized him from a photo in their living room, but she still couldn't hide her shock, nor could Isa hide her surprise.

"Is that your dad?"

Isa was clearly struggling not to giggle, or to blush, as she said, "I guess a tiger can change its stripes after all."

"It looks as if he's changed his to rainbows."

Then Isa did laugh, and when Lilith glanced back in the direction of her father, he waved at her, grinning widely and not looking the least bit ashamed to be where he was. Yes, he had changed quite dramatically, and not in a way she would want to complain about.

The woman officiating cleared her throat and opened the book of poetry she was set to read from for the ceremony. She began to read the words they had chosen together, two months ago, her voice ringing clearly out over the crowd. Lilith barely heard her speak, though. She was looking at Isa all along, completely lost in Isa's beautiful, love-filled eyes.

Lambda Literary Award finalist **Carsen Taite** is on a mission: spin tales with plot lines as interesting as the true but often unbelievable stories she encountered in her career as a criminal defense lawyer. Learn more at www.carsentaite.com.

This story features characters from *The Best Defense*.

BORN TO RIDE
CARSEN TAITE

"If you polish that chrome any harder, you'll put a hole in it."

Skye looked up from her Harley and squinted into the sun. Her best friend, Parker Casey, stood in her driveway, dressed in a sleek suit. A total contrast to her own cargo shorts, tank top, and sweat. She looked down at the torn T-shirt rag in her hand and compared it to the fancy leather briefcase Parker held. They'd first met as fellow cops. Now she was a P.I. and Parker was a lawyer. They still worked on cases together, but she rarely saw Parker in lawyer drag outside of the office. She must've come straight from the courthouse.

Skye's stomach twisted in panic, and she deflected whatever business Parker had come to discuss by pitching the rag at her. "I could use some help. Take the rear fender and make sure you can see the evil in your eyes when you're done."

Parker shook her head but set her briefcase down, rolled up her sleeves, picked up the rag, and elbowed in. "You plan on riding in a parade or something?"

Skye grabbed another rag and went back to work. "Nope. I'm selling her. Got a guy coming by this afternoon to take a look."

Parker stopped rubbing. "No way. You've had this bike as long as I've known you. Does your wife know you're getting rid of your favorite possession?"

"It's not my favorite possession."

"Liar."

"Shut up, Casey. If you don't want to help, get lost." The banter was playful, but Skye meant what she said. She didn't want to talk about it.

Parker threw the worn rag back at Skye. "Well, now that you mention it, I didn't come over to polish the chrome on your ride. We have a hearing scheduled for Thursday. I came by to go over the paperwork. Aimee's office said she was working from home this morning."

Skye's stomach rolled and she struggled to keep the panic from her voice. "Thursday? Next week?"

Another voice interrupted Parker's answer. "What are you two up to?"

Skye tamped down her anxiety and turned to face her wife. Aimee, like Parker, wore a suit, but they couldn't have looked more different. Instead of navy wool with hard lines, hers was bright red and showed off sexy curves. Normally, the sight of her wife all dressed up was arousing, but today it only fueled her sense of foreboding. "Hey, babe, did you know attorneys make house calls?"

"Ours does, anyway." Aimee gave Parker a big hug. "Parker, why don't you come inside where my wife will fix you a drink instead of making you baby her favorite possession." Aimee led them into the house. The moment her back was turned, Parker mouthed "see" and Skye responded by punching her in the arm. The two continued their silent but physical argument until they reached the dining room. When Aimee turned back to them, they froze like two five-year-olds caught in the act.

Aimee cast them a wary look before addressing Parker. "I assume you have the paperwork with you? Why don't you set up in here, and we'll be right back."

Skye watched Parker open her briefcase and line the table with several stacks and rows of paperwork before she followed Aimee to the kitchen. As soon as she crossed the threshold, Aimee swept her into a tight embrace. Skye looked over her shoulder and started to push away, but Aimee murmured, "She's not coming in here. Let me hold you for a minute."

Skye stopped resisting and allowed the warmth of Aimee's closeness to flood through her. The soft waves of Aimee's hair brushed lightly against her cheek and the calming scent of lavender soothed her worries. She breathed in time with Aimee's smooth and steady heartbeat and after a few moments, felt her anxiety fall away. "How do you always know what I need?"

She felt rather than saw Aimee's smile. "Magic."

"Seriously." She didn't know why she had to know, but suddenly it was very important.

Aimee leaned back and stared deep into her eyes. "The same way you know what I need. Love." She grinned and added, "Oh, and you get this panicked look in your eye when you need a little escape."

Skye opened her mouth to reply, but a loud cry pierced the air. Both of them turned to the kitchen counter and stared at the monitor.

"Speaking of need," Aimee said, "you go. I'll get our drinks and meet you in the dining room."

Skye felt the tension come back the minute she left Aimee and started up the stairs. When she reached the top landing, she broke into a run. Despite Aimee's calm, she still hadn't gotten used to these episodes and they never failed to bring her to the brink of panic. She rushed into the room and pulled up short at the railing of the huge mahogany baby bed Aimee had insisted on. As she grasped the frame and stared down at the red-faced, mouthy occupant, she silently thanked her wife for buying the most expensive, sturdiest crib on the market.

"Shh," she murmured as she lifted Olivia into her arms. "You're going to wake the people in the next state with your crying."

As she bounced Olivia, the screams subsided into gurgles and grunts. Skye urged them along with aahs and oohs she would only voice in the privacy of her home. Her daughter reduced her to a pile of mush.

Her daughter. Not quite a reality yet, but Parker was sitting downstairs with the paperwork that would make it happen. Two weeks ago when Skye had gotten the call that Olivia was on the way, she'd rushed to Aimee's side and held her hand through every second of her labor. She held Olivia while the doctor cut the cord and spent hours standing outside the hospital nursery, staring at the wonderful new life that she knew would turn theirs upside down. Now it was time to take the final step to adopt her daughter, and she couldn't be more excited. Or more scared.

She rocked Olivia in her arms until she fell back to sleep. Hard to believe the howling baby now basked in peaceful drool. Things could change so drastically in an instant.

Aimee and Parker looked up as she walked into the dining room. Aimee flashed a radiant smile, and Skye stuffed her fear.

"Parker says we can get the home visit done on Tuesday, and

we already have a hearing date for next week." Aimee glowed with excitement. She'd been glowing since the moment she'd learned she was pregnant and she'd been giddy the entire time. While she reveled in the excitement of it all, Skye had installed safety locks on every window, cabinet, and door in their home, and read every article Google coughed up on the dangers that could befall an infant.

"Thursday, right?" If she kept saying it, maybe it would sink in.

"Yes. Can you believe it?"

Skye flashed the smile she knew was expected and sat down at the table. "No. That's great news."

The paperwork Parker pushed in front of her appeared blurry, the words floating off the page. For the next half hour, while Parker explained how the hearing on second-parent adoption would work, she managed to grip a pen, and sign and initial more blanks than she had when she and Aimee had refinanced their home. When Parker finally stacked the signed paperwork and placed it in her briefcase, Skye silently congratulated herself on fooling the two of them into thinking she was calm and cool about the situation. But her mind was already ticking ahead to the home visit. First step, get rid of what her mother had always called the machine of death. Her 1995 Harley Softtail.

"Stuart, I can't believe you let her buy that machine of death."

Skye's father's reply was swift and adamant. *"She's an adult and it's her money."*

Skye had listened to the exchange. It was the first time her mother had ever treated her differently than her brothers. The boys in the family all had motorcycles, and no one had ever voiced a concern that they might die in a fiery wreck, but according to her mother, she was doomed to a horrible death if she chose to ride that "monstrosity."

Skye's Harley had been her primary mode of transportation most of her life and she'd never had a wreck, but she wasn't about to take a chance that the caseworker assigned to do the home visit was a worrywart like her mother. She mentally challenged the caseworker to find a single sharp object or toy with small parts, and the only bike present on her visit would be the sparkly purple tricycle with fringe on the handlebars that Olivia would have to wait several years to ride.

Later that afternoon, when she handed over the keys and the title to her Harley, she remembered the first time Aimee had ridden with her. Wearing an expensive tailored suit and Skye's helmet, she'd wrapped her arms around Skye's waist and squeezed the breath out of her as they sped up I-35 from Austin to Round Rock. When they'd stopped at the Harley-Davidson dealership, Aimee squealed and wanted to know when she could ride again. They'd spent an hour at the store while she selected the most stylish helmet, boots, and leather jacket, and then begged to ride again. Her excitement had been intoxicating.

Skye didn't need the bike for excitement. With Aimee, every day was an adventure, and their most exciting adventure was upstairs in a crib, relying on them to keep her safe.

❖

"Tomorrow's the big day." Aimee bounced on the edge of the bed.

Skye held up a finger and strained to listen. That noise again. She picked up the monitor on their nightstand and placed it against her ear. "Shh, can you hear it?"

"Did you just call our daughter an it?"

"Not even. Seriously, Aimee, I swear I heard something in there." She swung her legs off the side of the bed. "I'll go check."

"Uh-uh. I don't think so." Aimee pulled her back down onto the bed. "I was just with her. She's fine. If you go in there you're going to wake her, and you'll ruin my plans."

Skye recognized the tone and she felt an instant surge of arousal. "You have plans?"

"I've had plans for a very long time, but it's hard to carry out a good plan when you haven't had any sleep. I slept like a baby, no pun intended, after the home visit yesterday, and now I'm ready to implement my strategy."

Skye leaned up on one arm. Aimee was irresistible when she had her mind made up about something. "I might be interested in hearing about your strategy."

Aimee began to slowly unbutton her silk nightshirt. "You'll have to watch and learn. It's more a show than tell kind of thing."

Skye forced herself to wait as her wife slowly stripped down to lacy silk panties. "If your plan is designed to distract me, it's working."

"My plan is designed to make you scream."

"What if we wake Olivia?" Skye glanced at the closed door.

"She's not going to come walking in, if that's what you're worried about." Aimee pointed at the monitor. "If she needs us, she'll be sure to let us know."

"I don't know. As I recall, we can get kind of lost when we're, you know…" The last nine months had been an awkward dance. As Aimee's pregnancy progressed, Skye had become more and more attracted to the glow of her pregnant wife, but ever cautious about the life growing inside her. She'd curtailed her work so she could spend more time by Aimee's side and turned down the more dangerous assignments in favor of the computer searches and paper reviews she normally despised. In the month before Olivia's birth, when Aimee was diagnosed with preeclampsia and on bed rest, she'd started working from home so she could be no more than a few feet away in the event of disaster. After all, the house was full of danger. Stairs, balconies, slick wood floors. She'd do anything to protect her lover, the mother of their child, and "anything" had extended to keeping her hands to herself.

She'd assumed everything would change once Olivia was born. Aimee would be healthy again. She'd resume her regular work schedule, and the only changes to their lives would be bottles and car seats and tiny little clothes to wash. But, if anything, her worry was worse now. Concern about Aimee's health was one thing, but Olivia was tiny and completely without skills. She relied on them for her every need, and she required the kind of protection that could only be provided by a vigilant parent.

"Skye Keaton, do you want to make love to me or not? Because I'm as hot for you as I was the very first time, and I'm not about to let an eight-pound, drooling, screaming mess come between me and my hot wife. If it hadn't been so long, you wouldn't have to say things like 'as I recall.' Now, let's have some torrid sex that neither of us will ever forget."

Aimee had always been able to read her mind. She gasped as Aimee punctuated her demand by yanking Skye's shirt over her head. Skye's breath hitched as the memory of every intimate moment they'd ever shared came rushing back. They could have this and be parents too, right? As Aimee's lips grazed over her nipple, she answered her own question by casting one last look at the monitor on the nightstand before arching into Aimee's embrace.

❖

"Stop fidgeting, you look great."

"I look stupid." Skye stood in front of the full-length mirror and frowned at the image staring back. Wasn't the first time she'd worn a suit, but every time was just as uncomfortable as the last. Too many layers, too many buttons, too much fuss. Every other time had been, like today, for some special occasion, usually something related to Aimee's successful real estate business or one of her many social causes: black-tie dinner, office holiday party, dinner with Aimee's wealthy and very formal Highland Park parents. Today, she'd wear whatever it took for the judge to think she was worthy.

"You can take it off the minute we get home."

"What about the party?" While they were at the courthouse, caterers would be preparing their fete in celebration of Olivia officially belonging to both of them.

"What about it? You can wear cut-offs and an old T-shirt, for all I care. And if you think Olivia will care, you haven't been paying attention. She spends most of her time in a onesie." Aimee lifted Olivia and held her up in the air. "But not today, right, little one? Everyone's dressed up today!"

Olivia, covered in pink lace and ribbon, screamed with delight as Aimee whirled her around the room. Skye smiled on the outside, but inwardly she strained against the image of Olivia falling through the air and landing with a thud on the hardwood floor.

Aimee's sharp voice jerked her from her fatalist imaginings. "Skye, I'm not going to drop our daughter. And if you don't wipe that look of horror off your face, the judge is going to think we're crazy and give Olivia to a whole different set of parents."

So much for her ability to mask her emotions. "He might do that anyway. Parker isn't a family law attorney. Maybe we should have hired someone else."

"You said yourself she's one of the smartest people you know. She consulted with a board-certified family law specialist about our case. She found a judge who has granted over a dozen second-parent adoptions, and she's like family." Aimee set Olivia back in her crib.

When she turned, Skye recognized the formidable, hands-on-hips, stern-jaw look and braced for a rant.

"I think you're amazing. Hell, I married you. The caseworker couldn't have written a better report and I think if I weren't around, she'd marry you herself. If you're having second thoughts about," she jerked her head in the direction of Olivia's crib, "speak now or forever hold your peace."

Pain lanced Skye's heart and she swept Aimee into her arms. "No, no, no," she murmured into her ear. "No second thoughts. Not a one. It's just…I feel so out of sorts. Like I don't have a clue what I'm doing." She waved at the crib. "She's so tiny. Helpless. If anything ever happened to her, I don't know what I'd do."

"Is that why our house is suddenly Fort Knox? I locked myself in the bathroom yesterday because I couldn't figure out how to turn the handle with the huge rubber thing you've installed. You realize it's going to be a while before she can even reach drawers and door handles and outlets, right?"

Skye felt her face redden. "I know, but there was the home visit and I didn't want the caseworker to think I was irresponsible. I mean, she knew I work as a private investigator and I'm sure she had some preconceived notions about that."

"Is that why you sold your bike?"

"What?" She hadn't mentioned the sale to Aimee. She'd had a feeling she might get flack for it.

"Parker told me."

"Some attorney she is. Way to keep information confidential."

"Shut up," Aimee said. "She's our friend. I think she was half-mortified and half-impressed that, how did she put it? That you were acting like an adult. You should've told me. That bike was the first thing I noticed about you."

Skye flashed on a memory. She had just ridden up Cedar Springs and parked outside Hunky's, a popular hamburger joint. While she contemplated whether she wanted to spend her last few bucks on lunch, a gorgeous blonde in a fancy SUV pulled up beside her and practically undressed her with her eyes. Never in a million years did Skye expect she would one day marry that woman and have a baby with her, but here she was.

Things change. Giving up the bike had been the right thing to do.

❖

The courtroom was already packed when they arrived. Skye scanned the room. Aimee's family and hers lined the first two rows. The rest of the seats were filled with their family of choice. Assistant District Attorney Cory Lance and her partner Serena Washington. Parker's wife, Morgan Bradley. Aimee's best friend, Mackenzie Lewis, and her partner Dr. Jordan Wagner. Megan and Haley.

She took her seat with Aimee and Olivia next to Parker at one of the tables inside the court railing. She was no stranger to the courtroom, having testified both as a cop and more recently as a private investigator, but today was different. Today she was on trial, or at least her fitness as a parent was. Parker had assured her Judge Lucas was fair and friendly, but until he signed the order stating Olivia was legally hers, she wouldn't be able to breathe.

When the judge took the bench, Parker offered the motion for second-parent adoption, the home study, and letters in support. Judge Lucas commented on the glowing report from the caseworker, said a few words in legalese, smacked his gavel, and then asked if he could be included in the first official family photo. As he made his way toward them, Skye looked from Parker to Aimee and back again, certain she'd missed something. The whole thing had lasted no more than fifteen minutes.

"Close your mouth, Keaton," Parker said, lightly punching her in the arm. "It's official. Olivia has two moms."

Skye turned to Aimee, who held their sleeping daughter, who was apparently immune to the sound of smacking gavels. "It's for real."

Aimee whispered in her ear, her breath soft and sweet. "It was always for real. It's just legal now." Aimee handed Olivia into her arms as the judge took his place beside them for the photo. "Now wake up your daughter. I have a feeling this is the first of many pictures today."

Almost an hour later they'd finally managed to please everyone's need for photos and were in the car on the way home for the party. Skye pulled into the driveway and reached for the garage door opener, but Aimee placed a hand on hers. "Park in the driveway for now."

"Why? Didn't you just get the car washed?"

"Trust me. I cleared out some space for the caterers to put their equipment, and there's nowhere for you to park in there."

Skye shook her head. "You know they could have figured out what to do with their own stuff." Aimee was a socialite on the surface, but she had never been above chipping in on a project, and this party had been quite the undertaking. "But I love you for making this day special." She parked the car and kissed Aimee on the lips. "We'd better get inside. Our guests will be arriving soon."

They worked together to get Olivia out of the car seat. It became easier every time. As they stepped though the side door to the garage, Aimee pulled Skye into an embrace.

"I want to talk to you about something."

"Here in the dark? Sounds ominous." Skye couldn't quite read Aimee's tone.

Aimee cast a look down at Olivia. "I just want you to know that there's no one I'd rather spend the rest of my life with. And no one I'd want to raise this little girl with. You are going to be, you already are, a wonderful mother."

"Okay." Skye stretched out the word, still uncertain where this was going.

"But as much as I want you to keep her safe, I also want you to challenge her. One of the things I love about you the most is your fearlessness. I want her to learn that from you, whether you are teaching her to ride this," she flicked on the light switch and gestured to the sparkly purple tricycle in the corner, "or this."

Following where Aimee pointed, Skye shook her head in disbelief. A Harley—her Harley stood in the center of the garage with a big red bow on the seat.

Aimee kissed her. "I have a feeling Olivia is going to take after you in a lot of ways—she's already told me she was born to ride."

Lesley Davis lives in the West Midlands of England. She is a die-hard science-fiction/fantasy fan in all its forms and an extremely passionate gamer. When her Nintendo 3DS is out of her grasp, Lesley is to be found seated before the computer writing.

This story features characters from *Playing Passion's Game.*

THE GAME CHANGER
LESLEY DAVIS

"Tell me again why we're here?"

Juliet Sullivan laughed at her best friend's exasperated tone as they were bumped and jostled by pedestrians on one of Chicago's busier streets. Juliet tightened her hold on Monica Hughes's arm as she helped steer her through the crowd.

"We're here to support the Baydale Reapers as they take one step further in fulfilling their ambition to be the number-one clan in their league." Juliet's gaze drifted over the group of people she and Monica were following. "I, however, am really here to cheer on that gorgeous hunk of butchness that is my lover as she does just one of the many things she excels at."

Monica snorted back a laugh. "Oh, I'm well aware of her many talents, courtesy of your inability to keep that sexually fulfilled look off your face."

Juliet's answering grin was unrepentant. "I'll freely admit there are things my Trent can do that don't require an audience. She's amazingly gifted." She watched Trent walking with the others. She stood head and shoulders above everyone except her friend Elton. Six feet tall with a lean, muscular build, Trent was dressed head to toe in black and cut a handsome figure that never failed to set Juliet's heart racing.

"Will you stop cruising your girl while we're fighting against the tide of humanity here? We're just trying to get from the damn parking garage to the hotel, for heaven's sake. Whose dumb idea was it to stay in one that didn't have the garage attached? These heels aren't meant for strenuous walking." Monica bumped Juliet with her hip. "And you can just quit it now. That look in your eyes is bordering on indecent."

Juliet smiled at Monica's teasing. She wasn't embarrassed at being caught checking out her lover's body. "I can't help it. I'm admiring her swagger and enjoying the view of her ass in those jeans."

Monica shook her head. "Well, it's no wonder you're salivating over her if you've been subjected to the same treatment I've had to put up with this past week."

Curious, Juliet reluctantly pulled her gaze away from Trent. "Subjected to what?"

"The 'no sex before a big tournament' rule," Monica said. "I swear if I wanted to be left high and dry, I'd have dated the sporty type and not the geeky pirate king." She gestured toward her boyfriend, who bore a strange resemblance to Captain Jack Sparrow with his wild long hair and plaited beard.

"Elton said you two couldn't have sex before this competition?" Juliet wanted to be sure she was hearing this correctly.

"He's been up all hours 'playing,' and not with me!" Monica shot Juliet a suspicious look. "He hasn't been up all night online with Trent?"

Juliet shook her head. "No, Trent has been by my side every night." She couldn't help herself from adding saucily, "Or above me, or under me…"

Monica visibly fumed. "You've had sex?"

Juliet knew her grin was only infuriating Monica more, but she was powerless to stop it. "Yes, several times, all week, *every* night."

"Fuck me," Monica growled. "Or not, as it happens."

Juliet hugged Monica. "I'm sorry, Monica. I guess my Trent subscribes to a different set of gaming rules."

"Great. You got the gaming geek who still plays with your *joystick* while I got the one who pulls a Zen Master Jedi mind trick on me."

"I guess everyone has their own way of preparing for an important tournament." Juliet smiled, aware of Trent's attention shifting to her as she finished her conversation with Elton. Trent had been doing that periodically—catching her eye—from the moment Elton had split them up to talk "team tactics."

"And don't think I haven't noticed she's keeping an eye on you, while the man of my dreams probably hasn't taken a break from his team-building spiel."

"She always looks after me." Juliet winked at Trent to reassure her

she was okay. She got a smile in return that made her ache to be beside her. But the weekend wasn't about them being together, it was about the Reapers and their gaming. She could afford to let the Reapers play with Trent for a little while.

"Rick's holding hands with Zoe while Elton's droning on," Monica pointed out with a grumble.

"They're on the team and they are together. It doesn't count."

"I bet they had sex too."

"Be sure to ask them over dinner tonight," Juliet commented dryly, more than amused at her friend's peevishness. She wondered how she would have coped not having Trent touch her for a week. She craved the connection with her all the time, a look, a touch, a kiss that lingered just a little too long before they had to go to work. She'd have been just as put out as Monica was now if she'd not had that closeness. "If the Reapers win, you'll know your enforced celibacy was worth every minute." At Monica's disbelieving look, Juliet said, "Elton's probably going to want to celebrate."

"I packed his favorite black corset of mine," Monica said, feverishly planning ahead. "He likes how it lifts everything up." She cast a wicked look at her chest, which was decoratively displayed in a frilly white gothic shirt. Monica's face suddenly fell again.

"What now?" Juliet was losing patience with her friend's mercurial mood swings.

"He'd better be giving them a rousing speech because I need this team to damn well win. I need some post-gaming sexcapades!"

Juliet's laughter brought Trent's attention back to her.

Win or lose, babe, Juliet thought, *we'll celebrate because you're always a winner in my eyes.*

❖

The hotel lobby was busy and Trent let Juliet lead while she carried their suitcase. She tried not to smirk at Elton, wheeling two large cases behind him. Monica's signature gothic style obviously meant an extra case for just the weekend. While Elton was listening to Monica, Rick and Zoe were talking with Chris and Eddie.

"He'll cramp my style, man," Chris whined. "What if I find myself a fine young lady? I can't bring her back to my room if I'm sharing with Eddie. He watches pay-per-view porn paid for by his mother, for Christ's sake!"

Eddie ignored the laughter at his expense. "She gives me her charge card to pay for my half of the room. I tell her I watch the sports channels."

Trent shook her head at him. "Eddie, we've got to get you a girlfriend."

"I would love that," Eddie said, "but it's hard for me to be noticed when *you're* the one the girl groupies trip over themselves to impress." He nudged Juliet. "Did she tell you about the one who bared her boobs while we were playing *Halo* at one tournament?"

Trent groaned inwardly at the pointed look Juliet gave her.

"No," Juliet said. "Oddly enough she didn't. I guess it must have slipped her mind."

Elton cut in smoothly. "Trent never missed a beat, she wasn't distracted at all. But the guys on the opposing team were busy swallowing their tongues and got slaughtered. It was awesome. We wiped them out while they were still wiping the drool off their chins."

"You weren't even a tiny bit distracted, Trent?" Monica asked as they all piled into the elevator.

"I was playing. No one distracts me when I'm gaming, except for a certain beautiful blonde."

Possessively, Juliet rested her hand on Trent's chest. "Just so you're aware, should any woman dare to flash her boobs at you anytime during this tournament, I swear I will rip them off and beat her to death with them!"

Everyone burst out laughing.

"They wouldn't even catch my eye, my darling. No one compares to you, Jule." Trent risked a peek at Juliet's ample cleavage before looking back up into Juliet's bright-blue eyes. She could tell by the intensity of Juliet's gaze that her desire had been easily read.

Juliet pulled back from Trent a fraction. "I do believe the groupies are all yours, Eddie."

He cheered and was still grinning like a fool when he was dragged from the elevator by a long-suffering Chris. Zoe and Rick stepped off too to find their room. The doors closed behind them.

"He is so not groupie fodder," Elton said. "I foresee a future of X-rated bills on his mother's card."

Trent disagreed. "Hey, if I can find my soul mate, maybe Eddie can too."

Elton sighed dramatically. "Juliet, you have turned my best friend into a hopeless romantic. I hope you're satisfied."

The elevator reached their floor and Juliet stepped off first.

"I'm perfectly satisfied, Mr. Simons," she said. "Which is more than can be said for your girlfriend."

Monica high-fived her as they walked down the corridor to their adjacent rooms. Elton and Trent got off the elevator and hung back as Elton struggled with his cases.

"What am I missing here?" Elton asked, looking truly perplexed.

"A word to the wise, my friend," Trent said, patting him on his shoulder. "The whole celibate, purifying your gaming aura before a big tournament was okay when you were single. But you have a girlfriend now." She waited for Elton to get what she was hinting at. He still looked puzzled. "No sex pisses her off, dude."

He sighed gustily. "Having a girlfriend alters everything."

"It's a game changer, that's for sure. But it's worth it." Trent followed Juliet's path down to their room where she stood waiting with a smile on her face. *It's worth every change you make to be with the one you love.*

❖

The hotel room was spacious, light, and clean. Trent placed their case by the bed and shucked off her backpack. She turned to find Juliet right in front of her. The look in her eye rooted Trent to the spot.

"You know Elton is going to expect everyone to just drop their bags off and head out to the venue." Trent's voice held a note of warning, but Juliet's intensity made her skin tingle and her hands itch to reach out and touch.

"He can wait a moment." Juliet slipped her hand behind Trent's head and pulled her down for a searing kiss.

The familiar warmth of Juliet's lips stole Trent's breath away. She moaned as Juliet's tongue tangled with hers, tasting her, teasing her, as the kiss grew deeper. Trent grasped Juliet's hips, tugging her closer, relishing the press of Juliet's breasts against hers. Unable to resist, she slipped Juliet's blouse free from her jeans and sought flesh. Trent was hungry for her, needing to get as close as possible. She craved every inch of her. Desperately, Trent tried to temper her roughness. The urge to take Juliet where she stood raged through her. Her kiss grew more feverish as she worked at the button on Juliet's jeans. She was seconds away from her goal when her phone rang. Trent tore her mouth from Juliet's.

"Goddammit, Elton!" She recognized his familiar ring tone and snatched the phone from her pocket. Gruffly she answered, "What?"

There was silence on the other end of the line for a moment and then Elton asked, "Testing out the hotel bed already?"

Trent rubbed her cheek on Juliet's hair while Juliet held her tightly. "What do you want, Elton?"

"We're going to check out the venue. Are you going to join us?"

Trent was torn. She wanted to experience the thrill of seeing their gaming venue for the first time, but she also wanted to stay with Juliet and finish what they had started. "We'll meet you in the lobby," she said finally and ended the call. She tossed the phone aside and wrapped her arms around Juliet. "We have to go play with the other kids."

Laughing, Juliet ran her hand through Trent's short hair, ruffling the piece that fell across her forehead. "That is why we're here, after all."

"But I liked what we were doing here," Trent admitted softly, her hands trailing gently across Juliet's back.

"So did I, and we'll continue later. For now, you need to be Gamer Williams and not my sexy lover."

"I can be both," Trent argued.

"I know you can, but I'm not sharing the sexy part with your fellow gamers." Juliet pulled free from Trent's arms. "Let me go fix my lipstick, and we'll get out of here before Elton sends a search party."

Reluctantly, Trent tucked her T-shirt back into her jeans and stuffed her phone in her pocket. They rode down to the lobby in silence, but the air was full of promises to come. Juliet never let go of Trent's hand. The connection soothed Trent's soul.

Monica was leaning against the wall as they stepped off the elevator. She took one look at Juliet's bruised lips and rolled her eyes. "Girlfriend, I could really learn to hate you two."

❖

The Annual Chicago Gaming Convention was a gamer's paradise. Rows upon rows of monitors, consoles, and computers lined the stages.

"Glad I didn't have to help lay those cables," Elton commented, his eyes shining as he took in the large rooms laid out for their pleasure.

Trent was impressed by the hard work that had gone into filling two conference rooms full of gaming equipment. She couldn't wait to get started.

"So where will you be playing?" Juliet asked.

"There's no seating arrangement here. You and Monica need to just pick a spot and hope we're somewhere in your eye-line." Trent shrugged apologetically. "Sorry. With so many teams competing it's a massively choreographed dance to get us all in here at one go."

"Any chance that groupie will be here this year?"

Trent sent Juliet an exasperated look. "I have no idea. Groupies have a habit of switching allegiances the higher the clan rank or the more prestige the top-ranking player has."

"So you wouldn't recognize her if you saw her?"

"Juliet, to be honest, it's not like anyone was looking at her face. I certainly won't be looking for her. I didn't pay attention to her last time and I sure as hell won't be interested in anything she has to offer this time. I've got you. No other woman stands a chance."

Juliet snuggled into Trent's side. "You're a charmer, Trent Williams."

Trent lifted up her shirtsleeve, exposing the new tattoo inked onto her upper arm. A stylized pink rose bloomed there, emblazoned with Juliet's name inscribed in an incredibly fancy font. Trent had chosen the *Bayonetta* lettering because the Umbra Witch from one of her favorite games oozed a raw sex appeal she recognized in her lover. Trent firmly believed that Juliet had brought her own special magic into her life. She trailed her finger over the artwork, tracing the magical symbols that framed the rose. "I have your name on my skin and your love keeping my soul alive. I'm not going to look at another woman, be she bare-breasted or otherwise."

Juliet touched her name on Trent's arm and was just about to lean up for a kiss when Elton bounded over to them, effectively shattering the moment.

"Come on, it's time to play. They're letting us practice."

Trent brushed a kiss over Juliet's smiling lips. "I'll win for you," she promised and let herself be dragged away by an excitable Elton.

❖

The day sped past in an endless stream of one match after another as the clans battled it out to get their names higher on the leader boards. Trent had already led the Baydale Reapers to victory in a button-mashing *Tekken* tournament and now she was watching Elton lead the charge in a capture-the-flag game against a formidable foe. In her mind's eye she was playing the game along with him, seeing where she would have taken chances and silently cheering when Elton's skill at the game shone through and he scored points in spectacular fashion. She could see Zoe and Rick's characters flanking Elton's every move as they fought alongside him. Chris was taking part in a dance-off elsewhere that wasn't part of the actual competition, but he boasted some very serious moves and he enjoyed the attention. Eddie, however, was talking in whispers not far behind her. He was earnestly holding a conversation with a young woman who seemed totally enamored by his every word. *Will wonders never cease?* Trent hoped this was the start of something good for him. She was drawn back to the game just as a rousing cheer erupted, led by Elton's distinctive Reaper roar.

"That's my Elton, ever shy and retiring." Trent watched him tower over everyone as he shook hands with the team the Baydale Reapers had just beaten. Then, like a huge puppy, he hurried over to Trent and hugged her tightly, swinging her around like she was a child.

"Awesome game, dude." Trent barely managed to get the words out once he finally let her go from his bone-crushing hug.

"Did you see how I managed to totally obliterate three in one go there? That was so cool. They learned the hard way not to congregate in that spot when I have grenades and the perfect aim." Elton draped his arm around Trent's shoulder as he turned her toward the main stage. "We're edging higher up on that leader board, my friend. The top three get the big prize money. If we rank, what are you spending yours on?"

Trent looked around her to make sure no one could overhear. "I want to put it toward the medical costs of getting Juliet pregnant."

Elton's eyes widened to almost comical size. "No fucking way! You're really going to have a baby?"

"It's what we've dreamed of. We've looked into all the details, the insemination stuff, and all the hospital costs. We think this is our time to go for it. I want my share of the prize money to go toward us having a baby to love."

"Shit, Trent," Elton whispered in awe, his eyes unashamedly teary. "That makes my wanting a new bigger, badder HDTV sound pitiful in comparison." He hugged her to him again. "Oh my God, you're gonna be a mama."

"*If* we can have a baby. There's still so much to go through first." Trent knew she was grinning like a fool but she didn't care. This was what she wanted with Juliet more than anything. The knowledge that Elton was as excited merely confirmed what Trent already knew: he was going to make an awesome uncle.

"Well, if I ever needed the incentive to win this competition, you've just handed it to me. We're going to play even harder to succeed now." Elton slapped her on her shoulder as he broke off the hug. "We've got a baby Reaper to make!"

❖

The end of the first day's competitions had weeded out many of the weaker teams, and the last game played had been a furiously fought battle. Trent and the rest of the Reapers had taken up their guns to play *Call of Duty* until their team had beaten everyone else. It had been a satisfying conclusion to an enjoyable day for Juliet. She had seen Trent playing her best and bring her team to victory. She looked over her shoulder to where Monica sat with her headphones on, blissfully tuned out to all around her as she listened to music and tapped away on her iPad. Juliet had already told Monica where she was going, now she just had to get past the throng of gamers congratulating the winning team so she could put her plan into action.

Trent was still in her gaming chair, and Juliet waited until the crush had eased a little before moving in behind her, laying a hand on Trent's shoulder, and whispering in her ear. "That was a fantastic way to finish the day off." She made sure her lips brushed the curve of Trent's ear and felt the shiver that ran through Trent's body in reaction. Trent turned to face her, her smile triumphant.

"You saw us win?" Her eyes shone with pride.

"I've been watching you all day, following your every move." Juliet ran her fingertips over the back of Trent's right hand. "You have marvelous hands." Juliet smiled. *It's time to play a different kind of game, gamer girl.* "I've been watching all the other women gaming here today, but none of them can compare to your...admirable skills."

Juliet leaned forward, deliberately drawing Trent's gaze to her cleavage. She had popped an extra button open for just that purpose. She was so close, she effectively pinned Trent in her chair. "I'm sure you get told this a lot, but watching you play really turned me on."

Trent's eyes darkened to a deep rich chocolate. They never once strayed from Juliet's face.

"Would you like to play...with me?" Juliet asked softly, running her tongue over her bottom lip. She noticed how quickly Trent's breathing accelerated. She could see how tight Trent's hands were clenched on the chair's armrests, physically stopping herself from reaching out and taking what was already hers.

"I play to win," Trent warned, her voice low, just the way Juliet liked it.

"Oh, you won me over right away." Juliet eased back and let Trent get to her feet. The way she towered over Juliet always made her feel safe. She immediately linked her arm through Trent's and led her away from the masses.

"Do I need to tell anyone where I'll be?" They passed Elton holding court with a crowd of eager listeners.

"I'll deliver you back in time for dinner. You won't be missed in all the postgame celebrations." Juliet looked up. "Unless you'd rather stay?"

"I'd rather see what games you have in mind for me."

"Good." Juliet led them back toward their hotel.

"Juliet..." Trent's desire-roughened voice nearly made Juliet stop in her tracks and kiss her there and then. She placed a finger over Trent's lips to stop herself from giving into the temptation.

"Not now, sweetheart. I need to get us back to the hotel in one piece. This game's only just beginning."

"And if I don't want it to end?"

Juliet held on to Trent's arm a little tighter as they hurried across the road. "Then it's lucky for you I'm the kind of girl who plays for keeps."

❖

Trent felt like she would explode if the elevator didn't hurry and reach their floor. Juliet's hand was rubbing up and down Trent's thigh, not close enough to her buttoned fly but near enough to make her clit tighten with every pass. She was grateful there were no cameras inside the elevator and no one else had stepped inside with them for the ride. She watched the floors count off and muttered "Thank God," when the doors finally opened. Juliet led the way, taking her time opening their door, which only served to drive Trent more insane. Once inside Trent made a grab for Juliet but instead found herself pushed back against the wall right by the door. Juliet very deliberately locked it and tossed the key card on the table behind her. She pressed into Trent, kissing down her neck. Trent was too wound up for soft and light, and began pulling at Juliet's top.

Juliet stopped her. "I know that before me, when some girl picked you up after a game—"

"It didn't happen *that* much," she argued weakly.

Juliet put her fingers against Trent's lips to hush her. "Before me, you wouldn't let anyone touch you. You'd go to their room, give them what you thought they wanted, and leave." She slid her hand up under Trent's T-shirt, to rest over her heart. "This time is for you, babe."

Trent sighed. "Where were you when I was so lost, Jule?"

"Just waiting until it was truly our time to be together." Juliet cupped Trent's breast and kissed her.

Trent's knees nearly buckled, and she was grateful for Juliet's body keeping her upright. She lost herself in the kiss as Juliet's fingers slipped under her bra and brushed across her nipple. Trent began fumbling for her T-shirt to remove it so Juliet could do whatever she wanted with her. She might not have let many touch her before, but she craved Juliet's hands on her with a hunger she could never satisfy. Juliet helped her remove her clothes and sucked a hard nipple into her mouth, biting gently. Trent gasped and speared her fingers through Juliet's long blond hair, pushing into Juliet's eager mouth. Juliet switched to Trent's other breast and licked at it roughly, knowing exactly what gave her the most pleasure.

Trent fitfully plucked at Juliet's shirt.

"This is for you, sweetheart, remember?" Juliet said.

"I want you naked against me," Trent begged, desperate to feel Juliet's skin against hers. To touch her, kiss her, taste her.

"Soon, lover, I promise." Juliet traced her tongue down Trent's chest, nibbling at the muscles there, licking over her abs.

Trent's whole body jumped as Juliet unsnapped the first button of her jeans, jolts of electricity streaking through her with each subsequent button. Juliet slid the jeans down as far as she could and Trent kicked off her Nikes and socks. Her jeans followed and Juliet, on her knees, pressed her lips to Trent's black boxer shorts, her tongue flicking against Trent's clit. Legs shaking, Trent braced herself as Juliet's licks became more insistent; each suck through the material made Trent writhe.

"Let's take these off, shall we?" Juliet pulled down the soaked shorts and Trent hurried to step out of them.

Then Juliet was back between her legs, her tongue sweeping over her. Trent's head banged off the wall behind her, but the pleasure between her legs was all she felt. Juliet hooked Trent's leg over her shoulder and opened her up even wider. Trent grasped for Juliet's hair, anything to keep her grounded as Juliet's mouth captured her and drew her in. Her hips bucking to the rhythm of Juliet's tongue, Trent gritted her teeth and held back a moan. Juliet tweaked Trent's tight nipples, her nails trailing down Trent's chest. Her tongue delved deep inside Trent, fucking her, before slipping out to swipe through Trent's soaked folds. She nuzzled at the swollen labia, then circled her tongue around Trent's rock-hard clit before sucking it in. At the steady, rhythmic pull of Juliet's lips around her clit, Trent began to come undone. Juliet's name left her throat on a whisper, repeated over and over in litany, as the pleasure and intensity grew.

Juliet didn't let up—her tongue seemed to be everywhere all at once, and her fingers pinched Trent's nipples in sync to the pulsing rhythm in Trent's sex. When Juliet pushed two fingers deep inside, Trent exploded. Hoarsely crying out Juliet's name, she came, quivering and shaking.

Juliet continued lapping gently at her clit, easing her through the orgasm. Trent moaned when Juliet finally eased her fingers free. She led Trent to the bed and guided her down.

Trent watched as Juliet undressed for her, her desire reigniting at the sight of Juliet's pale skin. She sighed with unashamed bliss when

Juliet got in bed and lay on top of her. Trent kissed the curve of Juliet's breasts, pleasure building again when Juliet pressed between her thighs, thrusting gently.

"It has to be said, you make the best groupie ever," Trent declared, kneading Juliet's breasts gently, rolling her thumbs over the taut, hard tips.

"I'd better be the only groupie in your camp, Trent Williams." Juliet kissed her swiftly, staking her claim.

"You're my one and only," Trent promised, loving how her wetness was mingling with Juliet's as they rubbed against each other in a lazy rhythm. "You'll always be my Player Number Two."

Juliet grinned down at her. "And to think some people don't think that gamers are sexy when they are talking geek speak."

"They don't know what they're missing." Trent licked her way around the pebbled skin of Juliet's areola before taking the nipple between her lips and sucking it in deep. Juliet's hips began to move faster. Trent let the nipple slip from her lips. "You know you're going to make me come again."

"I know your body better than my own, sweetheart. You're always good for another round right after the first."

Trent flicked the edge of her tongue off Juliet's nipple as it plumped for her, begging to be played with. "Are you going to come with me this time?"

Juliet nodded, her hips pumping faster as her need grew more desperate. She smiled down at Trent, love and need brimming in her eyes. "You really are the most beautiful woman I have ever seen."

"Just as long as I'm the only player in your game," Trent teased her softly.

"You're the only one I'll co-op with." Juliet's voice broke as she began to come in Trent's arms.

Trent held her close as she came, lost in the sounds of her pleasure, how her body shook with each spasm that rocked through her. When Juliet opened her eyes, Trent smiled smugly.

"Do not give me that look that says we're going to make love all night," Juliet said. "You have a big game tomorrow to prepare for."

"I don't play by Elton's rules. I follow my own."

"Which are?"

"To love you every second I breathe." Trent kissed her. "And I want to make the most of our time together before someone calls and demands we go eat pizza."

Juliet shot a look at the clock and slid her hand between Trent's thighs. "We have plenty of time before they start ordering food."

Trent knew by the wicked glint in Juliet's eye she had well and truly met her match. Come victory or defeat at the tournament, with Juliet by her side, she was always on the winning team.

Barbara Ann Wright runs a home for lost and abandoned books between writing fantasy novels and ranting on her blog. Her work has made recommended reading lists on Tangent Online and Tor.com. She'd love to hear from you at barbaraannwright.com.

This story features characters from *The Pyramid Waltz*.

THE LIGHT IN HER EYES
BARBARA ANN WRIGHT

Starbride sipped her wine, relaxing on the balcony of Countess Nadia's suite. Unlike most of the high-ranking nobles, Countess Nadia didn't move to the interior of the palace when the weather began to turn cold. Her ancestral lands were far north, near Farraday's mountainous border, and she preferred a chill in the air.

A handful of bejeweled boxes sat on a small table between them, and Nadia showed off her pretties one by one. Starbride lifted a silk-covered box and gazed again at the strand of flawless pearls inside. It seemed a simple thing, no diamonds or other jewels, just a golden clasp. Each pearl was perfectly spherical, not a divot or imperfection. They nearly glowed white.

"Lanaster pearls," Starbride said in wonder.

Nadia nodded and sighed. "I seldom wear them because they're so rare. I'm terrified of losing them."

Starbride glanced at Nadia over the top of the box, a puckish feeling rising in her. "I was once promised the naughty story to go with these pearls."

Nadia winked and reached for the box. "Perhaps another time. What about you, child? How goes your life of late?"

Starbride couldn't hold in a sigh. Katya had been moody and depressive, but who could blame her? Cousin kidnapped, Fiend stolen, uncle set to murder her—anyone would be depressed.

"Ah," Nadia said, "problems?"

"Nothing we can't weather, though a lot has...gone wrong recently."

"It shall pass, never fear."

"Thank you, Countess." But now the mood had changed. Starbride had started *thinking* again. "I suppose I'd better go."

Nadia stood but gripped Starbride's hand before she could leave. "Have faith in yourself, and in the princess."

"I will. Thank you again." She left before Nadia could offer more words of encouragement. They only made Starbride dwell more. She wouldn't give up Katya for all the world, but the problems that haunted the princess gathered around Starbride too, hunching her shoulders as they had Katya's. And they weren't over yet. Roland was still out there, still alive.

And Katya had no Fiend with which to defend herself. A knot of worry tied Starbride's stomach. That had been her doing. She knew she'd done the right thing when she drained Katya of her Fiend, but without the strength to match Roland, how could Katya hope to defeat him?

The answer came to her in a flash. Rather than trying to give Katya another Fiend, someone else in the Order could carry one for her. Starbride nearly stopped in the hallway, astounded by the thought. Someone Katya loved and trusted could undergo the sexual ritual required to pass a Fiend from one person to another.

Starbride tapped her chin as she walked. But who? Brutal or Pennynail? Averie? Even if one of them consented, who would give them the Fiend? The king and queen couldn't do it, there were too many problems there. Katya's grandmother might have a heart attack at the idea. Brom would never consent. Reinholt would probably laugh at the idea.

A little voice in Starbride's head reminded her that she could take on a Fiend herself. But sex with King Einrich or Queen Catirin or Reinholt...all three made her shudder.

That left Hugo.

Starbride nearly burst out laughing. She'd have to get him drunk first, and that would put her square in the driving seat...where she had little experience. Besides, Queen Catirin was probably already searching for a new bride for Reinholt, someone who'd follow orders. Starbride smirked. Lady Hilda was available.

She had to put away such thoughts as she continued to Crowe's office. Since he'd been wounded, he'd insisted she train with him every day, and no amount of objection would sway him. He cared about her and the royal Umbriels, about their state of mind, but he wouldn't let anyone stop learning what they had to learn in order to survive. She could almost hear him saying, "Depression won't stop Roland."

He barked a gruff "Come in" when she knocked. But he'd been gruff before he'd been wounded. She wondered if he was grateful to finally have an excuse to bark at everyone.

"Reporting for duty," Starbride said as she entered.

"Have a seat." He continued to write.

"An important missive?" He had demanded she come. The least he could do was look at her. She sighed, ashamed of the thought as soon as she had it. Now who was using current circumstances as an excuse to be grouchy?

"Just a little something I've been working on." He finished writing, folded the paper, and added it to a small stack beside him. If he noticed the archness in her tone, he didn't mention it. He took the stack of notes and put them in a bottom drawer. "Now." When he looked up at her, his smile was sad.

"What is it?" she asked. "What's happened?"

"Nothing, my dear, nothing at all. Just thinking about the future."

"And it makes you sad?"

"Bittersweet, I suppose." He waved a hand. "Target practice today."

Starbride groaned. She wanted to learn something else, maybe start on pyramid construction, but day after day it was learning how to throw. She'd never been very athletic, and she didn't see how she could suddenly become so. Still, after all the times she'd seen pyradistés lobbing pyramids around, she supposed she should get used to the idea that she'd have to learn to do the same, especially as a member of the Order of Vestra.

He led the way, hobbling on a cane, to one of the sparring rooms that had been cleared for their use. Starbride offered to carry his satchel for him, but he only gave her a withering look. She shrugged the look away and dropped her hand. She should have brought Dawnmother, who would not only have insisted, she would have *taken* the satchel from him.

Windows high on the walls of the sparring room flooded it with light. She had first expected racks of steel weapons, but those were tucked carefully away somewhere. Even the wooden mock weapons weren't lying around for anyone to pick up and use. Like all sections of the palace, the sparring rooms had servants and section-housekeepers, and visitors found nothing without seeking assistance. Sometimes it seemed like the servants, rather than the masters, were the people with the power.

Today, by Crowe's request, a practice dummy stood at one end of the room. Its base fitted into a narrow track that ran the length of that end. Starbride crossed to a small table set up on the opposite end of the room. Wooden pyramids clustered at one end. Actual pyramids were too valuable to waste on target practice. Starbride lifted a few and held them in the crook of her arm. "Ready."

Crowe nodded and hobbled to a lever set in the wall. He pulled the handle down, and the dummy careened back and forth with the aid of springs. Starbride chucked her pyramids at it, one after another, staying behind a line on the floor. Archers used this same contraption to practice their skills, and Starbride wondered if they had the same difficulty she did. She didn't manage to hit the dummy until it began to slow, eventually coming to a stop. Once it did, she caught it on the head.

Starbride cried out in triumph. Crowe hadn't lost his frown.

"What? I hit it!"

"When it was stationary."

She put her hands on her hips and shrugged. "I didn't hit it at all yesterday. Besides, how many of your enemies were moving back and forth that quickly in the field?"

He pinched the bridge of his nose. "That's not really the point, is it? Your aim must improve." He nodded toward the dummy. "Reset."

Starbride trudged over, wondering if anyone in the palace was high-ranking enough to have the servants reset their practice dummies. Knowing Crowe, he would have made Katya do it too, maybe even King Einrich. Maybe it was a punishment for not doing well. Only winners got to have their dummies reset by someone else.

Starbride pushed the dummy back into place, forcing it against the spring until the latch clicked in place. She collected her pyramids and trekked back to the table. "Ready."

On and on it went. Throw the pyramids, miss the dummy, reset the dummy, and throw the pyramids again. Her shoulder began to ache, but she knew she had to keep at it. Unlike most pyradistés, her future work would include incapacitating those trying to attack the Order. She began to envy those pyradistés who worked for counting houses or chapterhouses. Most of what they had to do was make traps and then sit all day, nothing athletic for them.

"Enough," Crowe said when she'd finally hit the dummy in motion. Slow motion, but it was better than any hit she'd scored all day. "I'm getting tired, so you must be sore by now."

Starbride rubbed her aching shoulder. "My mother should have included this in her courtier training."

He pulled a flash bomb from his satchel and pressed it into her hand. "When you finally start using these for the Order, you'll need to learn to shut your eyes after you've thrown."

"Wonderful, another step to learn." When she caught his scowl again, she sighed. "I'm sorry I'm moaning so much. You're a good teacher, Crowe."

He waved the compliment away, but it did wonders for his scowl. "I'm privy to the same recent misfortunes as you. I understand."

"It's Katya I'm worried about."

"Hmm, I'm more worried for Einrich."

Starbride blinked at him. "But he's been through so much in life."

"My point exactly. Katya's young. She'll bounce back. How many disappointments in life can one person take?"

Starbride nodded but thought that applied equally to Katya, youth or no. She hefted the pyramid in her hand. "How many potential problems has this solved for you?"

"It's the pyradisté's best friend," he said. "It's not going to go out of control and kill anyone, and it catches most everyone unawares."

Such a simple thing, but she could feel its power. Anyone could use it. It only needed to be broken to blind an opponent, or an unwitting comrade, which was why a pyradisté usually shouted a code word before throwing it. "What does it feel like?"

"You've seen its effects."

"People stumbling about, grasping their eyes."

"Blinds and disorients, that's what it says in the pyradisté handbook."

She turned the pyramid over. "It must hurt."

He shrugged. "If you're that curious, you could find out, but I don't recommend it."

"Have you ever—"

He chuckled. "Turned it on myself? Well…"

Starbride brightened. "You didn't!"

"I was young and foolish once too. It was a bet while at the Academy, and I didn't want to look cowardly in front of…well, someone I once knew."

"A sweetheart?"

He just shook his head. "I stood entirely too close to it and broke it open, and ten thousand red-hot needles dug through my eyes and into my brain. At least, that's what I would have sworn to at the time."

Starbride set it carefully down on the table. "And the person you once knew?"

"Left with somebody else. But I won the bet."

"Which was?"

He thought for a moment before laughing. "I can't remember." He took the flash bomb back. "Still interested in finding out?"

"I'll take your word for it."

"Smart. Here, take it. Study it. When we begin construction, you should be familiar with how the various pyramids feel. You're very familiar with the light pyramid, but you should get to know the pyradisté's best friend, too."

Starbride nodded and took the pyramid back to her apartment. She dutifully reported her training to Dawnmother, who'd spent most of the day shopping in Marienne and fending off eager courtiers and nobles determined to win Starbride over with gifts.

"I'd rather have spent the time watching you practice," Dawnmother said. "But at least we now have soap and more of that silk you like."

"I wish you *had* been there. Crowe obeys you."

"Is he trying to do too much again?"

"At times." She let the flash bomb rest on the table in front of her and trailed one finger down its side.

"Is that really as dangerous as he said?" Dawnmother asked.

Starbride eyed her. "Do you want to find out?"

"No, I can learn from a fool's story as well as you can."

"He was probably in love."

"Fools can fall in love, often do."

Starbride laughed. "Well, I should fall into this pyramid and explore it as he asked. The better I do, the happier he is. Maybe it will make him live a little longer."

Dawnmother kissed the top of her head. "I shall be as quiet as dust."

Starbride smiled at Horsestrong's saying before she took the pyramid in hand and let her mind fall into it. Unlike a light pyramid, it didn't respond to her, but waited to be used. She felt its potential. She could almost see the pathways within it that had been manufactured by Crowe. No, not pathways, fractures, unseen by the eye but felt by the mind—like pieces being held together, waiting to splinter, wanting to break and let something out.

Starbride dug deeper until she reached the something, a giant nimbus of light, like the sun, but contained in this tiny pyramid in her hand. The light that flashed after it broke couldn't possibly be this big, though, this unfathomable. Nothing could contain such brightness, not even her. She couldn't pull her gaze away, even as she knew it was in her mind.

That was the problem. It was *in* her mind. The light pulled her closer, filling her mind, trapping her. "Dawn," she whispered, all she could manage.

The bright light began to burn, blinding her, sending shards of pain ricocheting through her skull, blotting out all sight, making her pulse pound in her ears. Still, she couldn't back away, couldn't do anything but be drawn inexorably forward. "Dawn!"

Something knocked into her hand, and the light pulsed even brighter, though that couldn't be possible. Agony filled her, and she screamed as she passed from light into darkness.

❖

Someone was shaking her shoulder. "Starbride." The voice was male, insistent. Her father? But he'd never sounded so stern, even when she'd gotten into his jewelry tools and scattered them over the carpet.

"Starbride. Wake up."

She opened her eyes; the voice wouldn't tolerate anything less. When she saw the white void, she gasped. She was back in the pyramid chamber underneath the palace, and Katya had just become a greater Fiend, turning the world to white. If that was so, then the male voice must be Roland's, it must. Starbride whipped her arm around. "Get away from me!"

"Softly now," Dawnmother said. Starbride would know her voice anywhere.

"Dawn?" If Dawnmother was calm, everything was well.

"Here." Soft hands gripped her shoulders. "You're safe, Star."

No, she couldn't be, not in the white void. She opened her eyes wider. "Where are you?"

"Do you see *anything*?" the man asked. Crowe, it was Crowe.

"White," she whispered. She knew by his voice that it shouldn't be so. "The pyramid." She couldn't stop her lips from trembling, but she couldn't let herself lose control, not yet. "Did it...am I...blind?"

Dawnmother's arms went around her. "Softly, now, dear heart, hush. We'll fix it." Her voice had steel at the end, and Starbride knew the look she gave to Crowe. If he didn't fix it, not even Horsestrong could save him. Starbride clung to her as if she were a raft.

"One in a thousand," Crowe said with a growl. "This happens to one in a thousand students, if that, and the only way to know it will happen is *after* it has happened!"

"And then they recover," Dawnmother said carefully. "These ones in thousands."

Starbride hung on that word, "recover." It was temporary, like a blindfold, a white blindfold, and soon it would fall from her eyes. "What happened to me?"

"Some students," Crowe said, "when they first encounter a flash bomb, like you did, get...sucked in by it, for lack of a better word. Most just fall into it, see how it works, then come out, but sometimes, there is a...chain reaction." Whatever she was lying on creaked as he got up, and she could hear his footsteps going up and down the room. "I should have been with you, I'm sorry. In the Academy, there's always someone around, and I never expected this to happen. A pyradisté could have guided you out, but Dawnmother…"

"Oh, Star, I broke it. I'm sorry."

"It's…Dawn, are *you* all right?"

"I looked away, but you were…"

Starbride hugged her tighter. "I'm frightened, Dawn."

Dawnmother patted her hair, too fast for comfort, a sure sign that she was frightened too. "What does this mean, Crowe?"

"It's not the first time it's happened," he said. "Not the first time someone has been drawn in with no one around to draw them out, but I'm afraid it might mean that the effect will last a little longer than usual."

The feeling of being blindfolded tightened, as if it would never go away, and pain pounded through Starbride's temples. "How long?"

He paused a heartbeat too long. "A day at most." But the pause told her he wasn't as sure as he sounded.

"I'll tell Katya," Crowe said. "So she'll know who to blame."

"No!" Starbride tried to sit up, but Dawnmother held her too tightly. "She can't know about this."

"Star?" Dawnmother asked.

"She's…already nervous about having me join the Order. She's already so protective." Starbride latched on to the excuse, her fear so sudden and immediate it almost choked her. "If she knows about this, she might forbid me from training."

"She can't exactly forbid you," Crowe said.

"Would you like to make another wager? I guarantee you'll lose this one." Yes, yes, that was it. If Katya knew, if she tried to forbid, things would become too tense between them. Katya already had so much on her shoulders, and a blinded consort would only add to that. And having Starbride continue her training would add even more anxiety. As Crowe himself had said, how much could one person take?

"I don't think this is wise, Starbride," Crowe said. "If you keep this from her and she finds out, it'll hurt her even worse."

"Then she can't find out."

"And how do we keep it from her? You almost live together, Star," Dawnmother said.

Starbride shook her head. "We'll have to think of something." They had to. Because if more people than the three in this room knew about her blindness... "We'll think of something," she whispered.

❖

"She's getting impatient," Dawnmother said.

Starbride nodded. She sat on the settee in her sitting room. She'd spent the entire day there. One down, who knew how many to go. "What did you say to her?"

"It doesn't matter. She doesn't want to hear anything from me. The princess either thinks you don't care for her or she thinks I'm holding you against your will."

"Katya knows I love her," Starbride said, but that didn't ease her guilt.

"You should tell her, Star."

"No," Starbride said softly, but she was beginning to see why she might have to. Her vision was still lost in a world of white, and how she could have used Katya's arms around her. She just didn't want...

She felt the settee dimple as Dawnmother sat. "I don't like leaving you alone to keep putting her off. I feel like I'm committing two betrayals."

"No word from Crowe?"

"You know as much as I."

Starbride nodded again. There was nothing he could do to help her, nothing a healer could do either. The blindness would either wear off or it wouldn't. She wouldn't be able to read or go anywhere alone. She'd never see Katya's beautiful blue eyes again.

Starbride mashed her lips together and curled her hands into fists. There was no use crying over something that would cure itself in time. She tried to summon every ounce of steel her mother had instilled in her.

Dawnmother's arms were around her. "She loves you, she wouldn't rob you of your ability to train, not if it means that much to you. Though...have you considered—"

"I still want to be a pyradisté, Dawn. It's incredible, even after this."

Dawnmother was silent, but Starbride could almost hear her

thinking. Finally, Dawnmother said, "So you wouldn't change what happened, if you could?"

"I'd be more cautious, that's all." But without her sight, could she even fall into a pyramid any longer?

"Whatever happens," Dawnmother said, "you won't have to go through it alone."

Starbride heard the warning in her voice. And she was right. Katya would have to be told of even temporary problems. "I should tell her before she comes barging in…"

"I'll explain it to her. If I take the brunt of her anger, you'll be left with the love."

"You are fearless, Dawn."

"For you."

After one more hug, she was gone. Starbride sat in the quiet room and waited. Would it always be thus? Hearing about adventure, but never seeing it again? Forget adventure. She wouldn't be able to see even the mundane. Could she fetch herself a glass of water? Was she truly helpless?

She stood. This had been her apartment for almost a month. She knew it. It was laid out similarly to Katya's, and she knew that one too. She took a hesitant step, feeling with her foot first and keeping her hands out in front of her. Maybe she could hire Hugo to guide her everywhere.

As she took a few more hesitant steps without incident, her confidence grew. Dawnmother always kept some water at hand, near a bottle of wine. Both perched on the cabinet in the corner, opposite the door, and both sounded ideal for her situation. Starbride headed in that direction, hoping to encounter the table to guide her.

She found the wall and frowned. That wasn't right. The table should have come before the wall. Starbride turned and walked a few steps away, but she suddenly feared leaving the wall behind. If she'd gotten turned around enough to miss the table completely, who knew where she could wind up? Better to feel around the wall until she encountered the cabinet. It had to be to her right.

When she found a door, she had to stop again. Was it the door to the bedroom or to the hallway? She couldn't very well go wandering into the hallway. She felt tears threaten again and forced them down. She wouldn't let a cursed door make her cry!

Maybe if she listened? Starbride put her ear to the door just as it opened. She stumbled forward, hoping it was Dawnmother catching her, but the person felt too tall for that. Familiar, calloused hands caught her under the elbows, and Katya spoke one of the first words she'd ever said to Starbride. "Steady."

Just the sound of her voice loosed Starbride's tears at last. Starbride threw her arms around Katya's neck and sobbed into her shoulder.

Katya patted her hair and made soothing noises until Starbride blurted, "I'm sorry I didn't tell you."

"Well, how can I be angry with you now?"

"It's the bedroom door," Starbride said through her tears. "You came through the passageway, and that's the bedroom door."

Katya's cool hands cupped her cheeks. "My poor Star. Let me help you sit."

"I've been sitting all day," Starbride said as Katya guided her through the white void.

"Why in all the spirits' names didn't you send for me?"

"Dawnmother didn't tell you?"

"I want to hear it from you."

Starbride breathed for a few seconds, trying to face what frightened her. She clasped Katya's hand and borrowed courage. "I was afraid."

"Of?"

"If you knew, I'd have to admit that it…it might be…"

"Permanent?"

Starbride choked down another sob and nodded.

"Even if it is, I will always be by your side."

Starbride shook her head. "You couldn't be, not always. You'd have your duties and your adventures, and I would be another burden."

"Never."

"You'd grow bitter having to wait on me, and I'd grow fat from never walking anywhere."

"You could walk."

"I couldn't even find the wine!" It sounded so absurd, even to her, that she hiccupped into laughter and pressed her forehead into the crook of Katya's shoulder.

"Don't blame the accident for that. You got lost easily before," Katya said.

Starbride laughed harder. "Oh, Katya, what am I going to do?"

"You're going to let me take care of you tonight. In the morning, we'll see how you are. If you're no better, we will scour the city for a solution. We'll talk to Master Bernard and every single pyradisté in the kingdom if we have to."

"And if they have no more answers than Crowe?"

"Then I'll care for you for the rest of your life."

"Your fat, easily lost burden?"

"My beautiful, brilliant, gifted consort."

"I don't want to add to your troubles."

Katya's lips pressed softly to Starbride's mouth. "Never, my love. Never."

Starbride didn't need her eyes to clasp Katya's cheeks and return the kiss. Why had she kept anything from Katya at all?

They parted gently, but Katya stayed close enough that Starbride could almost feel her smile. "Do you need something to take your mind off your troubles? Something you don't need sight for?"

"I always like looking at you."

"Tell you what." Katya took her hands and lifted her to her feet. "I'll keep my eyes closed, and then we'll be on equal footing."

Starbride chuckled and let herself be led, toward the bedroom, she was certain. On the way, she realized that Katya's voice had become less strained than she'd heard in weeks. It was as if having a problem she could care for had lifted some of the enormous burden Roland had put on Katya's shoulders.

Starbride smiled wider. Even after everything that had happened, even after she had drained Katya of her Fiend, Katya loved her still. Katya loved her enough to care for her when she was nearly helpless. Starbride's mild guilt over taking the Fiend away evaporated. Love was never a reason to feel guilty.

"Maybe I should blindfold you," she said as Katya closed the bedroom door behind them. "To make sure you keep your promise."

"Whatever pleases you, pleases me."

"A silk scarf, then, please."

In moments, it was pressed into her hands. Starbride took her time tracing her fingertips from Katya's waist to her face, eliciting a shudder that made Starbride's stomach tighten in anticipation. She tied the silk across Katya's eyes. "Can you see?"

"Not a bit."

Starbride pulled Katya down, kissed her, and then worked the buttons of her coat open. The body underneath, Starbride knew well, and by the way Katya's hands roamed over Starbride's own curves, it was obvious that neither needed their eyes.

Together, they stumbled toward the bed and half fell upon it, laughing. Starbride slipped out of Katya's grasp and felt Katya searching the sheets for her. Starbride scooted away, feeling for the other side so she didn't fall off.

"Come and find me." She moved again.

Katya let out a fake growl. "I am not above pulling off this scarf."

"That's cheating." Starbride felt the mattress shift as Katya pounced. She laughed with delight as Katya scooped her up.

"I've hunted traitors in dark forests. Think I can't find my love in her bedroom?"

"How many loves have you hunted in their bedrooms?"

Instead of answering, Katya kissed Starbride's throat and licked her way downward. Starbride groaned and grabbed at the knot in the silk scarf, moving Katya's head where she most desired it.

Starbride closed her eyes, but the white void remained. She filled it with memories of Katya's body, picturing her caresses and kisses, letting Katya's moans be her guide as she had the very first time they'd lain together. She spent her time on areas she knew Katya loved, ear nibbles and the soft undersides of her breasts. And she endeavored to find new territory, letting her hands and mouth explore without her eyes, kissing and tasting every bit of skin. When Katya cried out, Starbride imagined the glow in her eyes, pupils dilated, hunger dulled but never satisfied.

"I thought I was supposed to be caring for you," Katya said, nearly a slur of words.

Starbride smiled proudly. "You did, dearest, you have. Now all you have to do is keep up."

Katya laughed. "As my lady wishes it, so shall it be."

Starbride laughed as Katya tackled her again and cared for her over and over.

❖

When Starbride's eyes cracked open the next morning, her dark thoughts were waiting for her. She might be blinded for good, lost forever in a white void.

Then she frowned. Something wasn't right. The white void had become a blue one.

No, she thought as she stared. Blue and white blurred together. She lifted her head and reached toward the blue. It was the scarf, the silk scarf, now wadded among the sheets. Starbride lifted her head farther and saw a blurry mass of blond hair and a pale face that even as she watched opened a pair of beautiful eyes.

"Star?"

"I can see you! Not well, but I can see you." Happy tears started down her cheeks.

Katya wrapped her in a hug. "That's wonderful, Star."

"If I'm seeing blurs today…"

"You might be fully healed by tomorrow."

"It was your love," Starbride said. "Your love healed me."

"Well," Katya tossed her hair over her shoulder, "my skills have never healed anyone before, but I'll gladly take the credit."

Starbride hit her with a pillow. "You know what I mean."

"Does this mean no more silk scarves?"

Starbride snorted a laugh. "Whatever pleases you, pleases me."

Katya picked up the blurry scarf. "I think I can tie this loosely enough to just impair my vision. You know, if you want to keep the footing level."

Starbride laughed and hit her with the pillow again.

"Well, if a few hours of love can heal you partway, think what an entire day could do."

Starbride took the scarf from her and pulled it through her hands. "You might be right, but I'll tie this again. I like what you can do when you have to rely solely on your hands."

Karis Walsh, a Pacific Northwest native, is the author of the Bold Strokes Books novels *Harmony*, *Worth the Risk*, and *Sea Glass Inn*, as well as multiple short stories. Visit her at www.kariswalsh.com.

This story features characters from *Sea Glass Inn*.

CAROUSEL
KARIS WALSH

Mel, wake up." Pam shook Mel's bare shoulder. Nervous as she was about the day ahead, her body still responded to the softness of Mel's skin and the familiarity of her shape and texture. She and Mel had become friends, and then lovers. Now, nine months after Pam had moved into Mel's inn and into Mel's life, they were partners in more ways than Pam had imagined possible. She kissed Mel's neck. "Honey, wake up!"

"No." Mel rolled onto her stomach and pulled a pillow over her head. "I'm staying in bed," she said, her voice muffled by the down pillow. "If I have to do another load of laundry, I'm going to shoot someone."

Pam laughed and wrapped her arms around Mel's waist, pulling her out from under the pillow and flush with her own naked body. Pam stroked from Mel's ribs down to her thigh. No one else would have been able to make her relax enough to smile, let alone laugh today, but Mel always managed to make her feel better. Hopeful. Optimistic. She needed all of Mel's enthusiasm and support today.

"No laundry," she promised. The summer had been a whirling mass of color for them, with the guests filling the Sea Glass Inn and new paintings coming to life in Pam's studio. The first week of September signaled a slight easing of their workload. Busy weekends and quiet weekdays. The annual hush of the off-season. More time for the two of them to be alone and celebrating their love. But not today. "They'll be here in a couple hours."

Mel reached down and laced her fingers through Pam's. "Will you be okay?" she asked, her voice alert and wide-awake now.

"I don't know." Pam sighed. The small movement pressed her breasts against Mel's back and she saw wisps of Mel's hair stir when she exhaled. Every tiny movement, every small touch made her want Mel. Want to lock the door and make love to her all day, forgetting the rest of the world while she lost her mind and her heart over and over in Mel's arms.

Mel moved away and got out of bed. She picked up the two robes that had been tossed on the floor sometime during the night and threw one to Pam. "I'll shower and make us breakfast."

She went quickly into the master bathroom and shut the door, but not before Pam had a chance to see the worried expression on Mel's face. She had been hesitant when Pam had first brought up the idea of asking Diane and Kevin to visit the inn. Pam knew it wasn't because Mel was jealous or because she wasn't wholeheartedly behind a reunion for Pam and Kevin. But Mel, like Pam, wasn't able to forget that the last time Diane had ripped Kevin out of her life, Pam had been unable to paint for eight years.

Pam slipped her arms into the sleeves of her yellow robe. She had to take a chance, to gamble that she'd be strong enough to keep her creative spirit intact no matter what happened this weekend. When Diane had left with three year-old Kevin, Pam had been left alone. Now she had Mel, and she'd never be alone again.

Pam showered after Mel finished, and by the time she came upstairs, Mel and her son Danny were sitting at the table eating huckleberry pancakes and bacon. Pam's dog Piper was sitting at Danny's feet, her head on his knee as she watched every bite he took.

"This is why she follows you around all the time," Pam said when she saw Danny break off a small piece of bacon and feed it to the spaniel. She poured a cup of coffee and brought it to the table, certain she wouldn't be able to eat any breakfast today.

"Piper's going to be lost when you leave for school," Mel said to Danny.

Pam put her hand on Mel's knee under the table and gave it a squeeze. Danny had spent the summer with them, but he'd be leaving for college soon. He'd only be going to Eugene—close enough for regular visits—but it wouldn't be the same as having him here full-time. Pam knew the transition would be difficult for Mel, but she hadn't anticipated how deeply it would affect her as well. She'd never had children of her own, but she had grown to love Danny like a son, just as she had loved Kevin. If things didn't go well today, she might be losing both of them in a short week.

Pam set her coffee mug on the table, unable to swallow even that. She should have left well enough alone. What she had was more than *well enough.* She had a good friend in Danny, and even though he was moving away she'd be part of his life forever. She was painting again and loving it with all the fervor she had felt before Diane and Kevin left her. Most important, she had Mel. She shouldn't have dragged the past into their wonderful present and their promising future.

"I need to go for a walk." Pam kissed the top of Mel's head and whistled for Piper. Although the dog usually spent every moment of the day with Danny when he was at the inn, she jumped up and trotted to Pam's side without hesitation, as if she, too, understood the turmoil in Pam's heart. Pam glanced behind as she left the kitchen and saw Mel and Danny watching her with expressions full of concern and love. She smiled back to show she'd be all right, hoping it was true.

❖

Pam kept herself busy in her studio, rearranging easels and cleaning brushes. Doing mindless work, but not painting. She wouldn't know what to paint while her emotions were raging and chaotic, and she needed to experience the reality of this day before she could capture it on canvas.

She stood in front of her current work, its deep reds and blues glowing like embers as the mid-morning sunlight lit up the studio. Sunsets on the beach were such a clichéd subject, but she hadn't been able to resist. She and Mel had been walking alone last week, holding hands and talking about inconsequential matters when they suddenly stopped as one and watched the sun set. No words, no oohs and aahs. Just a silent communion with their home and each other. She'd never felt such a profound peace and connection, and she had sketched the picture as soon as they got home. The painting would sell easily if she put it in her gallery, but she wasn't about to let it go. It would be perfect in the bedroom she and Mel shared.

She felt a brief rush of relief. The sunset painting was almost finished, just in case Diane and Kevin devoured her desire to paint yet again. She hurried to block the negative thoughts from her mind. She was stronger now. She could take whatever trauma the day brought.

Mel tapped on the studio door. "They're here."

Pam nodded and walked toward her. Mel met her halfway across the room, hugged her tightly, and with her hands on Pam's cheeks, gave her a slow, melting kiss.

"Don't forget you have me and Danny," Mel said. "You have *family*. We hope Kevin will be like family, too, but even if he isn't, you're not alone."

Pam leaned her forehead against Mel's for a moment. Mel's kiss and words calmed her more than anything else could. She suddenly felt ready.

She held Mel's hand as they walked across the yard, but she went inside alone. She walked down the hall and paused in the living room doorway for a moment. Diane and a tall boy—nothing like the toddler she had known—stood with their backs to Pam, looking at the painting of a breaching whale that Pam had painted for Mel. Pam studied the tableau in front of her as if she were about to paint it. The splintered multicolored sea glass mosaic contrasted well with the dark mahogany elegance of the living room. The splash of red from Diane's graying auburn hair and Kevin's coppery tones provided an interesting focal point. Pam shook her head. The perspective of an artist gave her distance from the subject, but she needed to bridge that distance. She cleared her throat and entered the room.

Diane looked just as Pam remembered. A little more gray after nine years, with lines of tension around her mouth and eyes, but Pam had a feeling she herself wore the same apprehensive look. Kevin's face had lost the chubbiness and frank openness of childhood, and he had turned into a gawky adolescent. She had expected him to have grown, of course, but she had thought she would recognize him as the boy she had known. Instead, he seemed curiously unfamiliar.

"Hi, Pam." Diane walked over and gave Pam a stiff hug. "You look great."

"So do you," Pam said. The impersonal and shallow tone of the conversation mirrored her lack of feelings. She had expected anger or recrimination when she saw Diane. Tenderness and affection when she saw Kevin. Instead, she felt empty.

"Kevin, come say hello to Pam," Diane said, beckoning him

forward. She turned back to Pam. "I've been telling him all about you and about what an amazing artist you are. This whale is one of yours, isn't it?"

"Yes, it is." Diane shouldn't have needed to tell Kevin about her. Pam should have been part of his life so he'd have simply *known* her. "Hey, Kevin," Pam said when he came over. She offered her hand and he shook it with the awkward grip of a preteen unaccustomed to such formality. "It's good to see you again."

"Nice to meet you," he said.

Pam winced at the words. She hadn't just lost the past nine years with him. She'd lost the chance to be the mother to him she had once hoped to be.

"Why don't we sit down?" She gestured at the arrangement of sofas in the center of the room, trying to soften her tone so she didn't sound as stiff as if she were conducting a business interview. "So we can have a chance to catch up."

Pam spent the next half hour listening to Diane talk about her job teaching art at the university where she and Pam had met. Following Diane's prodding and Pam's questions, Kevin told her about school and his karate dojo and his neighborhood friends. Pam nodded and made the appropriate comments, but she felt so tightly wound she wanted to scream. Kevin was a stranger to her and she to him. She should have expected it. He had been a baby when she first came into his life and a toddler when she was forced out of it. Of course he didn't have any real connection to her.

She heard the front door open and close, and then Mel came into the living room. "I don't want to interrupt, but Danny brought home Fortuna's Pizza. Are you hungry for lunch?"

Pam jumped at the chance for a reprieve from their stilted conversation. "Thanks, Mel. Why don't we eat in here?"

Mel, Danny, and Piper came into the room with a flurry of energy and activity. Mel put napkins and cans of Coke on the table while she introduced Danny and Piper to Diane and Kevin. Piper swirled around Kevin, all tongue and waving tail, and he laughed and slid off the couch to play with her. Pam finally saw a glimpse of the child he had been.

Mel watched Pam's face transform as she looked at Kevin and Piper. She was glad to see some emotion in her instead of the flat, expressionless look she'd had when Mel had first walked into the room. She and Danny sat on either side of Pam, flanking and protecting her. She wanted to touch Pam, make sure she was okay, but she made herself settle for simply sitting close enough for their thighs to brush whenever one of them moved.

They started to eat in silence, and the distance between the two sides of the table seemed too much to bridge. Danny seemed to understand, and he engaged Kevin in a conversation about baseball and summer leagues. The boys chatted throughout the meal while the three adults ate quietly.

Mel forced herself to swallow bites of pizza, but she was too worried about Pam to relax. When they had first met, Pam had been broken, unable to paint. Mel had been there to watch as Pam had reconnected with her talent and as she had slowly and painfully picked up a brush again. The journey from Pam's isolated and barren life to her new one of hope and creation had been a long and difficult one. Mel didn't know if she could help Pam out of that dark place again, if she fell back into it.

The brief moment of emotion Pam had shown when Kevin was laughing with Piper had disappeared. Mel had worried about this reunion, but she had been optimistic that Pam could come out of it with her need to express herself through art intact. Maybe Pam would paint joy, maybe sorrow, but she simply wanted Pam to *paint*. The emptiness Mel saw in Pam's eyes scared her. Would Pam be able to create if she felt nothing?

Danny tossed a piece of crust into the empty pizza box. "Hey, Kevin, want to come outside and play ball with me and Piper?"

Kevin looked at Diane for permission, and she looked at Pam.

"Sure, Kevin," Pam said. "I'll bet Piper would love that."

Pam stood up as soon as they'd left the room. "I need…I think I need to take a walk." She put her hand on Mel's shoulder. "Okay?"

"Of course," Mel said as she started to gather their used napkins. "Take your time."

Diane picked up some empty pop cans and followed Mel into the kitchen. "That didn't seem to go well." She set the cans on the counter. "Maybe it was a bad idea to come here."

Mel looked out the window at Danny and Kevin as they played with the dog, and she struggled to get control of her anger. Diane had forced Pam out of Kevin's life, and now she was trying to wrest them apart again. Too soon. "Give them time," she said. "They haven't seen each other for eight years, so you can't expect them to become best friends in one hour. They have the weekend to get to know each other again."

"We'll see." Diane walked over to the painting hanging by the kitchen table. The watercolor was washed with pale yellows and blues—the beach at the height of a hot summer day—and two women sat with their backs to the artist, leaning toward each other with their hands intertwined where they rested on the sand. Mel and Pam. Pam had painted it based on a picture Danny had taken of them when they hadn't realized he was there. The original photo, enlarged and framed, hung in their downstairs bedroom.

"How do you live with it?" Diane asked, turning back to face Mel.

"Live with what?"

"Her talent. How do you live with someone so gifted and consumed by her art? How do you keep it from consuming *you*?"

Mel paused, uncertain how to answer. Diane's jealousy of Pam's talent had been what drove them apart, but Mel couldn't understand such pettiness. Pam and her gifts were interwoven. To love Pam was to love what and how she created. "She makes me *more*, not less. When I'm with her, I'm more myself. More the person I want to be. She never tries to overshadow me, and she always supports and encourages me, no matter what I do."

"But she never stops drawing, or thinking about what to draw."

She did stop, for eight years after you took Kevin away from her. Mel didn't say it out loud. She never wanted Pam to bury her desire to paint again. Mel loved the faraway look she'd get when she saw something that inspired her. The frantic search for a pencil and paper so she could capture a moment and later bring it to life.

"I hope she never does."

Diane shook her head. "I used to worry she wouldn't make time for me and Kevin. She let her art rule her life, and I always knew that if she had to choose us or a paintbrush, we'd have lost."

Mel made a pot of coffee so she'd have something to do with her hands besides strangling Diane. "She has never once let me or Danny down. I have no doubt we're her first priority, just like Kevin would have been if you'd let her stay in his life."

"You don't understand—"

Mel put the coffee filters on a shelf and slammed the cabinet door shut. "I understand perfectly well." She pointed out the window. "That is my son. His father and I are divorced, but I'd *never* try to cut him out of Danny's life. I want Danny to be surrounded by people who love him. I wouldn't let my own insecurity or jealousy get in the way of that."

Mel felt her hands shake with the ferocious need to protect Pam. She stepped toward Diane, her voice quiet and low, but sounding dangerous even to her own ears. "You made a mistake. Not in letting Pam go, because I know for certain you were the wrong partner for her. But you never should have stood in the way of her relationship with Kevin. Don't make the same mistake again. You're going to give them this weekend, give them as long as they need to form a bond, because it's the right thing to do for both of them."

"Ooh, I'm scared," Diane said with a laugh, but she took a step back. "Don't get all riled up. Kevin is old enough to make his own decisions. If he wants Pam in his life, I won't stand in his way. But he doesn't even remember her, so don't get your hopes up."

Mel looked out the window again. She saw Pam walk past the boys and go into her studio. No matter what Diane said, Mel had no choice but to keep her hopes up. Because more than anything, she wanted to see Pam become whole again.

❖

Pam moved through her studio with a sense of calm. The anxiety she'd felt in the morning, the emptiness of loss she'd felt when first talking to Kevin, were gone now. She chose a large canvas from a pile and picked up some paints, brushes, an easel. She lugged everything out the door and onto the stone path that curved through the garden. Without looking at the boys, who were still playing with Piper, she set up her easel and prepared to paint.

The surety of her vision gave her confidence to quickly spread and mix oils on her palette. She smeared a brush in some black paint and made an interlocking set of ovals down the center of the canvas. Some gold inside the shapes, and she had the twisted pole of a carousel. Next, she outlined the horse. Dapple-gray, with brightly painted saddle and bridle in shades of blue. Royal and navy and aquamarine. Tassels and gilded medallions made the frozen horse look worthy of a Bedouin warrior. And on his back was a young boy, his coppery hair a fine complement to his fancy mount. Pam's hand moved swiftly and easily over the canvas as she blended and outlined and brought the carousel to life.

She had started the background when she came out of her painting zone enough to realize she had an audience. She smiled at Kevin before returning her attention to the canvas. She took some liberties with her memory of the state fair, where she and Kevin had played and explored just days before her world fell apart and Diane took him away. Although the fair had been large and spread over several acres, she condensed the best parts into the space on the canvas. The goats and sheep, the ice cream and hot dog stands, the slats and tracks of an old wooden roller coaster.

"I remember that." Kevin pointed at the animals. "We got to pet goats and one tried to bite me. And we shared a big banana split before we went on the roller coaster, even though Mom said it'd make me sick."

"It didn't, though, did it?" Pam's brush almost rushed over the painting. She drew a mechanical arm with a gaudy red ring at its end. "Do you remember trying to grab rings as you went around the carousel?"

"I couldn't reach," Kevin said, looking at her instead of the painting now. "But you helped me get one."

"Yes, I did." Pam blinked away her tears as she continued to paint the memory.

❖

Pam turned the covers back and crawled into bed, pulling Mel into her arms. She burrowed her nose in Mel's hair and inhaled the scent of warmth and roses from Mel's shower. She moved slightly and her breasts rubbed over Mel's smooth back. Mel sighed and pressed closer, her hips nestling against Pam's crotch. Pam held Mel in the same position she had that morning, but this time they had nowhere to go for at least eight hours.

"Mmm." Pam nuzzled Mel's neck. "I thought I had dried off after my shower, but I seem to be getting wet again."

"I can help with that." Mel turned in Pam's arms and kissed her on the lips, her tongue tracing Pam's front teeth before she leaned her head away and laid her hand on Pam's cheek. "Are you sure you're all right, sweetheart?"

Pam understood the depth of the question. "Yes. It was…a good day."

And it had been. She had imagined this day thousands of times over the past eight years. Joyful reunions. Blame and guilt-ridden shouting matches. And everything in between. She hadn't anticipated the total emptiness she had felt at first, or the slow and tentative day of getting to know Kevin again. It hadn't been what she'd expected, but it had been good. Quietly, hopefully *good*.

"He's an interesting kid," Mel said. "Smart and athletic. And he has an artistic side. He reminds me of you."

"Me, too," Pam admitted. Once she and Kevin had reconnected through the shared memory in her painting, they had been able to make a new connection in the present. He had shown her a kata from his karate class, they'd tossed a baseball around on the beach, and he'd followed her with seeming interest as she showed him the paintings in her studio. Diane had even stepped aside and let him go to dinner with her, Mel, and Danny. She had discovered that as much as she had loved the toddler Kevin, she wanted to get to know Kevin as he was now.

"I couldn't have done it without you," she said, kissing Mel again and sucking gently on her lower lip. "You were right there every time I needed you. With the pizza, with baseball mitts. But also you were just *there*. Every little touch or smile or look you gave me today helped me feel less alone. And Danny was great, too. They sure got along well."

Mel laughed, her breath tickling Pam's ear. She swirled her tongue over Pam's earlobe. "He used to write letters to Santa asking for a little brother. Maybe he'll finally get his wish."

"Better late than never?" Pam gasped as Mel nibbled her neck. She rolled Mel onto her back and kissed her collarbone. The sentiment was a stale one, but it fit today perfectly. She had to stop mourning the loss of

Kevin as a toddler in order to appreciate the Kevin he was today. Mel's words to her this morning—that she and Danny were Pam's family— had been the catalyst for her new perspective. She had a family and a future, and she needed to live moving forward. Not looking back.

And right now her future, her hope, her love was sighing and squirming underneath her. Pam smiled as she kissed a trail over Mel's breastbone and toward her abdomen. Onward and downward. No going back.

Lee Lynch is author of *The Raid*, *Beggar of Love*, and *Sweet Creek* from Bold Strokes Books. Her work has been honored with the James Duggins Mid-Career, GCLS Trailblazer, and Alice B. Readers Appreciation awards. Her novel *The Swashbuckler* was first recipient of her namesake award, the Golden Crown Literary Society's Lee Lynch Classic Award.

This story features characters from *Beggar of Love*.

Dawn Knew
Lee Lynch

Dawn knew from day one that Jefferson was an excitement junkie, a quality that kindled her. In the past, Jefferson's fix was new, or at least illicit, women. The women were gone, but not the excitement.

One Saturday, they joined the tourists in downtown Wolfeboro. The bakery, as always, pumped out hot bread and cinnamon scents. They stopped to say hello to the owner of the hippie store, where the incense reeked more of balsam than the surrounding pine woods. Annoying little gift shops displayed windows stuffed with silly gewgaws, as her dad would call them, which they laughed at, arm in arm, as they passed.

Another of Jefferson's addictions went back to childhood, when she spent summers in New Hampshire at the vacation place that was now her home. Saturdays, the Jeffersons boated into town. There was an old restaurant on the pier where the tourist and mail boat, the *Mt. Washington*, docked. Ice cream cones were served from the restaurant's window. Fifty years later, Jefferson still enjoyed the hot summer excursions into town for cold ice cream.

Dawn went to town as a kid, but more often her family ate at home, much cheaper. Those were happy times with the whole family at the supper table, spooning ice cream from the small rice bowls her aunt brought over from Vietnam. U.S. ice cream and spicy fish sauce—just the thought of the unlikely combination of foods she'd grown up with brought happy tears to her eyes. She only wanted with Jefferson what her father and mother had—a long, fun, harmonious, even luminous marriage.

Watching Jefferson's pleasure as she sat in her boat, rocking on the water, licking the melting vanilla with that wonderful tongue of hers, Dawn wondered how to make her this happy all the time.

"What's the frown for?" Jefferson asked, touching her hand.

"I'm trying to figure you out, J, so I can keep you forever and ever," she said, exaggerating the frown with a squint and pursed lips.

Jefferson leaned over and gave her a quick sun-chapped kiss on the nose. "Am I going somewhere?"

"If you could, where would you go?"

"To bed. With you."

Why didn't Jefferson's quick response reassure her? Had she said that to a lot of women? Of course she had. Jefferson's tumultuous past love life haunted her more than it did Jefferson, who seemed to have moved on. Did Jefferson have regrets? Did she miss the longtime lover who died after leaving her? Did she carry invisible hurts?

The happy kid in Jefferson was showing in her smile and her eyes. What could be more reassuring?

They sat on blue lifesaver cushions on the stern bench of Jefferson's launch, watching runabouts, small sailboats, and yachts come and go. Jefferson wore white shorts, a black polo shirt, and white deck shoes, no socks. Dawn was in a white-and-yellow print cotton skirt, lace-trimmed tank top, and white sandals. Jefferson looked around, ice cream cone in one hand, with the other reached under Dawn's skirt.

"J, no!" She pulled back. The boat rocked.

"Why? No one can see."

"You're not in New York anymore."

"You're so alluring in that top," Jefferson said, grinning.

"You're embarrassing the town librarian."

"Aren't librarians allowed to have sex?"

Damn. She'd done it again, said no to something that excited Jefferson. And herself. But she couldn't enjoy those seeking, commanding hands in public. At least not this public, not where she worked. "Take the boat out a little farther," she whispered.

"The lady," Jefferson said, making her way to the helm, "wants privacy. I can do that." She turned the ignition key, deftly backed the launch, in all its polished mahogany glory, away from the dock, and bumped through the wake of a large white yacht as she brought the boat about and left the marina.

Dawn stayed where she was, the air cooling as they got farther out on the lake. She pulled Jefferson's white sweatshirt over her bare shoulders. Jefferson accelerated slowly, steadily, until the bow rose out of the water. Ignoring the posted speeds, she stood at the wheel and sliced through the water, her graying, overgrown hair brushed back by the wind. Dawn loved to watch Jefferson in her element like this, masterful, as if she was the actual source of the boat's power. God, she cherished this woman.

Minutes later, tucked in the boathouse, Dawn was more than ready.

Jefferson tied up and rejoined her. "Better?"

The boathouse was dark and cool, a world of wet. She shrugged the sweatshirt off and shivered a little. To the touch, her hair felt like lake grasses. She was sunburned and chilly, but refused to say no to Jefferson again, maybe ever again.

She locked eyes with her lover and lifted her foot to the gunwale. Her gauzy skirt fell back to the tops of her thighs. As Jefferson twisted to kiss her, Jefferson's strong fingers pulled aside the crotch of her panties and opened her to the damp air. She clenched inside. Then, to her surprise, she was coming, all limp against Jefferson's shoulder, Jefferson's free arm holding her up.

"God, J."

"Nice?"

She leaned on Jefferson, unable to sit upright. "Nice? I think you just turned me into something like that vanilla ice cream you devoured earlier."

"Did I devour you?"

"Is that what you call it?"

"I call it love," Jefferson said. "Come in the house so I can really love you."

She followed, a boneless version of herself, stepping in Jefferson's footsteps. The surprise of it, the way she'd let herself fling away control—Jefferson was her siren song: once heard, ever obeyed.

In bed, she had no will to resist her conquering lover. Was that when Jefferson left women, once she had thoroughly overwhelmed them? Dawn clung to her, empty of self, subsuming her consciousness into Jefferson's, living for a time only as part of this untethered, unaware being.

"Stop!" she breathed, wanting more, coming hard on Jefferson's fingers. Jefferson ignored her, using her mouth and fingers, licking her, driving her, seducing her into yet another orgasm and then another, slower, longer and powerful.

"Let me love you," she managed to demand, seeking, in her exhaustion, to maintain the ecstasy of her immersion in Jefferson, of her pleasure at merging.

But Jefferson simply held her, brushed Dawn's skin with gentle lips, and whispered, "Later."

After a brief nap, she struggled to place herself, to replace spaces left hollow when Jefferson withdrew. It grew more and more difficult to differentiate between herself and Jefferson after lovemaking. Naked, she joined Jefferson on the porch, still a bit frightened of her powerful emotions, and at the same time, grateful.

"Is it later yet?" she asked with an impish grin, tilting Jefferson's newspaper down so she'd acknowledge Dawn's offering. Dawn unbuttoned and unzipped Jefferson's white shorts. "Here? Can I touch you out here on the porch? I guess you're not worried someone will see us?"

Without a word, Jefferson eased her to her feet and then stripped. When they kissed, soft on soft, she still tasted of vanilla.

"Yes, here," Jefferson answered, guiding her onto her lap and easing a finger inside her. Dawn rocked on Jefferson's finger, hugging it while stroking Jefferson's wet clit, circling with a thumb until Jefferson's long exhale told her she was done.

"Don't wear me out," Jefferson said. "It's time for my swim."

Only once, for Jefferson. Always only once; no matter how insistent Dawn was, Jefferson could give herself over just once. Dawn was torn. How could she explain that Jefferson was withholding as much as Dawn gave? She smiled against Jefferson's neck, thinking there was a kind of balance in that. Was it possible that she would love Jefferson less if Jefferson didn't tie herself to some emotional mast to protect herself from Dawn's love, all love, and from betrayal? Would Jefferson, rather than leave because Dawn posed no challenge, stay to prove she could? Dawn had told her she didn't tolerate straying lovers. It was all or nothing with her.

"What makes you tick?" she asked.

"You, you sexy time bomb. You're always ready to go off."

Jefferson laughed as she bundled Dawn in one of her grandmother's afghans.

It was still warm on the porch, or maybe she was still warm with bliss. The pine trees gave off the heated aroma of real balsam. She said, "You'd make a good poker player, J."

"I'm not too shabby at poker."

"I can see why. Your face never shows what's going on inside."

"You're the only thing that goes inside me," Jefferson said with a glance at Dawn's hand.

Ignoring Jefferson's joke, she went on. "You're also very good at deflecting my questions."

Jefferson hung her head. "I'm sorry. That's left over from my drinking days. Honesty is hard."

Living on the lake hadn't done much to bring Jefferson peace, she thought. She was like a child who puts her fingers in her ears and makes noise so she can't hear. In Jefferson's case, so she couldn't hear what was going on inside herself.

"Do you have to swim today?" She heard the whine in her voice and could have kicked herself.

Jefferson was plainly all revved up and ready to go. "What's wrong with swimming?"

"It's not the swimming, it's these impossible challenges you set for yourself." At times like this, Jefferson's heedless distancing made her so angry she could just stalk off and never return. Let her drown in the lake the way she almost drowned in alcohol. Let her find some other dancer type like the one who turned her life upside down. Didn't Jefferson understand that Dawn wanted to help right her? A surge of love quelled her anger and frustration. She stroked Jefferson's hair. "I worry about you."

Jefferson kissed her hand. "I like that."

She'd never known a lover so courtly.

Dawn got dressed, still vibrating, and stood on the porch steps in time to see Jefferson, in her neon orange racer's swimsuit and cap, dive into the lake. Today she was headed to a promontory with an oversized new house and an acre of new lawn. The swim, round-trip, was about a half mile, Jefferson said, and added, "No sweat."

Jefferson, in the water, rolled on her back and waved like a playful otter. Dawn waved back from the porch, watching in case anything went wrong. Jefferson became an increasingly distant orange dot bobbing in the lake. She didn't seem to understand that her body was a piece of aging equipment, or maybe she did, and this was her way of refusing the loss of her powers.

Jefferson wasn't a deep thinker and just now, Dawn tried to shut her mind down too. She'd learned that there were times in life when you just had to go for it. The air before you becomes robust, as if it's taking a shape, your shape, and you must step into it.

She was still on the porch when two stand-up Jet Skis roared away from the promontory.

Kids, she thought, it must be kids because one of those one-person skis held two people.

"That's nuts," she said aloud to no one. And then, yelling, she ran across the lawn, down the stone steps, and out on the dock. She waved her arms, frantic with the thought that she'd called for this drowning not ten minutes ago. The Jet Skis were loud, crazy loud, even from this distance.

Jefferson heard them too, she was sure, but could she evade them? How many times had she told Jefferson it was crazy to be that far out in the lake without a spotter boat? She mimed swimming and gestured for the kids to veer west, but she was so far away. Would they see Jefferson in time?

The skiers were laughing and yelling as they circled and jumped over each other's waves. Jefferson was doing the backstroke now. Was she trying to make herself more visible or was she pretending invincibility, ignoring the danger? Why, Dawn wondered, did I have to fall for such a daredevil dope? She yelled again.

Bob and Bonnie, the straight couple in the next house toward town, called from their dock, asking if she was all right. She pointed.

"Is that little Amelia swimming out there?" Bob yelled.

She gave a vigorous nod. They'd watched Jefferson grow up.

"You'd better go get her!" Bonnie said.

Dawn glanced at the boathouse. Her family had cows, not boats. Jefferson kept saying she would teach Dawn to run the launch, but hadn't.

Then it happened. She heard Bonnie scream and looked back at the lake in time to see the Jet Ski that carried two people barrel over into the water, throwing the passenger and taking the driver down with it.

Where was Jefferson?

Bob cast off in his small motorboat. His engine was smaller than Jefferson's, but it was obvious he was running full throttle.

She saw the orange bathing cap then. Jefferson was treading water. Had something hit her? She ran to the porch for binoculars and focused from the front steps. Jefferson was holding someone up. The lone skier dove again and again, searching for the third person.

Jefferson helped put her charge, who appeared to be eight or nine, in the neighbor's boat. The missing skier surfaced. He floated on the surface and his friend towed him in.

Bonnie arrived carrying binoculars too.

"What's Amelia doing way out there?" she asked.

Bob was cruising toward the new house. Jefferson swam beside him.

Bonnie said, "She must be exhausted."

Dawn was surprised to hear herself speak with pride. "She'll see it through."

"My Bob is the same way. Has been since the day we met. When he's set on something, nothing and no one will stop him. He scares me sometimes, but I wouldn't have him any other way. That's the guy I fell for forty-odd years ago."

Dawn wanted to ask how long it took. How many of those forty years did Bonnie worry herself sick over Bob's stubborn risks?

Bob must have given his cell phone to one of the kids, as the parents were waiting on their brand-new dock. The mother held a hand over her mouth, the father smacked the eldest kid in the head and yanked the wailing youngest across the lawn by his scrawny arm. Jefferson hoisted herself into Bob's boat. He handed her what looked like a moth-eaten army blanket. Dawn breathed her deep relief, the clean lake air soothing her throat, scratchy from yelling.

When the two adventurers tied up, she helped Jefferson into her blue terry robe with the sense she was wrapping herself around her. Bonnie invited them for barbecue, but Jefferson looked wan, her shivers interrupted by shudders. Dawn asked for a rain check.

Her anger was gone. She could no more accuse Jefferson of foolhardiness at that moment than she could have stalked off earlier.

This wasn't her folks' marriage, how could it be? She'd chosen the excitement that was Jefferson.

Dawn led her home to shower. She tested the water's warmth and stepped into the shower to lather Jefferson's strong swimmer's shoulders. Forty years. The thought made her light-headed with happiness.

Ali Vali is the author of *The Devil Inside*, *The Devil Unleashed*, *Deal with the Devil*, *The Devil Be Damned*, and *The Devil's Orchard*. Her Forces Series includes *Balance of Forces: Toujours Ici* and *Battle of Forces: Sera Toujours*. Her stand-alone novels are *Carly's Sound*, *Second Season*, *Blue Skies*, the two Lambda Literary Award finalists *Calling the Dead* and *Love Match*, and *The Dragon Tree Legacy*.

This story features characters from her long-running Devil Series.

The Devil You Know
Ali Vali

"Are you sure you want to be seen with me?" Emma Casey asked as she sat in the bathroom putting on her makeup.

"Is this pregnancy making you lose your mind or something?" Mob boss Cain Casey toweled off after a long shower. Emma had her head cocked back slightly as she applied mascara, but she stuck her tongue out at her in the mirror anyway.

They were getting ready for the costume party Marianna Jatibon hosted every year at the Piquant for her husband Ramon's birthday. With encouragement from the Piquant's owner and old family friend Poppy Valente, it had become an annual event that kicked off the fall social season in New Orleans. Poppy had lost her first partner, Carly, to breast cancer, so along with a few events she hosted throughout the year, Ramon's party raised a tremendous amount of money for breast cancer research in Carly Valente's name.

"I don't know why I'm bothering with all this stuff." Emma finished with her eyelashes. "We'll have masks on the entire time."

"First," Cain said, kneeling next to Emma and running her fingers from her knee up her thigh, "it'll always be a privilege to escort you anywhere, and I don't take that lightly." She continued touching along Emma's stomach to the underside of her breast. "And you bother because you'll take your mask off at midnight, and the thought of being in public without makeup on will make you nuts, though I'm not sure why. My prediction is you'll be the sexiest and most beautiful woman there, war paint or not."

"It's a good thing you're so loyal. You lie so well." Emma grabbed her hand. "But we don't have enough time for me to put all this stuff back on, so behave, mobster."

Emma balanced herself when she stood by putting her hands on Cain's shoulders. They were close enough that Emma's midsection pressed against Cain's lips, so she kissed the surface, hoping the baby somehow knew how much it was loved and wanted. "You've got a few months to go, so don't wear out your welcome, buddy. And take it easy on your mama."

"Casey babies seem to only come in extra-large." Emma groaned when Cain licked her nipple. "I should be over the crazed sex phase of this pregnancy, but I'm not, so keep your tongue and those grabby hands to yourself until we get home."

"I could relax you without going anywhere near your makeup, scout's honor."

"You were never a scout, honey, though you're always prepared. You might've shaken up the ranks if your mom had signed you up, and your cookie sale numbers would've been legendary."

"So how about some R-and-R before the party?"

"Remi and Dallas will be here in a little while to pick us up, so you're going to have to exhibit some of that patience you're known for." Emma leaned her bottom against the marble counter and smiled up at Cain as she stood. "Tonight I want to have fun," she said, putting her hand between Cain's legs. "I want to dance and have you whisper in detail what you're going to do to me when we're alone again."

Emma's fingers stroked through her growing wetness and got her instantly hard. Cain spread her feet slightly. "Eloquent words to get me to behave, but your hand isn't in agreement, lass." Emma squeezed her clit between her index and middle finger, and the pressure almost made Cain come.

"Sometimes I can't look at you without wanting you," Emma said and let up a little. "Do we risk my makeup or can you wait?"

Cain lifted Emma a little more on the counter and covered her sex with the palm of her hand, only dipping one finger down to see how wet she was. "I can wait if you can." Emma's hips jerked and she came close to changing her mind. "It can be like our dating days when you worked me into a lather, then sent me home in a desperate state."

"Good things and waiting, baby, you know the old saying." Emma circled Cain's diamond-hard clit with a feather touch. Cain was about to beg for her to finish what she'd started when they'd gotten in the shower together. "We can pretend it's like those old wonderful days, but when we get home, I promise to teach you a whole new meaning for desperate."

"Fuck," Cain said as Emma got wetter and she got harder.

"I promise you it'll come to that," Emma teased as she pushed her back a step.

❖

"Mama!" Hannah slammed her hands against their bedroom door. "Can I see you?"

"Aren't you glad we decided to wait," Emma said, stepping into her panties and slipping on her robe as Cain headed into the walk-in closet.

"You know I work well under pressure."

"Go put something on, troublemaker." Emma opened the door to their daughter and their son Hayden.

"Can we say hello to the baby?" Hannah asked.

Emma opened her robe a little and Hannah and Hayden went through their ritual of whispering something and kissing her big tummy, as Hannah called it. This daily exercise had started when the children had seen Cain doing it.

"Let me." Cain took Emma's stockings from her and knelt to put them on for her. "You're going to be good, right?" she asked the children as she got the first leg done, her fingers resting on Emma's thigh longer than necessary before she started on the other leg.

"I should ask you the same thing." Emma tapped the end of Cain's nose.

"Did you tell the baby something special?" Hayden asked as he sat with Hannah on his lap.

"I told them I saved some toys so we could play in the bathroom when they get here." Hannah stood on his lap and leaned back as far as Hayden's reach would go. "What did you say?"

"I let them know how great it is to be the big brother, and what a wonderful big sister they're lucky to have." Hayden slowly stood as Hannah walked her feet up his chest and fearlessly flipped over and landed on her feet. "Are you going to help Mama get dressed and I'll take Mom?"

Dallas Montgomery walked in without knocking and pointed at

Hayden and Cain. "I volunteered for that job too, so clear out, you two."

"Who are you, Aunt Dallas?" Hannah asked.

"Tonight I'm the reformed Genevieve."

"Reformed?" Cain asked.

"My Arthur's downstairs, and she looks so hot in that armor, Lancelot doesn't have a chance." Dallas made them all laugh, playing with Hannah as Emma tied Cain's bow tie.

"We'll be down in a few. Try not to forget the list of stuff you have to do later," Emma said to Cain.

"It's going to be an eventful night, and not just for us."

"Those are the best kind."

"I doubt everyone agrees with you." Cain kissed Emma's cheek, followed by Hayden.

"That's because they haven't seen you naked."

"A little work, a lot of fun, and then naked. I promise a memorable night," Cain whispered.

"You always deliver those in stunning fashion, so I'm glad the fun and naked part will be all I'm involved in," Emma murmured as Cain gathered the rest of her costume and left.

❖

The Piquant's main ballroom was packed and everyone in attendance seemed happy to have an excuse to leave their Katrina-related repairs behind for the night. Most of Cain and Emma's friends had come through the storm okay except for Vinny, whose house had been severely flooded. Katrina had only cost them part of the roof over the sunroom and kitchen, some trees, and all of Hannah's playground equipment. That Cain had replaced before the roofers even showed up.

"You picked a costume that makes it hard to kiss you in," Emma said as they danced to the old Spanish love song Ramon requested every year. The one he said had been played at his wedding.

"I thought my choice was perfect since I'm sure our surveillance team and your mother believe I seduced you to a dark underworld." The Phantom mask was making her hot and itchy, but it was important to keep it on until Ramon blew out his candles. "You're my young impressionable Christine tonight, and I intend to seduce you."

"You know I can't sing worth a damn, right…much less opera?"

"No, but you will scream when I put my tongue—"

"Have mercy on me, mobster." Emma bit her chin softly. "I'm already at the breaking point, and we've got a few hours to go."

"I thought you wanted a detailed description of how your night will end?"

"Right now I want you to walk me to the restroom *again*." Emma leaned on Cain when Cain put an arm around her waist to make sure no tipsy dancers ran into them. "While we're in there, maybe you can convince baby Casey into swimming clear of my bladder for a little while."

"I'll see what I can do about all the promises I made to you."

❖

"Someone's getting lucky tonight," Special Agent Joe Simmons said into the mike at his wrist. "But don't let the lovebirds fool you. Casey loves nights like this to cover up some plan or another, so maybe we'll get lucky in return."

Claire Lansing sat in the small conference room next to the one where the party was raging. "So far I'm thrilled with the new equipment." Earlier they'd mounted the new high-powered, electronically easy-to-aim microphones. "The new stuff does a fantastic job of dropping out the background noise, so of course, the only thing on Cain's mind is getting her partner to go home early. Actually hearing her voice and not some hideous song her evil mind comes up with is a blessing."

Shelby Phillips had to agree with that. They weren't sure how she did it, but songs like the theme from *Bonanza* could drive you insane after a few hours and would stay lodged in your brain for weeks. "At least we know this all works and so far haven't been jammed," she said, standing up so the bathrooms were in sight. "It was a good time to test it."

"Shut up and pay attention," Special Agent Brent Cehan said when the door opened and the Caseys came out. "I hope she does try some shit tonight before I go."

"Back off and bring it down a notch," Shelby warned as Brent paced close to where Cain and Emma were walking. "After tonight this won't be your problem anymore, and the only reason you're here is some of the agents assigned to the other families are out sick. I'm sure the good citizens of Anchorage will love you, but I've had enough of your mouth for a lifetime." Shelby smiled when Brent made a rude gesture in her direction, but after he'd gotten it out of his system, it seemed that he'd do as he was told.

She scanned the room again for anything out of the ordinary, but so far this was what it seemed—a party and nothing more. The music stayed slow and the dance floor full, including the Caseys, but she had them in sight as Cain kept up her flirting with Emma.

One of the waiters dropped a tray of glasses that made her look as they cleaned it up, but that was as exciting as it got for the next hour. Aside from testing their equipment, this night was a total waste of time.

"But I'll take that any day," she said softly as she hummed along with the band's next selection.

❖

After another trip to the bathroom together, the Caseys joined in to serenade Ramon after he'd handed the representative from Susan G. Komen a check that'd she seemed overwhelmed by. Emma helped Cain clean her face of the mild adhesive that'd held her disguise in place, and Cain was finally glad to get rid of it.

"How much do you want me?" Emma said as they swayed to the last song they were dancing to.

"Enough that I can't make it home." Cain turned Emma around to greet Poppy and Julia Valente. "Good thing the owners are good friends and have lots and lots of comfortable beds at their disposal."

"The suite you ordered," Poppy said as she handed over the envelope with a slight bow. "And congratulations on the new addition."

"It's time to add to your brood, or so your mother tells me," Cain said as Poppy took her hand.

"She's finally found her niche for sure," Julia said, touching Emma's midsection. "Being a grandmother is her calling, and she's trying to make it a full-time job. You're giving me the itch, Emma. I'm jealous."

"You know me, I'm ready for ten." Poppy smiled. "You two enjoy the rest of your evening and have the staff call me if you need anything."

Cain waved to their watchers as they got in the elevator and kissed Emma to celebrate that the work part of her evening was done.

"Don't you love a good party?" Emma pressed Cain to the elevator wall.

"I do, especially when it's for a good cause." She clasped Emma's hips as Emma slowly pulled her bow tie undone. "You, on the other hand, are very good at being bad."

"Me?" Emma unfastened the three top buttons of her shirt. "If I am, it's because I've learned from the master." Just as Emma put her hand in her shirt, the doors slid open and Lou, waiting in the hall, cleared his throat. "Do you have something else to do?" Emma asked Cain in a way that would start a fight if she said yes.

"I have plenty to do, but they all have to do with you. The only thing on my mind is getting you alone." Cain led Emma to the end of the hall and another elevator.

"I'm right below you if you need me." Lou pointed to the door next to the elevator. "I already checked upstairs, so have fun and relax. Our exterminator went through it with me. It's bug-free."

"Thanks, and that's all for tonight. Don't open your door again unless the hotel is on fire. If you need me, use the phone."

Emma followed her inside and Cain placed the key Poppy had given her in the slot to make the doors close. "Where are we going?" Emma asked.

"It's my last surprise of the night." The doors opened to the Carly Suite, which was really more of an apartment Poppy and Julia had lived in while their house was being renovated.

"This place is gorgeous," Emma said as Cain led her to the master suite.

"We can sightsee later. I've got plans for you."

"After a night of your driving me insane, I should apologize for all those nights I sent you home hard as rock." Emma turned so Cain could start on the long row of buttons at her back. "How'd it go while I was dancing with Muriel?"

Her cousin Muriel Casey was the family's attorney, and as far as Shelby and her team knew, she was in Las Vegas on business. "Did she blush when she turned on the recording in her breast pocket?"

"I probably blushed more than she did. She was more worried you'd punch her in the nose for holding me so close, but I told her I'd protect her." Emma leaned her head to the side so Cain could kiss the spot where her neck and shoulder met. "You were gone and I was curious about your surprise. Spill it."

"How long do you think it'll take Shelby and her crackerjack agents to figure out Brent is missing in action? A few broken glasses shouldn't divert your attention away from your target, but they don't work for us, thank God." Cain finished with the buttons but didn't take the dress off yet. Ever since they'd stripped to get in the shower she'd been ready, but this was about Emma right now.

"Is Brent permanently missing?" Emma tugged on her sleeves and the dress came off her shoulders. "I did say it's what I wanted for my birthday."

"There *are* worse things than death, lass, especially if you've got a good imagination." She pulled the dress down a bit more and unfastened Emma's bra. Her breasts had swelled along with the rest of her, and while she knew Emma became self-conscious during the last months of every pregnancy—this was when she thought of Casey baby number four. "You are so incredibly beautiful."

Emma, as she had the first time they'd made love, covered her chest with her forearm. "I'll take your word for it since I can't see much past this bulge." She circled her stomach with her other hand.

The innocent gesture made Cain smile as she quickly stripped. "Believe me, I never tell stories when it comes to how I feel about you." She moved behind Emma and pushed the dress completely down and out of her way. She cupped Emma's breasts and smiled when her nipples came to full attention.

"I'm not sure how you can find anything remotely beautiful about me now," Emma said with a short laugh.

"Let me show you." She walked them back until they reached the bed. "When I asked Poppy for a room, she suggested this one."

"I'm surprised she allows guests up here after you first told me about it." Emma sat on her lap, facing their reflections in a large, ornate French antique mirror propped against the opposite wall.

"She said it reminded her of all the blessings in her life, and she knows what a blessing you are in mine." Cain took Emma's hands and moved them out of the way to expose her nakedness in the reflection. "Poppy found love and tragically lost it when Carly died." When she leaned back slightly, Emma went with her and spread her legs. "The loss made her feel lost in return." She braced herself up with one hand and squeezed Emma's breast gently with the other. Too much pressure was painful now, so she was careful.

"I don't know how she survived it. I'm not sure I could," Emma said.

"We survive the pain and loss by taking a chance on happiness again." She rubbed her hand slowly along Emma's belly until she reached her thigh. "Poppy's new love has brought her back from the hell she was in and given her a life she adores now."

"They're as lucky as we are, then." Emma took her hint and opened her legs wider. "Because of you, I love my life too."

"Put your knees outside mine." Emma was completely open to Cain, and even in the dim light, her wetness was easy to see. "So I thought this room would be a good place for me to show you how beautiful you are to me, in a way that'll prove it to you." Cain spread Emma's sex open, making Emma moan softly. "While I can't wait to welcome our baby into the world, this is what I was looking forward to the most when we got pregnant."

"What?" Emma squeezed her arm as if to make Cain touch her where she needed her.

"You like this?"

In answer, Emma covered Cain's hand with hers and encouraged her to squeeze her breast harder than she would've dared to.

"I see you with our baby growing inside you, and it turns me on."

"Me too," Emma said as she massaged her other breast herself.

"You look so lush that I have to control myself." Cain put her finger at Emma's opening and dipped it in to the knuckle. They both stared at her hand and Emma encircled her wrist. "But tonight I don't want to hold back." She glided her wet fingertip over Emma's hard clit.

"Please, baby." Emma leaned back against her as if to bring her body into full view. "I need—"

"Keep your eyes open. You're mine and I love you, but right now I have to have you." Cain slid from Emma's entrance to her clit in fast, hard strokes until Emma closed her eyes and screamed as she came. The orgasm didn't seem to soften her clit or her desire, but Emma pulled her hand away anyway.

"We need one of these suckers at home," Emma said to Cain's reflection in the mirror. She turned and carefully got on her knees. "I know you love me, and you know I belong to you, but what about you? Who do you belong to?"

"All yours."

Emma blew on Cain's sex, her cool breath a fire starting in Cain's groin and shooting to the top of her head. She'd never craved anything or anyone as much as she did Emma, and it only increased with time.

Emma put her tongue at the base of Cain's clit and licked upward with a flat tongue, starting a rhythm that'd make her come fast if she didn't ease up. Cain dug her toes into the rug and gripped the edge of the bed, but never took her eyes off the reflection of Emma's ass and the back of her head.

"Fuck." The word spat out of her mouth when Emma changed her tactic and sucked her in, plunging two fingers deep in a fast move that caught her by surprise.

"You want my tongue or do you want me to suck you?" Emma gazed up at her with a sweet expression that didn't really match the question.

"You decide on technique," she said, about to go mad that Emma had stopped.

Emma sat back on her heels, watching her fingers go in and out as she caressed Cain's clit with her thumb on every downward stroke. "If seven months of pregnancy turns you on this much, I'll be ready again at the end of the year."

Thankfully Emma sped up her hand and sucked her in until the orgasm started and raged through her, extinguishing the ache that'd built for hours.

"We're getting one of these mirrors for sure." Emma laughed and rested her head on Cain's thigh.

When she took her fingers out, Cain was ready to go again, but she had to get Emma off the floor.

"Thank you," Emma said.

"For what?"

"I believe you." Emma reached for Cain's hands and brought them to rest on her belly. "You make me feel beautiful, and no matter how much I protest, I really do love being pregnant."

"Enough to try again?" She laid Emma down and hurried around to the other side of the bed.

"Why not? Getting pregnant with you is fun, and being pregnant with you is even more fun." Emma pouted when she didn't seem to be able to stop the yawn at the end of her sentence.

"Let's get some sleep so we can see how the magic mirror works in the daytime." The phone rang as she said it, and Emma groaned. Cain listened to Lou for a minute and laughed. "Tell her she can come up if she promises not to move five feet past the elevator."

"Who picked the short straw?" Emma asked as Cain got up and put on a robe.

"Shelby the mighty is on her way up. She told Lou it was important."

"They noticed their lost lamb is gone already?"

"If he was a lamb it'd have taken days, but he's a loud, obnoxious jackass, so the sudden silence must've tipped them off." She tied off the robe and kissed Emma. "Keep my side warm. This won't take long."

❖

Shelby appeared annoyed but she stayed quiet. Cain really was surprised they'd noticed Brent's absence this quickly, and she hoped it wasn't because Lou and Merrick missed a surveillance camera in the ballroom. That worry died as quickly as it came since there'd be a team of smiling agents behind Shelby if they had taped evidence of her kidnapping Brent from the party as Muriel traded places with her on the dance floor. Besides, Lou and Merrick really were that good.

"Yes?" she said, ready to do more dancing than she'd already done that night.

"Do I really need to spell it out?" Shelby lifted her hands and let them drop.

"Even if I knew what you were talking about, the answer would be yes." Shelby looked better than the last time they'd talked, as if she was more relaxed despite her late-night visit. "You should save time by deleting that question forever."

"I like you, Cain, but I can't save you from killing a federal agent." Shelby stayed as close to the elevator doors as Cain had asked.

"I killed a federal agent?" Cain smiled as she laid her hand on her chest. "In case you're recording this, that last statement was in question form, not to be confused with a confession of any kind. What special federal agent was it? And I don't really understand why you include the word 'special' in the title. From my perspective, there's very little special about all but a few of you."

"I understand that about you, but your witty sarcasm won't make Brent reappear, will it?" Shelby crossed her arms and glared at her. "Before you get defensive—I'm not accusing you of anything. We're questioning everyone at the party."

"And I'm touched you started with me."

"You don't know that."

"Yes, I do, and if you tell me why you and your merry band of idiots were here tonight, I'll answer your question."

"You know why, Cain, and you know we'll play this game until you lose. For surveillance to work it has to be constant and unrelenting, and because it is, you're guaranteed to lose."

"Then refer to your notes. I was helping my good friend and his family celebrate his birthday. I danced with my wife a little, I flirted with her a lot, then I came up here." She mirrored Shelby's stance as she tapped her bare foot on the cold marble floor. "I noticed you and Agent Simmons. If anyone else was there, and they didn't have a good excuse to beat me without cause, I didn't see them."

"Do you think I believe that?"

"You don't? Does that mean you don't like me anymore?" Cain laughed and headed for the bar. After a night of champagne and finger foods, she was thirsty for a sparkling water. She opened one without offering Shelby anything. "Do you ever ask yourself what'll come next if I ever do lose our little game?"

"After, as in after the big party we'll have when you're locked up, you mean?" Shelby finally smiled. "I'll move on to the next egotistical thug who thinks they're smarter than everyone who works for the FBI."

"Be careful, Agent Daniels." Cain drained the bottle and placed it in the sink. "The world is a dangerous place, so perhaps you should heed a very old Irish proverb."

"Which one?"

"Better the devil you know than the devil you don't. You have nothing to fear from me, and in this case neither does Cehan, if that's who you're missing. The next devil that comes along might not be so nice." Shelby flinched when Cain walked toward her and pressed the call button. "You have my word I didn't kill Cehan or anyone else tonight." And technically that was true. It was a godsend when the FBI always thought the worst of you—there was no reason to lie.

"You didn't see anything?" Shelby asked when the soft ding of the elevator cut through the silence that followed.

"Nothing that comes to mind except how good Emma looked in her costume." She pointed to the open door, then waved. "Everything else I didn't care about."

"I might have more questions." Shelby put her hand on the elevator door to keep it open.

"You always do." She removed Shelby's hand from the door and waved as it slid closed. "You're a devil I know too," she said when she was alone.

"Only you'll always be better than all of them together," Emma said from behind her.

"I don't like to rub their faces in it, lass." Cain laughed.

"Come on, you've got a big day tomorrow."

"Yeah, tonight was Ramon's night, and tomorrow is Brent's coming-out party."

❖

The next morning Cain and Emma had breakfast at the outdoor café at the Piquant. Lou and Merrick sat at the table next to them. Joe Simmons and Claire weren't too far away, appearing pissed. None of them loved Brent Cehan, but he was one of them and he was missing.

"Those stares should keep your coffee hot," Emma said as she put her juice down.

Cain turned and stared back. Shelby called this a game, and while that was true, the rules had changed when Brent had cuffed her on a bullshit charge, then beat her. She didn't often feel bone-deep fear, but the seizures from the blows to her head had scared her. The terror had stayed with her until they'd finally subsided, but the fear was still not totally erased. The doctor couldn't promise that the seizures were gone for good, so she'd thought of a way to return the favor to Brent.

"Those looks are about to cool when their human scavenger hunt comes to an end. Only it won't be pretty," Cain whispered directly into Emma's ear.

"You did take the hotel's security into account, right? I don't want to insult you, but I also can't recreate last night with a thick sheet of Plexiglas between us."

"Brent made it to a room with a nice lady from out of town who's in the entertainment industry, and he's been there ever since. Like Lou's, his door will show that it hasn't been opened except when his companion left."

"Did the nice lady entertain him?"

"Even I'm not that cruel, lass. She tucked him in and gave him a gift that I'll tell you about later. Right now we're expecting a guest about the evening's shenanigans." She kissed Emma's cheek.

"Someone you invited?" Emma threaded their fingers together and leaned back.

"Shelby isn't someone I want to keep to myself, but she keeps turning up." Cain pointed to the door that opened to the lobby.

"Can I speak to you a minute?" Shelby stood close enough to be heard, but far away enough to not appear intimidating.

"You *may* speak to us, but any more than that and we might have to charge you." Emma pointed to the empty chair across from her.

"I thought you'd want to know we found Agent Cehan."

"Thank God, we were worried sick," Cain said and Emma laughed. "Who was he trying to strong-arm? Whoever it was probably got a big load of his charming personality before he ran and hid behind the giant blue wall that is the FBI." She forced a smile. "Brent Cehan is a gorilla with a badge, and I'm never going to change my mind about him, but I'm sure his mother's glad you found him."

"He trashed a room here last night and tried to beat a team of security guards when they attempted to remove him. All that while he was high on crack. We just posted bond for him at central lockup." Shelby folded her hands and rested them on the table. "Amazingly, the security team was able to land their punches in the exact spots Brent hit you."

"And the coincidence makes me responsible?"

"Seems odd, doesn't it?"

"Aren't you glad someone brought him down before he did any more damage?"

"I should thank you, is that what you mean?" Shelby asked.

"Not me, but the security staff here would probably appreciate a fruit basket."

"Maybe it's karma for scrambling Cain's head." Emma nibbled on her muffin. "Now he might see how important a clear head and his health really are. It took a while before Cain's seizures went away, so I'm sorry if we can't work up any sympathy for him."

"Once his high wore off a bit, he swore the blows to the head came from you," Shelby pointed to Cain, "and the staff here simply Tasered him."

"When did I supposedly do this?"

"Last night, which we can disprove since Joe Simmons and I as well as the other surveillance tools at our disposal back up your alibi. Brent knows that, but he still swears you beat the crap out of him and forced drugs on him."

"Isn't that what addicts do?" The waiter came, refilled her coffee, and seemed bright enough to know Shelby wasn't staying. "Blame anyone and everyone but themselves, I mean."

"That's all you have to say?"

"That sums it up," Cain said.

Shelby left, mumbling what sounded like curses.

"You might drive them all to drugs and alcohol before it's all over." Emma waved to Claire and Joe, who followed Shelby out.

With time Cain figured Brent would get over the cravings from the hits they'd given him the night before, but he'd probably lose his job. That should've happened way before now and would save someone down the line from Brent's temper. Last night was about paybacks, and it was satisfying to know he'd never forget their brief encounter where she'd reversed their roles. Brent had looked like a scared little boy when it was him tied down and at her mercy.

"That would've been a good trick, you have to admit."

Emma laughed. "What, teleporting yourself magically out of your body, beating Brent, making him attack the staff, and popping back in without even me noticing? You're right, but like you said, you're the devil they know. If you did have an out-of-body experience, they'll never figure out how you pulled it off. You could headline in Vegas with talent like that."

"I could tell them my secrets, but what'd be the fun in that?"

"True, baby, but for today, they can sit in the dark and wonder how you got another one past them."

Gun Brooke (gbrooke-fiction.com) resides in the countryside in Sweden with her very patient family. A retired neonatal intensive care nurse, she now writes full-time, only rarely taking a break to create websites for herself or others and to do computer graphics. Gun writes both romance and sci-fi. Connect with her on Facebook (gunbach), on Twitter (redheadgrrl1960), and on Tumblr (gunbrooke).

This story features characters from *Fierce Overture*.

FIERCELY YOURS
GUN BROOKE

The SUV skidded across the road, swerving over to the opposite lane and back. Helena gripped the steering wheel tightly and stomped on the brake. The snow whipped at the windshield like bullets as she fought to keep the vehicle on the road. Next to her, Noelle gasped as they nudged another snowbank.

"Damn it!" Helena tried to slow the car down, but it behaved like Noelle's little Lotus Elise. At least nobody else seemed to be out at this late hour.

"Carolyn and Annelie must be getting worried. I'll give them a call." Noelle pulled out her cell phone. "Oh, great. No signal. Guess that's what you can expect this far into the Adirondacks."

Helena didn't dare take her eyes off the road to look at the gorgeous woman next to her. Noelle, worshipped by millions of fans for her music, was, unfathomably, Helena's miracle. Their start had been rocky, but the attraction was undeniable, and love had grown very quickly. Now they were on their way to visit their closest friends, another famous couple, Carolyn, an award-winning actor, and her wife Annelie, producer and publisher. Why the two of them insisted on living this far away from civilization was anyone's guess.

"Still nothing," Noelle sighed. "At least the GPS is working so we don't end up in—oh God!"

Helena tried the brakes, hoping the ABS system would help keep them on the road. The car seemed to do a slow-motion dance routine, and suddenly another snowbank was looming over them. Everything came to an abrupt halt. The seat belt dug into her upper body, and the airbag deployed with a startling sound, muffling her cry.

"Helena!" Noelle's voice was pitched high with fear. "Are you all right?"

Helena shifted, blinking against the strange dust whirling around them. It was freezing cold and the engine had stopped. The pounding of her heart filled her ears. "Noelle?"

"You blacked out for a few moments." Noelle ran her hands up and down Helena's body. "We slammed into a snowbank and something else, something harder. The windshield is in a million pieces."

That explained the cold. "L-let's see if it'll start," Helena murmured. "Are you okay?"

"I'm fine. Your side of the car took most of the impact."

Helena turned the ignition key with trembling fingers. The engine coughed once and then died. Despite her attempts, the car would not start. "Terrific. Your cell?"

"Still no signal." Noelle leaned to the side and felt for something on the floor. "Hey, the GPS is still working. At least we know where we are."

"How far to Carolyn's cabin?"

"I can't judge distance exactly, but it looks doable. We're both dressed properly for this weather. Well, almost. We have to change footwear."

Helena probed the tender spot on the side of her head. She must have hit it against the door—she had a growing bump to prove it. "I guess you're going to force me into those horrible things you insisted on bringing for both of us."

"If you're talking about the Uggs, then yes, I am. If you think I'm going to let you make your way through this blizzard in your Blahnik ankle boots, you're dead wrong."

"I like when you take command." Helena winced as she smiled at her own words. Her head really was hurting now.

"And I'll remind you of that." Noelle sounded teasing, but her hands were gentle as she cupped Helena's chin and turned her head. "Oh, honey. That's got to hurt." She placed whisper-light fingertips against the bump. "Ouch." She kissed Helena's cheek quickly and then crawled into the backseat. She sorted through their luggage and returned with two pairs of black Uggs. Noelle helped Helena out of her beloved Blahniks and into the soft, warm boots. "There. You need this too." She wrapped a wool scarf around Helena's neck. "Got your gloves?"

"Hey, you're not my mother." Helena frowned.

"No," Noelle said calmly, "but you're decidedly dazed and perhaps concussed. I'm not taking any chances with the woman I love."

Helena had to smile, even if it hurt. "Sweet-talker."

Noelle checked her ever-present tote bag. "I think I have everything. Phone, GPS, water—no doubt it'll freeze—and the first aid kit with the survival blanket and stuff."

"I'll never tease you about that bag again. I'll have to get out on your side—mine is blocked by the snowbank." Helena moaned as she slid over to the passenger side of the car. Outside, she pulled her faux fur closer, grateful that it reached her calves. "God almighty, it's cold."

As they walked, Noelle checked the GPS every few minutes.

"I bet they'll be surprised when we arrive on foot." Helena chuckled mirthlessly. "I know Annelie is quite outdoorsy when they're up here, but Carolyn is more like me. A fire, some brandy or red wine, and a good book."

"Or, as I recall," Noelle said in a sultry voice, "a fire, some warm, spicy body oil, and…me."

"Darling, you know how to keep a woman warm on an icy-cold winter evening." Helena glanced over at her lover. "This year we've had together—I've never been happier. I never knew there was such… such contentment. I know it might sound boring, but I can't remember ever feeling such bliss. Coming home after a day's work to you is wonderful. I don't dread it any longer."

"You used to dread coming home?" Noelle pulled Helena closer as they made their way through the drifting snow. "You never told me this."

"It's nothing you just say, since it sounds utterly pathetic. It wasn't as bad when I went to my house in the Hamptons. There I had my dog and my housekeeper, and sometimes friends like Manon would visit. If I ever entertained, it was acquaintances or business associates more than friends." Helena shook her head. "Speaking of Manon, I think you see more of her and her group than I do these days."

"Only because we've been cutting a few tracks for my new album, sweetie." Noelle rubbed Helena's arm. "You're shivering."

Helena smiled at the thought of the four women in the famous improvisation group, who were now close friends. "I'm a little cold. Tell me about the new songs again." The Chicory Ariose group didn't normally record Noelle's type of music. They were instead famous for their special style of creativeness, never sounding quite the same twice. "How's it working for you?"

"Actually, it's working out great. I stick to the melodies and the lyrics as I wrote them. Manon, Eryn, and Mike play them beautifully, but it's Vivian's voice that makes them soar. She's added some brilliant tracks. She keeps joking that she loves being a backup singer, which is crazy, of course. Vivian Harding, world-renowned mezzo-soprano, is nobody's backup singer."

"Neither is Noelle Laurent. Our friends in Chicory Ariose love working with you. They consider you the most amazi—oh!" Helena's feet lost their grip, Uggs or no Uggs. Flailing with her free arm, she tried to keep her balance but knew she was going down. She tried to not drag Noelle down with her, but her lover was clearly not about to let go.

"Helena!" Noelle tugged at her, but they still tumbled into a snowdrift.

The ground seemed to give way and Helena rolled down a slope into the trees, moaning as her already bruised body took yet another beating.

❖

Noelle felt around in the snow for her bag and the flashlight. Perhaps it was broken, as it certainly didn't light up anything around her. "Helena, are you all right? I can't see you." Helena didn't answer and Noelle tried to swallow the panic that rose in her throat. "Helena, please, where are you?"

The snow reflected enough light to see a little way into the woods, but not enough to make out specific details. Noelle had no idea from which direction they'd fallen. The area around them was a series of slopes, and the drifting snow was covering their tracks quickly. *And Helena.* If she was unconscious, it wouldn't take very long for the snow to cover her. Noelle's heart pounded in fast, painful contractions.

"Helena. Talk to me. Whistle. Anything!" Sobbing now, Noelle dug through the snow with her hands, not caring one bit that she was getting colder with each passing moment. She crawled on hands and knees, shoving her gloved hands through the snow, frantically searching for

Helena. Suddenly she felt something and gripped it tightly. "Helena? Oh, God." But it was only her purse. "Where are you? Why aren't you answering?"

Noelle kept calling out, but she needed to see! Remembering her phone, she pulled it out, opened her start screen, and found the flashlight app. Holding the phone aloft, trembling in the cold, Noelle scanned the area. Tall pine trees obscured her vision, but they also gave her an idea where Helena might have ended up as they tumbled off the road.

She was just about to move farther to the right when something glimmered in the snow. Sliding down through the powdery snow, she clung to her purse and the all-important phone, not taking her eyes off the sparkling object. As she came to halt, she recognized Helena's diamond-studded watch. A black leather glove showed it was still attached to Helena, who was almost buried in a pile of snow. Shoving the phone back into the purse, Noelle bent down and laid her cheek just above Helena's mouth. Small puffs of air against her skin told her all she needed to know. Helena was alive.

"Sweetie. Please. Can you look up at me? Helena?" Noelle couldn't tell how badly Helena was injured and was afraid to move her. "Please, sweetie. Can you hear me?"

Miracle of miracles, Helena slowly opened her eyes. She was shaking badly now, but at least she was conscious.

"Noelle?"

"Oh, thank God." Noelle pressed her lips to Helena's. "Are you in pain? Can you move?"

"I...No, I'm not hurt any more than before. I don't think so, at least. Help me up?"

Helena sounded so unlike her normal assertive self, Noelle hardly recognized her voice. She supported Helena as she stood on wobbly legs.

"Where's the road? Are you all right? You...you're bleeding!" Helena gently touched Noelle's left temple. "Did you hit your head?"

Noelle looked at the dampness on Helena's gloves. "I don't know."

"We have to get back up to the road."

"I guess we can just follow our tracks back up. We better be quick. It's coming down hard again."

Small, whip-fast snowflakes hit Noelle's face as she looked up to locate the furrows in the snow. She lost track of time as she held on to Helena and waded through the knee-deep drifts. She could hardly feel her feet anymore despite the warm Uggs, and she was worried sick about Helena's less-than-proper winter attire. "How are your legs and feet?"

"Don't ask. I'm afraid to look. I don't feel much of them."

Noelle forced back sobs of panic. She knew they were in deep trouble. If they didn't come across a house soon, or even a shed, they were at risk for developing hypothermia. She'd read horrible accounts of how people had started to undress in the bitter cold, the confusion of the later stages of hypothermia making them think they were burning up. She would not allow this to happen to Helena. They had so much to live for. And what would her mother and sisters do without her? She was the breadwinner in the family. They relied on her, and they loved Helena. They would all be heartbroken if something happened to either of them, let alone both.

Finally they reached level ground.

"This must be the road," Noelle said, although the snowfall was so dense now it was hard to know for certain. "Let's keep going the way we started out. Hold on to me. I'll carry you if I have to." Noelle doubted it was possible, but she would die trying.

"I think I'm hallucinating," Helena murmured, staggering toward Noelle. "Is…is that a helicopter? Or perhaps…a wolf? That'd be all we need. P-predators."

Noelle whimpered, pulling Helena closer to make sure she didn't go down. She didn't think she would be able to get her up again if she did. It scared her that it was even the slightest bit tempting to lie down in the snow to rest a little while. And yes, she did hear a distant roar, growing in strength by the second. Perhaps it was a wolf. A large Adirondack beast that would dig its fangs into them and tear them to shreds…

A bright light shone from behind and the roar came closer. Nearly falling, Noelle tried to push Helena out of the way. No monsters with bright, shiny eyes would get their paws on her lover.

"Hey there! What're you two gals doing out in this kinda weather?" A rumbling male voice broke through Noelle's fearful imaginings. "That's got to be your car I found mangled back there."

"Oh, my…" Helena clung to Noelle. "A plow. A tractor and a plow."

A plow? Really? Noelle squinted at the figure jumping out of the growling vehicle and hurrying toward them. A short, stocky man dressed in bright orange coveralls wrapped his arms around their shoulders and pushed them toward the tractor. "Come on, gals. We gotta getcha into the warmth before you croak."

After some effort on the driver's part, they were soon huddled on a ledge behind the driver's seat in the blessedly heated cabin of the tractor.

"I'm Hugh," the man said as he took his seat, flipped some levers, and continued plowing. "I'm cranking the heat up to max. You'll be toasty in no time."

"Thank you, sir." Noelle trembled so badly now, she could barely remain upright.

"No need to call me sir. Just Hugh is fine."

"Thank you, Hugh." Helena slumped against Noelle. "Do you know where Carolyn Black and Annelie Peterson live? We were driving to them when our car hit a snowbank."

"Annie? Sure thing. Those lovely ladies are my next-door neighbors. Their cabin is only about a mile from mine. I'll take you right there, unless either of you need medical attention. My missus is a registered nurse."

"We just need to get warm. Thank you again, Hugh." Helena closed her eyes and pushed her face against Noelle's neck. "Thank God."

"Good thing I came along when I did." Hugh shook his head. "You looked like you were about to fall over."

Noelle nodded, too tired to reply. She couldn't wait to get to the cabin and get warm. A bath and a cup of hot chocolate would be heaven. With Helena. Thank every single deity. With Helena.

❖

Helena, wrapped in an angel-fleece blanket, sat on the floor with her back against a love seat. She wanted to be as close to the fireplace as possible and clearly so did Noelle, as she hadn't left Helena's side since they finally arrived at Carolyn and Annelie's. Across from them, Piper, Annelie's little sister, sat watching them intently.

"You look more pink now," the little girl said. "That's good, right, Annelie?"

"It sure is, honey." Annelie, a blond, statuesque woman, sank down next to them on one of the large floor cushions. She handed Helena another hot chocolate and gazed up at her wife, Carolyn, who brought one for Noelle. "You scared us half to death when it got so late and we couldn't reach you. Piper overheard us talking and wouldn't go to bed until she was sure you'd arrived safely."

"And then Mr. Hugh came and he carried Aunt Helena. That was almost scary." Piper chewed on her bottom lip. "It *was* scary. I thought she was dead. Just like—just like…"

"Oh, baby girl." Noelle opened her blanket and let Piper snuggle in between them. "Were you thinking of your mama?"

"Yes. She was still like that. I couldn't wake her."

"I'm so sorry, Piper. But Helena is doing much better, and we'll both be fine. Thanks to Hugh. We're going to have to go visit him before we go back and thank him again."

"Can I come?" Piper looked up at Helena now.

"Of course." Helena smiled and sipped her hot chocolate. "Mmm. Who knew hot chocolate could be this good? I haven't had this since I was in my teens. I wonder why."

"Maybe you forgot how good it is?" Piper frowned. "Sometimes grown-ups seem like they've never been kids."

"You realize this child is smarter than all of us?" Helena chuckled. "Piper, you're absolutely right."

They all sat on the floor in silence for a while. Helena combed her fingers through Noelle's long hair, feeling the heat radiate off the woman she loved, but she could also feel her shivers. They'd nearly lost everything out there in the snow. The idea of spending her days without Noelle was a physical, overpowering pain. If she lost her, if somehow Noelle was ripped from her life, she would never recover. Helena thought of how she had spent her days before Noelle. Alone, claiming she was so self-sufficient, she didn't need anyone. The truth was the loneliness had choked her, and she still couldn't believe how she'd been able to fool herself for so long.

❖

Noelle slipped into bed, humming with pleasure when she felt how well the electric blanket had heated it. The sheets, silky and soft, engulfed her. Helena came out of the en suite bathroom and hurried into bed.

"Oh, this is wonderful." She snuggled close to Noelle and pressed her lips to her cheek. "And you're here."

"We're here." Noelle embraced her and pulled her closer. "And I wouldn't want to have it any other way. When I couldn't find you in the snow…" She shuddered.

"But you did. You saved my life and then Hugh saved us both."

"Yes." Noelle sobbed against her neck. "I'm sorry."

"It's all right." Helena rocked Noelle gently. "Have a good cry, darling. It was very stressful and now that we're going to be okay, all that tension has to go somewhere. Tears are good in this case."

Noelle pulled Helena on top of her. "I need to feel you really close. Your heart against mine. Your warmth. Your heat." She ran her hands up and down Helena's body.

Her palms were certainly hot enough, scorching Helena's skin and warming her through her satin pajamas. "I'm here. Yours. All yours."

"Helena." Noelle cupped her bottom.

Rolling her hips gently into Noelle's, Helena groaned. "I need you. I always want you."

"Helena, you're so beautiful. You're hurting my eyes, you're so beautiful."

"No, no. You're the beautiful one. Inside and out. And God, I need to be inside you." Helena shifted impatiently. She made sure the duvet covered them and then unbuttoned Noelle's pajama shirt. The sight of her beautiful breasts made her moan. She wanted to go slowly, but as soon as she had one of Helena's plump nipples in her mouth, the frenzy was back. She shoved Noelle's pajama pants down as far as she could reach, baring the curly black hair framing Noelle's sex. Cupping her, Helena felt how wet she was already. "May I?"

"I need to feel you inside me. I need to feel *you*. Warm. Alive. Here." Noelle shivered, and for the first time all evening, not from cold. She kicked off her pants and parted her legs. "Take me."

That was it. That was all Helena needed to hear.

"With you. Always with you." Helena swirled her middle and ring fingers in the copious wetness and then pushed inside. She filled her, amazed at how tightly Noelle gripped her fingers.

"Helena!" Arching, Noelle cupped her bottom again. "Yes, yes. Like that. Oh, yes."

Helena pressed her thumb to Noelle's clitoris, circling it in unison with the thrusts. Noelle babbled softly, the way she did when she was so deep into the pleasure, she became completely incoherent. Nearly bursting with happiness, Helena stroked faster until Noelle went rigid, arched higher, and cried out. Ready for her lover's pleasure, Helena kissed her firmly, catching her screams in her mouth.

Noelle whimpered, slid her tongue over Helena's, and then rolled them over, ending up on top. Her hips still pumped in lustful waves, seeking contact, but her hands were busy elsewhere. She pushed at Helena's pajamas, baring her stomach and breasts first. Then she simply slipped a hand into her pajama pants, cupped her, and parted her folds. Noelle filled Helena just as Helena still filled her.

"Kiss me," Noelle whispered.

"Gladly." Helena brushed her lips across Noelle's over and over until Noelle finally delved inside Helena's mouth. Then their tongues echoed the thrusting of their fingers.

Helena knew now she was finally warm again. Striving for the perfect moment of bliss, the fact that they were here together, creating heat, meant everything. Noelle knew just where to add pressure and how to stimulate her, opening her as she twisted her hand back and forth.

"Coming." Helena drew a trembling breath. "I'm coming for you, darling. Coming…"

"Me too. Again. Baby, oh, my baby." Noelle whimpered, convulsing again and again.

Helena sucked hard at Noelle's neck as her orgasm tore through her, the fire racing to every part of her. Forgetting she ought to be quiet, she screamed Noelle's name.

"I have you," Noelle said, gasping. "I have you. I have you."

"Don't let go."

"I won't."

Slowly, Helena came down from the heights of pleasure. The warm cocoon under the duvet was so safe and warm. She snuggled close to Noelle. "I love you, Noelle. I love you so much."

"And I love you. I adore you, Helena. I don't want to lose you. Ever. I couldn't bear it."

"Then marry me?" The words, completely heartfelt and infused with all the love Helena felt for this beautiful creature in her arms, came out so naturally.

"Marry…Marry you?" Noelle's mouth described a perfect "O" for a few moments. Then she pulled Helena into a heart-melting hug. "Yes. Oh, of course, yes. Yes, yes, yes."

"I'm sorry I don't have a ring," Helena whispered, her heart thundering. "Yet. That's my number-one priority when we get back to civilization." She hugged Noelle. "Just when I thought I was the happiest I've ever been, you go and make me even happier."

"You should talk. You take my breath away on a daily basis and now…I don't think anything can ever top this. Possibly with the exception of knowing we're meant to be together, always."

"Yes," Helena murmured, inhaling the soft scent of her lover as she closed her eyes. "Always."

Radclyffe has published over forty romance and romantic intrigue novels, dozens of short stories, and has edited numerous romance and erotica anthologies. She is a three-time Lambda Literary Award winner and an RWA Prism, Lories, Aspen Gold, and Bean Pot winner.

This story features characters from *When Dreams Tremble* and *Homestead*.

BAD GIRLS AND SWEET KISSES
RADCLYFFE

I thought you were going out on the lake with Mike," Tess said to Leslie as she watched her pull on a pair of hip-hugger jeans and thick-soled black boots. "I think you're going to be too warm out on the water in that."

"I told Mike I'd catch up with him later," Leslie said, leaning toward the mirror hung on the wall over the small vanity opposite her bed. The window was open, and the warm June afternoon breeze, carrying the scent of pine needles and lake water, ruffled her shoulder-length, sun-kissed blond hair. She caught it back in a careless ponytail that made her sculpted cheekbones look even more model worthy and met Tess's gaze in the mirror. Her aqua blue eyes sparkled. "Dev promised me a ride around the lake on her motorcycle this afternoon."

"She's the one who brought you home last week when you were late working on the school paper, isn't she?" Tess remembered the dark-haired girl in the leather jacket on the big motorcycle. She'd only seen her for a few minutes, and when Leslie had asked the girl to stay and meet Tess, she'd shaken her head, muttered something that Tess hadn't been able to hear, and roared away.

"Yes, she's the one."

"Did she work on the paper too?"

"Dev? No, if Dev had her way, she wouldn't even show up at school." Leslie laughed and rummaged around on the vanity. After opening a tube of lipstick, she swiped her full lips with the light pink gloss and smiled as if enjoying a private joke. "Dev is kind of a bad girl. Hopefully she'll stick around long enough to graduate."

"I can't believe it's over sometimes." Tess doubted her experience in the small rural high school compared to Leslie's, but the ending represented the same thing—the first step toward the future and a life of her own.

"I am just *so* glad that's all over." Leslie swung around and grabbed the big leather bag she carried everywhere. "I don't know why we have to go a week longer than all the other schools around here. You're so lucky you got out early."

"I'm just glad I had this job waiting and could move up here right away," Tess said, the feeling of freedom something she hadn't known she'd wanted until she'd arrived at Lake George to work for the summer at Lakeview, the resort Leslie's family owned. She loved the farm and got along all right with her distant, somewhat sullen stepfather, and she'd never really thought about being anywhere else. But now that she was here, living in her own apartment—even if she was sharing it with another girl working there for the summer too—she'd come to savor the sense of being on her own, making her own decisions, and experiencing the excitement of meeting new people in a matter of days. Leslie Harris was practically an instant friend—they'd connected the moment they'd met, even though Leslie was the daughter of the resort owner and not a chambermaid like Tess. Leslie was warm and funny and open and welcoming, and Tess already looked forward to all the time they would spend together before Leslie went off to college and she went home to go to the community college and work the farm.

"Well," Tess said, squeezing out of the way as Leslie hurried past her toward the stairs, "sounds like a blast."

Leslie sent her a blazing smile over her shoulder. She didn't act this excited when she was going out on a date with Mike. "It's going to be great. I've really been looking forward to it."

Tess heard the sound of the motorcycle roaring down the drive and followed Leslie out on the wide wooden porch. As Leslie hurried across the grass, Dev slowed the bike, putting a leg down on either side to steady it while Leslie climbed on behind her. Dev handed her a helmet she'd detached from a clip on the back, and Leslie slipped it on, wrapped her arms around Dev's waist, and leaned her cheek against Dev's shoulder. Tess got a funny feeling in her stomach watching them, and for a second, loneliness crept in. She'd recognized the low ache in her midsection, having felt it most of her life. She had no siblings, had always been too busy for friends, and had quickly learned her hopes and dreams were something only she could understand.

"Bye, Tess!" Leslie waved, her expression joyous.

"See you!" Tess waved back and shook away the melancholy, enjoying Leslie's pleasure secondhand.

Climbing back to the porch, Tess leaned on the railing and looked down the sloping green lawn to the lake where speedboats made graceful curves on the surface as they navigated around the islands that dotted the broad expanse of water. She hadn't had a chance to spend much time on the water, but she loved the way it looked and sounded and smelled. She loved everything about the lake, its constantly changing colors, the dense evergreens that grew right down to the waterline, the still-wild nature of the undeveloped forest preserves all around it.

Other than the few guests, early arrivals to the season, she had the lodge to herself. As soon as she and the other girls had finished cleaning the cabins and lodge rooms for the day, the girls had left to meet their boyfriends in town. With Leslie gone and her work finished, Tess didn't have anything to look forward to for the rest of the night except her own company, which she was used to, after all.

She'd picked up a book in town the other day and was looking forward to reading it. The cover had caught her eye—two young women leaning close, as if they were sharing a secret, or about to kiss. The blurb on the back intrigued her—something about the way it was phrased made her think the women had a romantic relationship. The idea was exciting, and had been for a while. She just hadn't been ready to think about it too hard. Now it seemed she thought about other girls all the time.

Ready to see if she was right about the book, she headed down the steps to the basement door of her apartment. She stopped at the door when the sound of the motorcycle returning caught her attention, wondering what Leslie had forgotten. A low-slung motorcycle slashed into sight, its rider bringing it to a sharp halt at the end of the footpath, kicking up gravel and bits of grass. The rider was about Dev's size, but not as lean, and dressed in the same black jeans and boots. Dev had worn a black leather jacket, but this person wore only a black T-shirt.

This person, Tess realized as she slowly walked down the path, was a girl.

When the girl pulled off the motorcycle helmet and shook back thick dark brown hair that fell to her collar, Tess stumbled a step in surprise. The girl, who couldn't be much older than her, smiled at her as if they were good friends and not strangers, and she was—well, she was gorgeous…the unruly hair made her look a little wild, and her chestnut eyes glinted with bits of gold in the sun, like a big cat's, and her face was all angles and soaring lines and…oh God, Tess realized, she was staring!

Blushing, Tess halted a few feet away. "I'm sorry, are you looking for Leslie?"

"No—Dev."

"Oh, she just left. They were going for a ride somewhere around the lake."

The rider rested her hand on her thigh, her fingers fanning along the inside of her leg. She leaned forward casually with her opposite elbow on the handlebar of her motorcycle, regarding Tess as if she was an object of infinite fascination.

"Who are you?" the girl asked softly, making the question sound like an invitation.

"I'm Tess. I work here."

"Doing what?"

"I clean." Tess felt her chin lift of its own volition. That ought to finish whatever curiosity this girl had. You didn't ride a motorcycle unless you had the money to buy it and keep it running, something she would never have—at least not for a very long time.

"Are you done for the day?"

Tess frowned. "What? Why?"

"Well, I wouldn't want to take you away from your job."

"I don't know what you're talking about."

The girl twisted around on the bike and unclipped a black helmet with a narrow leather strap and held it out to Tess. "You need to put this on if we're going for a ride."

Tess stared at the helmet as if it might bite and automatically put her hands behind her back. The other girl laughed and Tess pressed her lips together. "I'm not going riding."

"Come on, it's safe enough."

"The helmet probably is, but I'm not sure you are," Tess said smartly. What was it Leslie had said about Dev—that she was a bad girl? Now she understood—this cocky, way-too-sure-of-herself girl was one too. A bad girl who was already more interesting than anyone Tess had ever met.

The girl grinned, shafts of sunlight dancing in her eyes. "Oh, I'm definitely not safe. I'm Clay, by the way." She held out her hand. "It's nice to meet you, Tess."

Exasperated, annoyed that she would look foolish if she didn't shake her hand, Tess returned the handshake. Clay's hand was bigger than hers, her fingers thicker, warm and smooth and strong. Before Tess could resist, Clay tugged her a little closer to the bike. "Don't forget to put your helmet on, Tess."

"I'm not going anywhere with you."

A dark brow winged upward. "Why not?"

"I don't know you."

"Well, this would be a good way to start."

Tess couldn't turn away, caught in the dazzling light from Clay's eyes, and Clay's gaze skimmed over her face and down her body in a way that no one's ever had before. She felt exposed, and oddly, inexplicably, excited.

"Come on, Tess. I promise I'll return you safe and sound."

All her life, she'd been reasonable and cautious and careful. She'd grown up on a farm where the weather was fickle, and only meticulous planning and the vagaries of luck allowed for success. She'd been taught to be frugal with money, painstaking with her judgment, and close with her private thoughts. She wasn't adventurous, she didn't take risks, she didn't long for excitement. Until she looked into those dark eyes and saw a world she'd never dared to imagine.

Jamming the helmet onto her head, Tess took two steps toward the big motorcycle. "All right. What—"

Clay held out her hand. "Climb on behind me, put your feet on the foot pegs, and wrap your arms around my waist. Lean when I lean, and get ready for the best thing you've ever felt."

Tess didn't think. She just held on and let go.

Clay wasn't exaggerating. Every sensation was amplified—the smell of the woods, the brisk purity of the wind in her face, the startling blue of the sky, the heat of the sun on her bare arms. As Clay spun them around the lake on the twisting narrow road, the bike slanting into the curves, the sun glinting through the trees, Tess was one with the world the way she was alone on the farm at dawn, when all the world was fresh and new.

"Like it?" Clay called, glancing briefly over her shoulder. Her grin made Tess's heart lurch in the best way ever.

Tess tightened her hold around Clay's firm waist. "Yes. It's wonderful. You were right."

Clay covered Tess's hand with hers, squeezing lightly. The contact sent a thrill through Tess's chest and into her stomach. Her cheek was against Clay's shoulder, close to the back of her neck, and she could smell her—tangy, sweet, fresh, and oh-so-exciting. Clay was the most breathtaking girl she'd ever known.

❖

"If we get caught taking this boat out, I'm going to get fired." Tess looked back up the hill to the lodge. The big porch was crowded with guests enjoying the sunset, but no one seemed to be paying them any attention.

"Don't worry," Clay said, "I'll have you back before anybody even knows we're gone. I brought sandwiches. We'll have dinner on the island. There's supposed to be a meteor shower tonight. And a full moon. It'll be great."

"Well, Mr. Harris did say we were free to use the boats if none of the guests were using them. So I guess technically it's all right."

"See? Nothing to get bent out of shape about." Clay held out her hand. "Come on. Climb in."

Tess settled in the bow of the outboard while Clay maneuvered them away from the dock. Clay rowed them out twenty or thirty feet from shore and started the motor. The outboard was not that large, and with plenty of boats still on the water, no one was likely to notice the sound of their engine. Tess turned her face to the wind and stopped worrying.

Soon they were bouncing over the waves as the sun sank lower, headed for one of the many uninhabited islands that dotted the lake. A few minutes later, they pulled up along a narrow strip of sand, and Clay tied the boat to a tree. She helped Tess climb out of the boat, and they found a clear spot under the pines to spread out their blanket.

"Hungry?" Clay asked.

Tess stretched out on her back, watching the sky turn pink, then red, then deep purple. "Not just yet. It's so beautiful I just want to look."

Clay lay beside her and propped her head on her hand. "Yes. Gorgeous."

Tess smiled, the skin at her throat warming under Clay's gaze. Clay had been looking at her that way a lot lately—like she was special. And sexy. Clay didn't have to say anything to make her feel that way—she just had to look at her with eyes that grew dark and deep. Tess touched Clay's face. "You're not looking at the sunset."

"I know." Clay's grin faltered as she drew a strand of Tess's hair through her fingers. "I've seen lots of beautiful sunsets, but I've never seen a girl as beautiful as you."

"You know," Tess said softly, brushing her fingers over Clay's shoulder, "it seems like I've known you for a lot longer than just a couple of months."

"It feels like you're the only one who knows me," Clay whispered, and she kissed her.

Tess had been waiting for this moment, wondering what she would do, how she would feel, forever, it seemed. To be alone with Clay, wanting to touch her, having Clay touch her. No one ever had. She wasn't scared, wasn't nervous—well, not too much. Everything about being with Clay felt right. Clay was right—they knew each other.

Tess tugged at the back of Clay's T-shirt and pulled it out of her jeans. Clay's skin was hot, soft and smooth. She ran her hands up and down the strong muscles in Clay's back, and Clay groaned softly. The sound surprised her—Clay was always so strong and self-assured, but the sound, almost helpless, struck at Tess's heart and made her want to hold Clay, to protect her. She stroked Clay's back, and Clay moved on top of her. Their legs entwined. Tess turned liquid inside.

"Tess," Clay whispered, her breath hot against Tess's ear, "I want to touch you everywhere. It's all I've been thinking about forever."

"I want you to touch me," Tess whispered back, and then Clay was unbuttoning her shirt, kissing her neck and her throat and the valley between her breasts. Tess pushed at the waistband of Clay's jeans, wanting Clay's naked belly pressed against hers.

"You feel so good."

"I've never—" Tess gasped.

"I know. I know. It's okay." Clay braced herself on her arms and smiled down at Tess. "You're perfect. You're beautiful. I—I'm crazy about you."

And then she kissed Tess again, so gently, so tenderly, Tess's heart shattered.

Half-undressed, completely naked—body and soul—Tess held Clay close. As the summer sun blazed out in the blue-black waters of the lake, Tess knew what she wanted. Had always wanted.

She wanted this bad girl with the sweet, sweet kisses, and now the bad girl was hers.

ABOUT THE EDITORS

Radclyffe has written over forty-five romance and romantic intrigue novels, dozens of short stories, and, writing as L.L. Raand, has authored a paranormal romance series, The Midnight Hunters. She is an eight-time Lambda Literary Award finalist in romance, mystery, and erotica—winning in both romance (*Distant Shores, Silent Thunder*) and erotica (*Erotic Interludes 2: Stolen Moments* edited with Stacia Seaman and *In Deep Waters 2: Cruising the Strip* written with Karin Kallmaker). A member of the Saints and Sinners Literary Hall of Fame, she is a RWA/FF&P Prism award winner for *Secrets in the Stone*, a RWA FTHRW Lories and RWA HODRW winner for *Firestorm*, a RWA Bean Pot winner for *Crossroads*, and a RWA Laurel Wreath winner for *Blood Hunt*. She is also the president of Bold Strokes Books, one of the world's largest independent LGBTQ publishing companies.

Stacia Seaman has edited numerous award-winning titles, and with co-editor Radclyffe won a Lambda Literary Award for *Erotic Interludes 2: Stolen Moments*; an Independent Publishers Awards silver medal and a Golden Crown Literary Award for *Erotic Interludes 4: Extreme Passions*; an Independent Publishers Awards gold medal and a Golden Crown Literary award for *Erotic Interludes 5: Road Games*; the 2010 RWA Rainbow Award of Excellence in the Short/Novella category for *Romantic Interludes 2: Secrets*, and a Golden Crown Literary Award for *Women of the Dark Streets*: *Lesbian Paranormal*. She has essays in *Visible: A Femmethology* (Homofactus Press, 2009) and *Second Person Queer* (Arsenal Pulp Press, 2009).

Books Available from Bold Strokes Books

Homestead by Radclyffe. R. Clayton Sutter figures getting NorthAm Fuel's newest refinery operational on a rolling tract of land in upstate New York should take a month or two, but then, she hadn't counted on local resistance in the form of vandalism, petitions, and one furious farmer named Tess Rogers. (978-1-60282-956-5)

Battle of Forces: Sera Toujours by Ali Vali. Kendal and Piper return to New Orleans to start the rest of eternity together, but the return of an old enemy makes their peaceful reunion short-lived, especially when they join forces with the new queen of the vampires. (978-1-60282-957-2)

How Sweet It Is by Melissa Brayden. Some things are better than chocolate. Molly O'Brien enjoys her quiet life running the bakeshop in a small town. When the beautiful Jordan Tuscana returns home, Molly can't deny the attraction—or the stirrings of something more. (978-1-60282-958-9)

The Missing Juliet: A Fisher Key Adventure by Sam Cameron. A teenage detective and her friends search for a kidnapped Hollywood star in the Florida Keys. (978-1-60282-959-6)

Amor and More: Love Everafter, edited by Radclyffe and Stacia Seaman. Rediscover favorite couples as Bold Strokes Books authors reveal glimpses of life and love beyond the honeymoon in short stories featuring main characters from favorite BSB novels. (978-1-60282-963-3)

First Love by CJ Harte. Finding true love is hard enough, but for Jordan Thompson, daughter of a conservative president, it's challenging, especially when that love is a female rodeo cowgirl. (978-1-60282-949-7)

Pale Wings Protecting by Lesley Davis. Posing as a couple to investigate the abduction of infants, Special Agent Blythe Kent and Detective Daryl Chandler find themselves drawn into a battle over the innocents, with demons on one side and the unlikeliest of protectors on the other. (978-1-60282-964-0)

Mounting Danger by Karis Walsh. Sergeant Rachel Bryce, an outcast on the police force, is put in charge of the department's newly formed mounted division. Can she and polo champion Callan Lanford resist their growing attraction as they struggle to safeguard the disaster-prone unit? (978-1-60282-951-0)

Show of Force by AJ Quinn. A chance meeting between navy pilot Evan Kane and correspondent Tate McKenna takes them on a roller-coaster ride where the stakes are high, but the reward is higher: a chance at love. (978-1-60282-942-8)

Clean Slate by Andrea Bramhall. Can Erin and Morgan work through their individual demons to rediscover their love for each other, or are the unexplainable wounds too deep to heal? (978-1-60282-943-5)

Hold Me Forever by D. Jackson Leigh. An investigation into illegal cloning in the quarter horse racing industry threatens to destroy the growing attraction between Georgia debutante Mae St. John and Louisiana horse trainer Whit Casey. (978-1-60282-944-2)

At Her Feet by Rebekah Weatherspoon. Digital marketing producer Suzanne Kim knows she has found the perfect love in her new mistress Pilar, but before they can make the ultimate commitment, Suzanne's professional life threatens to disrupt their perfectly balanced bliss. (978-1-60282-948-0)

Trusting Tomorrow by P.J. Trebelhorn. Funeral director Logan Swift thinks she's perfectly happy with her solitary life devoted to helping others cope with loss until Brooke Collier moves in next door to care for her elderly grandparents. (978-1-60282-891-9)

Forsaking All Others by Kathleen Knowles. What if what you think you want is the opposite of what makes you happy? (978-1-60282-892-6)

Exit Wounds by VK Powell. When Officer Loane Landry falls in love with ATF informant Abigail Mancuso, she realizes that nothing is as it seems—not the case, not her lover, not even the dead. (978-1-60282-893-3)

Dirty Power by Ashley Bartlett. Cooper's been through hell and back, and she's still broke and on the run. But at least she found the twins. They'll keep her alive. Right? (978-1-60282-896-4)

The Rarest Rose by I. Beacham. After a decade of living in her beloved house, Ele disturbs its past and finds her life being haunted by the presence of a ghost who will show her that true love never dies. (978-1-60282-884-1)

Code of Honor by Radclyffe. The face of terror is hard to recognize—especially when it's homegrown. The next book in the Honor series. (978-1-60282-885-8)

Does She Love You by Rachel Spangler. When Annabelle and Davis find out they are in a relationship with the same woman, it leaves them facing life-altering questions about trust, redemption, and the possibility of finding love in the wake of betrayal. (978-1-60282-886-5)

The Road to Her by KE Payne. Sparks fly when actress Holly Croft, star of UK soap *Portobello Road*, meets her new on-screen love interest, the enigmatic and sexy Elise Manford. (978-1-60282-887-2)

Shadows of Something Real by Sophia Kell Hagin. Trying to escape flashbacks and nightmares, ex-POW Jamie Gwynmorgan stumbles into the heart of former Red Cross worker Adele Sabellius and uncovers a deadly conspiracy against everything and everyone she loves. (978-1-60282-889-6)

Date with Destiny by Mason Dixon. When sophisticated bank executive Rashida Ivey meets unemployed blue-collar worker Destiny Jackson, will her life ever be the same? (978-1-60282-878-0)

The Devil's Orchard by Ali Vali. Cain and Emma plan a wedding before the birth of their third child while Juan Luis is still lurking, and as Cain plans for his death, an unexpected visitor arrives and challenges her belief in her father, Dalton Casey. (978-1-60282-879-7)

Secrets and Shadows by L.T. Marie. A bodyguard and the woman she protects run from a madman and into each other's arms. (978-1-60282-880-3)

Change Horizons: Three Novellas by Gun Brooke. Three stories of courageous women who dare to love as they fight to claim a future in a hostile universe. (978-1-60282-881-0)

Scarlett Thirst by Crin Claxton. When hot, feisty Rani meets cool vampire Rob, one lifetime isn't enough, and the road from human to vampire is shorter than you think… (978-1-60282-856-8)

Battle Axe by Carsen Taite. How close is too close? Bounty hunter Luca Bennett will soon find out. (978-1-60282-871-1)

Improvisation by Karis Walsh. High school geometry teacher Jan Carroll thinks she's figured out the shape of her life and her future, until graphic artist and fiddle player Tina Nelson comes along and teaches her to improvise. (978-1-60282-872-8)

For Want of a Fiend by Barbara Ann Wright. Without her Fiendish power, can Princess Katya and her consort Starbride stop a magic-wielding madman from sparking an uprising in the kingdom of Farraday? (978-1-60282-873-5)

Swans & Clons by Nora Olsen. In a future world where there are no males, sixteen-year-old Rubric and her girlfriend Salmon Jo must fight to survive when everything they believed in turns out to be a lie. (978-1-60282-874-2)

Broken in Soft Places by Fiona Zedde. The instant Sara Chambers meets the seductive and sinful Merille Thompson, she falls hard, but knowing the difference between love and a dangerous, all-consuming desire is just one of the lessons Sara must learn before it's too late. (978-1-60282-876-6)

Healing Hearts by Donna K. Ford. Running from tragedy, the women of Willow Springs find that with friendship, there is hope, and with love, there is everything. (978-1-60282-877-3)

Desolation Point by Cari Hunter. When a storm strands Sarah Kent in the North Cascades, Alex Pascal is determined to find her. Neither imagines the dangers they will face when a ruthless criminal begins to hunt them down. (978-1-60282-865-0)

I Remember by Julie Cannon. What happens when you can never forget the first kiss, the first touch, the first taste of lips on skin? What happens when you know you will remember every single detail of a mysterious woman? (978-1-60282-866-7)

The Gemini Deception by Kim Baldwin and Xenia Alexiou. The truth, the whole truth, and nothing but lies. Book six in the Elite Operatives series. (978-1-60282-867-4)

Scarlet Revenge by Sheri Lewis Wohl. When faith alone isn't enough, will the love of one woman be strong enough to save a vampire from damnation? (978-1-60282-868-1)

Ghost Trio by Lillian Q. Irwin. When Lee Howe hears the voice of her dead lover singing to her, is it a hallucination, a ghost, or something more sinister? (978-1-60282-869-8)

The Princess Affair by Nell Stark. Rhodes Scholar Kerry Donovan arrives at Oxford ready to focus on her studies, but her life and her priorities are thrown into chaos when she catches the eye of Her Royal Highness Princess Sasha. (978-1-60282-858-2)

The Chase by Jesse J. Thoma. When Isabelle Rochat's life is threatened, she receives the unwelcome protection and attention of bounty hunter Holt Lasher who vows to keep Isabelle safe at all costs. (978-1-60282-859-9)

The Lone Hunt by L.L. Raand. In a world where humans and Praeterns conspire for the ultimate power, violence is a way of life…and death. A Midnight Hunters novel. (978-1-60282-860-5)

The Supernatural Detective by Crin Claxton. Tony Carson sees dead people. With a drag queen for a spirit guide and a devastatingly attractive herbalist for a client, she's about to discover the spirit world can be a very dangerous world indeed. (978-1-60282-861-2)

Beloved Gomorrah by Justine Saracen. Undersea artists creating their own City on the Plain uncover the truth about Sodom and Gomorrah, whose "one righteous man" is a murderer, rapist, and conspirator in genocide. (978-1-60282-862-9)

The Left Hand of Justice by Jess Faraday. A kidnapped heiress, a heretical cult, a corrupt police chief, and an accused witch. Paris is burning, and the only one who can put out the fire is Detective Inspector Elise Corbeau…whose boss wants her dead. (978-1-60282-863-6)

Cut to the Chase by Lisa Girolami. Careful and methodical author Paige Cornish falls for brash and wild Hollywood actress Avalon Randolph, but can these opposites find a happy middle ground in a town that never lives in the middle? (978-1-60282-783-7)

Every Second Counts by D. Jackson Leigh. Every second counts in Bridgette LeRoy's desperate mission to protect her heart and stop Marc Ryder's suicidal return to riding rodeo bulls. (978-1-60282-785-1)

More Than Friends by Erin Dutton. Evelyn Fisher thinks she has the perfect role model for a long-term relationship, until her best friends, Kendall and Melanie, split up and all three women must reevaluate their lives and their relationships. (978-1-60282-784-4)

Dirty Money by Ashley Bartlett. Vivian Cooper and Reese DiGiovanni just found out that falling in love is hard. It's even harder when you're running for your life. (978-1-60282-786-8)

Sea Glass Inn by Karis Walsh. When Melinda Andrews commissions a series of mosaics by Pamela Whitford for her new inn, she doesn't expect to be more captivated by the artist than by the paintings. (978-1-60282-771-4)

The Awakening: A Sisterhood of Spirits novel by Yvonne Heidt. Sunny Skye has interacted with spirits her entire life, but when she runs into Officer Jordan Lawson during a ghost investigation, she discovers more than just facts in a missing girl's cold case file. (978-1-60282-772-1)

Blacker Than Blue by Rebekah Weatherspoon. Threatened with losing her first love to a powerful demon, vampire Cleo Jones is willing to break the ultimate law of the undead to rebuild the family she has lost. (978-1-60282-774-5)

Murphy's Law by Yolanda Wallace. No matter how high you climb, you can't escape your past. (978-1-60282-773-8)